UPON THIS PALE HILL

By Patrick Ashe

ISBN: 978-1-7348477-1-0

Cover Design: James Kenyon
Editing and Formatting: C&D Editing

With highest gratitude to Heather, Carina, Jim, and Jess.
Each of you gave me reasons to drive.

In the developed countries, there is a poverty of intimacy,
a poverty of spirit, of loneliness, of lack of love.
There is no greater sickness in the world today than that one.

Saint Teresa of Calcutta

October

TWO SHADOWS CUT ACROSS THE foundation of the hilltop house, cast away from the setting sun.

Brandon Marcel looked up at the clear blue sky covering the Carolina Piedmont. He heard the hum of the year's remaining crickets, the eight-bit chime of his cell phone's sent text, and the crunching footsteps of his one true friend.

The late afternoon air was clear with a scent of burning leaves. He took a deep breath and looked down upon the construction site. Wood, brick, and plaster sat in piles covered with tattered blue tarps. He thought about places, and he thought about people. Beauty and truth. Family. He thought about home. *Home.*

And then the sky and the ground reversed, as his anxious palpitations and whirling tinnitus picked up again. Home was where the heart hits.

"I . . ." Brandon started to speak. The average height and average weight of his average self stood pensively on the red dirt in a white T-shirt and blue jeans. He had gray eyes and neatly parted light brown hair, all soft and vulnerable in the ultraviolet light.

Most of his neighborhood could be seen from this lot. There were new and old houses along the Carolina hills, each punctuated by deciduous trees of varying autumnal colors. Many of these trees were small, young, and artificially planted. But when he looked closely, he could see a large, old maple tree by a dilapidated brick house and the old forest.

1

"Good leaves this year."

"Leafer," Jeremy "Germy" Kuhn responded as he texted away on his gunmetal gray phone. "Leafer madness." A whim later, he whipped back around toward the construction site. His lanky figure in anemic white skin skimmed around a spiral of copper wire. He leaped over a waist-high pile of lumber, knelt down, and gathered a pile of leaves. His brown eyes shot through tangled, chin-length black hair. Always clad in darker shades of gray, he looked like a modern-day Lewis Carroll stuck in a goth phase . . . with a side of pyromania. "I need your lighter."

"Do you ever settle down?" Brandon asked.

"I settle down right about the time you quit obsessing."

"Obsessing? I appreciate the little things. I'm . . . a dreamer."

"That's cute, John Lennon. But right now, I need Jim Morrison to light my fire."

Brandon laughed. "You really want my lighter? I think you used up your arson karma on the incident with the shaving cream. If East Hall didn't have sinks in the rooms—"

"Come on; that was freshman year. I've been good," Germy interrupted as he dug his thumbnail into the seam of his ratty jeans.

Brandon sighed. "We've both been good, Germy—that's the problem."

"Oh . . . but I've been *really* good."

Brandon chuckled and shook his head. "You know what I mean."

"Indubitably."

Spotting a box of nails, Germy's attention broke.

Brandon walked along the new cinder wall and turned again to see the old brick house. He covered his eyes with his hand again. The outer leaves were as orange as the late afternoon sun and almost as bright.

Taking in the moment, Brandon let himself marvel. His favorite moments were those that were more imagined than real, more within than without, and more possible than probable. But the aesthetic wonders of beautiful sights, sounds, and sentiments weren't enough, and he knew it. They weren't enough for his possible future, and they weren't enough for his impossible past. It was all potential withering away under the kinetic.

As foolish as he knew it was, however, he kept thinking about all that could be. He thought about the means and ends of purpose, meaning, family, and love. And he thought about a woman's face, one that he thought he would get to see one day, if only he was worthy of it. A face of many possible faces, but only having one.

If any.

Aisling.

Germy stuck the magnetic level into the ground and started building a tower of nails around it when his phone's industrial metal ringtone went off. He silenced it and returned to his destruction project.

Brandon sighed again. "Is it always going to be like this?"

"Like what, dreamer?"

"We have less than a year left of college, and this is what we're doing on a Saturday?"

"Speak for yourself. I've got a date tonight, and I'm not graduating until next December."

Brandon turned back toward the neighborhood. "I don't know about you, but I'm sick of being a . . . beauty scavenger . . . or whatever you want to call this."

"Dreamer, scavenger—whatever. You just need to learn to relax," Germy said as he sent a hammer flying through his nail-adorned effigy. "Quit worrying and focus on appreciating little things, as you said. I'm better at it than you are. I like picking through half-built houses."

"You like picking through half-worn underwear."

Germy laughed. "Hey, idle hands, you know. Gotta make sure everyone's satisfied."

Brandon shook his head. "Well, we're both idle. And that's my point. I think of a world that never was, and you want to give it a reach-around." He looked toward the sunlight. "And yet we both get big ideas, and then don't do anything about it. We're the inverse of the partiers, Type-A personalities, and adrenaline junkies. People who mistake motion for action, but at least, y'know . . . act! Even if we know better, we still don't do any better."

"Yeah, but you know the saying: insight's worth a thousand words? Action without vision is hell? Whatever. We're still young, so gimme that lighter. We've got time to burn."

"Some people say they've still got time all the way until their deathbed."

"Sure, but all your obsessing makes it worse. Relax." He scratched the side of his head through his mopped hair. "Besides, I don't want to nail the world more than I just did. I just want to nail some of its . . . ophidiophiles? Is that a word?" He felt a vibration, and then pulled out his cell phone again. "Oo . . . speaking of."

"Tell her we're busy."

"Busy doing what?"

"My point exactly."

As Germy texted, Brandon paced on the edge of the cinder block wall. His thoughts of maples, playing guitar, and a similar afternoon in his childhood abruptly changed into thoughts of cover letters and informational interviews. His ears rang.

He tried to distract himself with the sunset. His ears rang and the palpitations got harder.

Uncertainty, worry, anxiety, pain; within him, they all manifested in ways that garnered little sympathy and fewer solutions.

With eyes darting from one place to another, Brandon's mind kept running until it caught up with his eyes and stopped on a construction apron. It was just someone's apron, left after a day's work.

But then another thought occurred to Brandon, as it did from time to time. It was the most essential thought of omnipresent circumstance and his moral self: others. More specifically, the virtually unknown but assuredly factual reality: others who had it worse. Worse in any or all the ways things could be worse. Those whose ears whirled louder. Those who worried more. Those whose neighborhoods had bigger houses and fewer trees. Those whose neighborhoods had real crime. Those who didn't have even one friend. Those who slept in the streets. Those who slept next to monsters. Those who had no bed. Those who had greater dreams with even less probability of being realized. Those who had little food. Those who had little hope. The poor in wealth, and the poor in spirit. Those who thirsted for water, and those who thirsted for meaning, burning in all their pockets of the world and all of their intersections, with the sky beneath them and the ground above them. His ears stopped whirling for a moment.

He also knew that such thoughts and their accompanying emotions could only do so much. And he knew where good intentions that were not truly good led. Just as a home without a loving family is a house, faith without works is dead, and flesh without bones is pulp, emotion without reason is chaos. Without continuously refined reason, wanting to change even a small corner of the world would be a ruinous mission with a nightmare of unintended consequences, known and unknown. Emotion could build or destroy.

He knew this. He had seen this. It was absolutely critical, even if he couldn't remember when or where it was that reason had served him. Even more importantly, Brandon didn't know what he was going to do to convert all his personal anxieties into service for others.

Germy closed his phone. "About ready to be out? I gotta pick up something and head to Club Zigg and hope I don't set off my parents' alarm. They've been paranoid since they put that speedboat in the garage. Takes up the whole damn place, I tell ya."

"Sure. What time are we driving back tomorrow? I have a career counseling appointment first thing Monday morning."

"Counsel . . . what?" Germy laughed. "You go do that, and I'll check my ever-so-detailed schedule and see if I can fit you in. Come on; you know me."

Brandon scoffed. "Germy time as usual."

"So, what are you doing tonight?"

Brandon exhaled. "Read all of my dad's emails about cover letters, worry about what the hell I'm going to do with my life, try not to think about finding a girlfriend before I graduate so we can maybe have a home one day. Oh, and sneaking out to smoke." He looked down and shuffled his feet in the crimson dirt. "The stars should be nice tonight. Outside of town, anyway."

"Star peeping, huh? I hope that clears your mind. Otherwise, it's peeper madness."

The shadows spread under the last rays of the sun.

For Brandon, there was a new kind of satisfaction and even hope in the crisp autumn air. Wandering and wondering with his friend was a meaningful day. He would be doing much less the next day. Just as the days before, and just as the days after, and on until there was another day like this one. He almost always knew what he would be doing, and knowing made it worse. And yet, he still didn't know what to do about it.

The Morning Star watched.

***

AN EMPTY SILENCE WAS BROKEN by the *cling* of Waterford crystal against a Hancock dinner plate. Gravy and rolls were passed over the starched tablecloth in a triangular pattern around the mahogany table. The merlot was two glasses away from full, and the chardonnay remained unopened. Little air fluttered around the vaulted ceiling, and a dark blue from the twilight eased into the dining room. Sooner or later, one of the three would realize that no one had spoken, and that person was Brandon's father.

"So, you have a good time with, uh . . . Kuhn, right? Jeremy? You guys paint the town?"

Brandon lifted a fake smile. "Nah. We don't really go out much, Dad. I mean, he goes to bars sometimes, but . . . No, we just drove around for a few hours."

"All right. But hey, that's cool. That's okay. That's college. Best time of your life, you know? Best time of your life. Live it up before you gotta beat the streets."

"Yeah."

"Best time of your life, son. I'm sure you guys have a great time up there at school. Enjoy it while it lasts. Met your mom there. Right?"

She looked up with a small smile, finished chewing, and nodded. "Mm . . . Mmhmm . . . College years are probably the best. Oh, and the golf tournament. That was a good year."

"It was. So, did you check out that email, son?"

Brandon put down his fork. "Yeah. I was going to try writing that cover letter tomorrow."

"You should start tonight. That's how you stay ahead. Monday's the big day. You gotta stay ahead. You know that, right? You gotta write that. You can't keep working those third-shift security jobs at the hospital to pay off your student loans, you know. You gotta start."

"Dad, I wouldn't have to have student loans if I did trade—"

"No excuses, son. Write it."

"I will. Sorry, Dad."

"Don't apologize," his mother interrupted. "It's a sign of weakness."

"That's a good one to keep in mind," his father said. "You can't let people walk all over you. Your sister didn't score that position with Vazio & Leer by being meek. Now, she had a chemistry degree, so it's okay that she's shy, because she's a techie. Techies can be introverts. But you're an economics major; that's social science. You're gonna need to be even more of a go-getter to use that. Take it from me, business skills only mean something if you're a go-getter. You're denying some company out there a great mind if you keep doing that introvert thing. It takes people skills. You gotta break out of that introverted comfort zone stuff. Right?"

"He has to start talking to the right people," Brandon's mother said. "As they say, it's really all about who you know, not what you know."

"There's that, too," his father agreed. "Networking is the name of the game. You gotta play the game. You gotta get started."

"And like we keep telling you, appearances are everything," his mother added. "*Everything*. It wouldn't kill you to dress nice, dress stylish, every day." She gestured with her knife. "I mean, just look at that T-shirt. You've had that rag since high school. Throw it out."

"I do dress nice for work," Brandon responded. "I have a slightly different casual—"

"A slight difference is enough to cost you a job. These days, people will sooner tolerate a big difference. They don't like this nuance stuff. You never know when you'll run into a contact, so you always have to be presentable. Don't ever look weird or slobby. It's bad enough that you can't stick with an extracurricular, so don't cut off every chance you have."

"I . . ." Brandon started. "I know these superficial things help society function. They're small expectations needed to make larger things work. But . . . I don't think substance is limited to just techie things." He sighed and looked away. He felt a notch of anger ratchet up, but then he remembered the apron. "Besides, everyone is different to some degree. Not better, just different."

"Are you trying to say you're special? I mean, sure, but—"

"I'm trying to not let the style be more important than the substance. It's a style in itself, I think. Over time, those small expectations grow and overtake what's actually important. We're too concerned about designers and not enough about"—he thought for a second—"the style of substance—I don't know. What I see as beautiful, others see as mundane, and vice-versa."

His father laughed. "Don't be so pretentious; be productive. That's how we succeeded."

"Dad, that's exactly what I'm talking about. Even in public service, people are paying too much attention to pleasantries, flashy fundraisers, old methods, and that new fast fashion stuff instead of whether they're making a difference. People have this 'beautiful today, trash tomorrow' mentality. What about endurance? It's the aesthetic of old T-shirts and . . . old rock songs." He took a nervous sip of water. "Besides, people like feigning individuality, anyway, so it's all a wash. Hey, endurance means saving, cost-cutting, and efficiency . . . in the long-term, at least. That mentality can get me a job, right?"

"Wait—what?" his mother asked. She lifted her napkin off her lap and tossed it on her plate. "Jobs are about here and now, not the long-term, especially in your generation. It's about what's in."

"Son, you're in your mid-twenties," his father said. "Individuality's great when you're in school, questioning authority, having fun and all. Fight the man, right? But get ready for real life."

"Dad, I . . . I'm just . . . I'm trying to figure my life out. I know conformity is on the horizon, which means false comfort. Ultimately, conformity and nonconformity should be irrelevant. We should just do . . . what we should, live honestly, whether it's different from others or not."

"Oh, come on," his father scoffed. "Between your slobby clothes, weird diet, and that whole 'not driving' thing, it's pretty obvious that you're trying to be different."

"That's my point. I'm not trying to be different; I just am. Honestly, I'm not—"

"Yeah, you are trying, too. There's your whole playing guitar all alone thing. Too good for a band, huh? They're all just phases of trying to be different. Let 'em go already, son."

"I've been playing guitar for ten years. I just can't find a band—"

"Whatever. Fine. But you can't deny that you got this big thing with authority. You're always bent out of shape about your professors and bosses. 'He doesn't listen' this and 'the policy is arbitrary' that. You take it so personally. I'm telling you, it's time to let it go and grow up. Son, authority is authority for a reason, you know. People like your teachers know best."

"Yeah, authority. Teachers always know best." Brandon

10

shook his head. Then he looked up and left, gazing outside at the orange streetlights of the nearly featureless neighborhood. The houses could only be distinguished by pastel shades of the vinyl siding, lawn acreage, and patterns of planted trees placed in precise, lifeless patterns. "I know, I know. We need leaders for institutions to function. But when they lose sight of the purpose of leaders and institutions, then it's self-perpetuating. There's no room for innovation or differences. Whereas being free and open leaves room for natural differences to flourish and . . . well, society moves forward, evolves. Just having unquestioned authority stifles innovation. It functions without an ultimate function, driven by authority for its own sake." He shook his head. "Authority by itself is power, and power corrupts. Of course, each individual has to choose—"

"Oh, power this and individual that. You gotta have authority for discipline. And you gotta have discipline to do anything, son. Do you want to do something? Or do you want to just sit around all lazy and be all different, like some free-spirited hippie doing nothing?"

"Dad, all I want is to do *something*"—the panic started, and with it, his tachycardia; a mild episode, at least—"to do something meaningful. Is working third shift and going to school lazy? I mean, I'm not trying to be different. Some people my age are trying to be different, but I'm just trying to be mys—I want to do something. I just want to do the right thing. The good thing."

"As I said, you gotta have discipline to do anything, son."

"Well, Dad, I think true discipline comes from within."

Brandon's father blinked hard then looked away. "Huh." He blinked again, refocused on his plate, and then jabbed a moist piece of steak and stuffed it in his mouth. "Maybe."

"You didn't like pizza growing up, did you?" Brandon's mother asked. She shifted forward in her chair and put her elbows on the table. "Your sister and all the kids at school would be excited about

Book & Pizza Day, yet you wanted me to pack a sandwich for you. And you'd never play a sport for more than a season. Too many rules, I guess. Then there's the Clark Kent haircut you always insisted on." She picked up her knife and gestured with it. "And look, you still have that Clark Kent haircut, wear rags, and you stay up late posting lonely stuff on your Gold Pavilion profile. That drives people away, you know. I don't care if it's a 'substance' thing or being yourself, but like you said, it's all your choice." Her tone darkened. "Not fitting in with your peers has consequences. But you're smart, so do what you want. I just don't think you'll be happy working crap jobs and coming home alone for the rest of your life."

"Mom . . ." He inhaled and slowly exhaled. "It's okay. I know."

The quiet returned, as did the occasional *cling*.

Brandon checked his cell phone. He thought one of his would-be friends would have texted him by now. He considered texting a classmate that he tutored, but then he remembered his message sent: received ratio. He looked over his shoulder at the last hint of dark blue in the sky and tried not to think about anything else, especially tomorrow. Or the next day. He checked his phone again. His ears rang. The synth-heavy Rush song "Subdivisions" started playing in his mind to counter the invasive sounds and feelings.

"Always like having you home," his father said with a forced grin.

Brandon stood up. "Thanks for having me." He picked up his plate and headed for the kitchen.

As he scrubbed his silverware in the sink, his father took another bite of steak and his mother had a few more sips of merlot. She glanced out the dining room window, and his father coughed. The neighborhood sat in the quiet.

12

Hearing her son run upstairs, she gave her husband a look. "I still think it's the meningitis," she said. "He's always been . . . different after that."

***

BRANDON PULLED BACK THE COMFORTER and sat on the edge of his bed. The bare wall stared right back at him. The color wasn't quite pink; it was more like Advil. He tried not to think, but he always thought. Sometimes it was about an idea, moral, or ethic, which seldom gathered interest for anyone other than Germy. Other times, it was about music. At this stage of rumination, however, it was usually about people.

"Hey, Rachel, it's Brandon. I'm in town, so I thought I'd see if you were, too. I hope you're having a good weekend. See ya."

He knew she wouldn't return the call. Knowing made it worse.

"Hey, Andrew, it's Brandon. I was wondering how the Cost-Benefit exam went. I hope you're having a good weekend. See ya."

It was quiet. It wasn't peaceful.

He fell back against his bed and considered checking his email again as the incandescent light faded across the ceiling. It wasn't that different from his childhood. The room, the wall, and the light were all progressively larger iterations of the three previous houses in which his family had lived. He started to think about the intended utility of these iterations. Space to do . . . what?

He wasn't supposed to spend this weekend enjoying the late October foliage in his hometown, but prepare. It's always about preparing. He had been preparing for most of his life for the rest of it and probably always would. Preparing to prepare to prepare. This fact, and his email account's lack of responses from friends, and the overflow of cover letter articles were *all connected* somehow. Inevitably, preparation must give way to action. It was the difference between theory and practice, of thinking and doing. There were so many theories swirling through society and his mind, and some were plausible. As plausible as they were incomplete.

In his narcissism, so typical for an individual of growing aspirations and little clout, the thought occurred to him that he could be of great importance. What was less typical was that he immediately figured this thinking was born of comfort, much like conformity, and that he was probably an awkward mix of odd and ordinary; a humbler, wiser, and likely truer thought.

Still, some part of his subconscious was indeed seeking comfort. Desperately. Silently and surely, it clawed and clung to any sense of normalcy and health and goodness atop a sealed horror. As the defensive network of his mind had detected a grave threat that it could not target, it had set its resting crosshairs upon his very self, always waiting for provocations. It was the death instinct.

He pulled off his threadbare high school physical education T-shirt, one of his few vestiges of subtle belonging, and sat on the edge of the bed. With the fingers of his right hand, he ran them gently over his left then up his pale arm. The skin was smooth at first, soft and smooth, and then it wasn't. He slowed his two fingers to a crawl, falling in and out of the unnatural ridges, the topography of melancholy, the terrain of self-harm, one by one. The scars reminded him that the past was always with him. And it was always waiting for him.

The Morning Star watched closer.

***

" 'I WANT TO DO GOOD'."

Brandon sat quietly, waiting for the muscular career counselor in the striped Polo shirt to finish reading his form and provide feedback. He checked the buttons on his blazer, and then he let his hands rest softly on his leather portfolio. Average height and average weight somehow didn't fit in the suit quite right. His hair was brushed in a perfect part on the left side of his head.

He blinked hard. The bass intro from Queen and David Bowie's "Under Pressure" started playing in his mind.

"It should say, 'I want to do well.' You should visit the Writing Center if you have trouble with basic grammar."

"I mean, doing good in the world," Brandon clarified with feigned confidence. "To give back, you know? I want to make a difference. I have Scouts and volunteering, and I care—"

"Yeah, yeah, don't start the Miss America speech." The counselor put down Brandon's form and started typing. "There are opportunities. I mean, there always are. Know what I mean? Let's see what we have here." He typed for a few more seconds then propped his elbow as he read. "So, yeah, we have some information on social work positions, if that's your thing."

Brandon sat up. "Sounds good. What kind of positions?"

The counselor looked back at him. "Well, unless you get a Master's, you're not going to be making much. You have Stafford Loans, right?"

"Yes. I didn't qualify for Pell, even though I had a four-point and my parents don't—"

"You're looking at big payments. You're going to want to make at least fifty-k. You better make the most of that economics degree. Know what I mean?

"Because I'm out in December, and I've already got a ninety-k position lined up with my finance degree. This gig didn't hurt, either. People skills, you know? So, you should go corporate; that's where the money is."

"Okay." Brandon opened his folder, as if to check notes, but all he did was mentally ruminate. Then he looked back up and noticed the logo embroidered on the counselor's Polo shirt. It looked familiar. Brandon felt something like futility and tried to ignore it. "Where do we start?"

"Let's put together a list of companies." The counselor looked over the papers in front of him for a moment, and then he sat back and thought before he typed again. "Let's see here . . . yeah. We have econ alum all over the Triangle. Now, these contacts just have names and emails, so work through it until you have a lead. Call, call, call."

Brandon nodded and sat quietly, his posture awkwardly proper, and waited. Tension ran from his feet to his head. Then, in his mind, he started to hear the "Under Pressure" lyrics. Instead of describing his own feelings, they reminded him of others. They reminded him of the point. The least he could do right now to stow his inflamed insecurities was to focus on what he believed he needed to do going forward.

As the stock nervousness faded into a synaptic glow, Brandon considered the possibilities. Could he live in the Triangle? Yes. Could he take an entry-level corporate position? Yes. Could he use this position for service to others? Yes. In fact, his preliminary financial and time management algorithms seemed oddly congruent with these purposes.

"Here; I'll print this out."

Brandon looked over at the office printer as the counselor stood up. He caught a glimpse of another career counselor in an adjacent cube. She was wearing a gray college sweatshirt with yellow print and many jangling metal bracelets. The graceful brunette returned a brief, brown-eyed glance before she picked up the phone. His tinnitus faded, and he felt a sense of peace.

"All right, here you are, Mr. Marcel."

Brandon looked up at the paper being handed to him.

"I'll email you this, too. Keep it close by and remember to try something every day. Call, email if you have to, or look up more info on the websites. Then call! Network all the time. Practice interviewing and presentations with your friends.

Public speaking is big. I'm telling you, even in this economy, offering that skill is huge. I hear back from happy alums all the time."

Brandon opened up his leather portfolio and placed the papers in the front folder.

A tinge of nervousness came back. If there was anything he learned from his Public Speaking course, it was that he didn't like public speaking. But he was capable when he believed in his message.

And only when he believed in his message.

The counselor reached his hand out. "So, good luck, stay in tou—"

"Just a quick question," Brandon stammered. "I appreciate this list—I'll check it out, definitely—but are you sure I can't find entry positions for, like, United Way, or . . . Red Cross? Boys and Girls? And other nonprofits? I'd be willing to—"

"Man, I'm sure there are, but I'm telling you, you're not going to make much on entry. At least work for-profit for a decade or so, then find a nonprofit paying for someone coming into their management with corporate skills. Hell, even government pays better and has job security. Find a real position, make real money. You can still help people if you want. Just donate."

"Okay . . ." Brandon looked away for a second then turned back. He was confident in his intentions, but not in himself. There was a hole in that confidence becoming inflamed. But, before another high-strung moment of regret was complete, the counselor offered an unexpected alternative.

"You know, since you're a bleeding-heart kinda guy, I know a good networking group for you. Have you heard of the Campus Progressives?"

"I think I saw a flier," Brandon responded with caution.

"That's the stuff they care about. Helping people, changing things. You should really check them out. And hey, the girls like a nice guy just as a much as a well-off guy. Know what I mean?

17

Double-up. That's smart. Here, let me find something."

"Wait—they're all about party politics, right?"

"Like politics and helping people. Voting is a heck of a lot easier way to change the world than giving up making real money to work in some little nonprofit, am I right?"

"I guess," Brandon stammered. "I guess economic policy is interesting, but really . . . politics seem like power games to me. Like, authority . . ." Brandon tilted his head back and wrinkled his nose. "I mean . . . if it does really help, maybe . . . I'm not against activism, so long as it really is about making a difference, not . . . all for show. Substance, not style."

"Yeah, like . . . that's what the Campus Progressives are all about. Let me find that name."

Collecting his thoughts, Brandon weighed his kernel of interest against his bushel of doubt. He followed politics periodically, but the issue complexities often became muddled in his mind before he could take positions. While he shuddered at ideological tribalism, he figured he could use group membership to achieve his personal and professional objectives.

He had heard from his parents that extra-curricular activities weren't important in themselves but were a means to other ends.

Maybe the groups are means and people are ends, he pondered quietly. *And what if their policy activism actually does produce a measurable change, like increased standards of living, increased access to healthcare, or reduction in food insecurity?*

"Sarah Shea-Trivette," the counselor said. "She's the head of the CP. Look up their website and contact her."

"Sarah Shea-Trivette; got it. Sounds good," Brandon said. "I'll check that out."

"Two birds with one stone, huh? You could meet

someone there, man. And get a job. Just keep up those contacts. I'm telling you, call every day. There are always opportunities."

***

TAKING THE STAIRCASE TO HIS apartment door, Brandon turned his key and unlocked it. He flicked on the overhead light and tossed his leather portfolio on the battered wood coffee table. Removing his cell phone from his blazer pocket, he did another perfunctory and futile check then set it on top of his portfolio. Turning on the laptop, he sat back into his tattered computer chair and waited.

The operating system's audio theme blared as the desktop icons loaded. He reached for the mouse. *Click, click.* The browser spread out, sitting gray as the machine caught up. *Click.* Brandon opened a link to his email and waited. His *6stringmartin89* account had six new spam messages. *Click, click, click . . . click.* He sat still for a moment.

Refresh.

Although his nightly browser refreshing had just begun, he did have an uncommon sense of urgency. There was a sense that time would not drag on until eternity, that there could be a day of progress. Progress via the Campus Progressives, even. It required the typical, awkward introductions, but so be it. It was a means to an end. And this fact could carry him through all the necessary social interactions.

A hum.

Thankful that he was home, Brandon went for his first defense against the sounds. He plugged in earbuds and clicked open his mp3s. He pondered what bands would be most appropriate for an empty evening at the end of October. Maybe Pink Floyd. "Welcome to the Machine" seemed fitting for his life at this juncture. Blue Öyster Cult's "Veteran of the Psychic Wars" was even more fitting. Or King Diamond's "At the Graves" topped with Type O Negative to really drive the feeling of the season. Perhaps it was Depeche

Mode.

The ambient sounds of "Waiting for the Night" started, and Brandon slipped into his playlist. He let go of his mouse, letting his shaking and tinnitus fade away.

And there it was. For a mind made of chaos, a brief refuge could be found in a song. From the holy hymns from Hildegard of Bingen to Buddy Guy's impeccable Stratocaster tones, music across genres was a refuge and a salve. Distorted sounds annihilated emotional distortion and cleans cleaned it up, leaving a momentary peace.

Momentary.

Nearing the end of the playlist, Brandon felt palpitations again. And, as sure as the night had slowed and the webpage refreshing was getting old, the hum returned. They overpowered the final theme recapitulation in The Cure's "Homesick."

He removed his earbuds and sat for a moment. It was time for the second line of defense.

As he stood up, he realized he was still wearing his suit, so he removed the blazer and tie and hung them in the closet. And then he went to his bedroom.

The aged Martin dreadnought acoustic leaned against a ragged black guitar stand. Sitting on the edge of his bed, Brandon picked it up with ritual grace, trying not to think about that very fact. Such fake formality was typical. It was glib. And yet, he thought about it. But he didn't think about emails, nor did he think about phone calls. He didn't think about uploading pseudo-artistic pictures onto his Gold Pavilion profile or hitting refresh until some type of response to something had materialized in a small, orange notification icon. He didn't think about the ringing. He didn't think about his palpitations. Victory.

A chord rang. He wasn't sure what it was, but he called it F#m7. It worked. It wasn't precisely the secret chord that would be noticed on the quad, but it worked for him. Then he played a few others. A little simple progression. There was something beautiful in the tones. Perhaps the beauty of the woman's face.

Aisling.

Perhaps there would be someone at the meeting. Perhaps this person would find the melody interesting. Perhaps she would see how he wanted to use his economics degree to contribute to the world. Perhaps she would have her own glorious gift for the world and for him. Perhaps she would help. Perhaps they would do good together. Perhaps this was another string of futile speculation.

Perhaps it was getting late.

He found himself striking a Cm. A C . . . minor. First the chord, and then some arpeggios. The tips of his fingers plucked awkward yet true. There it was—the life behind the sound. The little resonance of each string, slowly singing, sustaining, lifting, drifting, becoming lost in the air.

It was an awkward performance of a piece written for piano. He couldn't quite remember each chord or pluck only the correct strings, yet he played it well enough, with heart. It was Beethoven's Piano Sonata No. 8, the Pathétique Sonata, second movement.

It was peace.

Aisling.

November

ALL SAINTS' DAY CAME AND went. The last brown leaves fell from the last maple tree. Cool air became cold air in the little mountain town. Brandon thought about emailing Sarah Shea-Trivette frequently as he walked to and from class.

On a cold and gray day, he realized that there weren't many meetings left in the semester.

"Come on; you don't need all these organizations and everything to do something," Germy told Brandon with a scoff. "Why don't you head over to the soup kitchen? Plenty to do there, especially around the holidays."

"Yeah, but . . . I want to take it to the next level, you know?"

"I guess. But organizations? Politics? All that order and rules? You don't need that level."

Brandon looked toward the street and tapped on his cigarette. Traffic sped by on all four lanes. It was almost rush hour, and even a small college town like theirs had a roadway mess at this time of day. "Okay, so if I don't join the Campus Progressives, I should just volunteer or something. Do-Gooder Brandon, huh?"

"You got it."

"But, y'know, at a club, I could meet someone who actually cares or understands—"

"You had it. Take a lap. I'll take a drink. I've got some

really nice Lagavulin whiskey, too. Tastes like a campfire. I know you like nostalgia and that's all the nostalgia you need."

Brandon shook his head but smiled. For all their arguments, Germy offered something other supposed friends and family did not—acceptance. No priority, nor personality clash had changed this. Yet, between so many individuals, even those whose values and backgrounds were more homogenized than theirs, acceptance was a fashion, not a way of life. It was a brand with no product. Brandon thought about this until it unearthed an unpleasant memory.

At the beginning of his third semester, Brandon had heard from Katie, who heard from Nathan, that there was a mud run to benefit AIDS research. He had asked Germy if they could go together, but Germy argued that it was better to exercise and donate rather than participate in a public event. Brandon had been annoyed by his friend's obstinate objection and had decided to go alone.

As it turned out, the starting time stated on their campus flyers was two hours later than the actual event, and no one had mentioned the actual time to Brandon. When he had arrived, he had laced up his old Converse All-Stars, paid the entry fee to volunteers who were packing up, and started running alone and far behind everyone else. The finishing horn sounded right before he reached the first mud pit at the end of the first kilometer.

He had walked, spotless, back to the beginning to find Katie, Nathan, and the rest of their group covered head to toe in sloshy wet mud, laughing and drinking beer. Brandon had tried to talk to Katie, but he couldn't get her attention. The next thing he knew, he was chain-smoking in the parking lot with Germy on the phone, who had made a sincere but dense attempt to comfort Brandon with the fact that overhead costs of the event ate up most of the proceeds, so the failed mud runner should have followed his less social friend's advice all along.

Of course, Brandon hadn't been comforted. He had attempted

to break out of his comfort zone only to discover that it had never existed. Comfort would necessitate a modicum of acceptance beyond the familiarity of Germy.

In the insular, cultural sphere of a college town, myriad beliefs and lifestyles ostensibly garnered understanding, tolerance, and even acceptance. But obvious differences were accepted with much greater ease than subtle ones, just as his mother suggested.

Anecdotal misadventures exemplified by failed mud runs aside, it didn't always seem to Brandon as though there was a substantive change in the righteousness fads. Perhaps some primary avenues of hate were closed only for back roads to take their traffic. After all, ignorance was masterful at metamorphosis, and hate was that and even more tenacious. Hate was a wild infection that grew between groups and individuals, especially when the need to control became blind and consuming, all the more empowered by the status quo of comfort and groupthink.

For all of Brandon's ideals about loyal friendships, benevolence, and acceptance toward others, he also felt resentment. Bitter resentment toward all the people whom he wished would look forward to seeing him at the mud run or at the get-together afterward. The stock response to his complaints echoed in his head, *you can't make people like you.* But, through all his wistful staring at pictures of rambunctious soccer teams and laughing couples, he couldn't control others to "make" them accept him as he accepted them. He couldn't even control himself. The vagaries of his experience screamed *control,* and yearning for social connection that simply didn't exist.

"Human nature is self-destructive, and people don't care," Brandon said to cool the intensity of his mind with something like certainty. Certainty is most comforting to those who know the least. "People don't care sincerely, anyway. Even if they donate or work at a charity or whatever, they're doing it to say they did it. To say that they're compassionate and all those smug badges of pride. And how effective are these little organizations? A soup kitchen just feeds someone for a day. I don't see what real difference it makes. For real change, you need bigger control, like a . . . government policy. Besides, free markets fail. Hate crimes happen."

"So, since people can do bad things to each other, we should concentrate their power?" Germy shook his head. "Don't be elitist. You have to really think your ideas through and be honest with yourself. We can talk about all your macroeconomics or all my postmodern philosophy, but in the end, it always comes down to the small stuff—the choice you make for yourself, the individual. That's real change. You don't need a government. Just life, liberty, and property."

"Oh, come on. It's . . . I don't know." Brandon looked back out at the street again. He puffed on his cigarette and exhaled with a sigh. "Hm. So, what are you doing for the break?"

"Finger Lakes tour. If you catch my entendre there. Ha. You know, there's nothing like a glass of seyval blanc after humping a pretty girl from a small town in Upstate New York."

"That's great, Germ. Flying?"

"Nope, driving. I hear the girls in Northern Virginia are pretty hot, too. Remember that girl from physics? I think she was from Alexandria."

Brandon sighed. "Physics, indeed. So, you're really going to have a road trip romp?"

"Ha, no. I was kidding. That plan is brought to you by the letters V and D. But hey, small-town girls and boys in Upstate New York. Smart, hot, and easy as—"

"Germy."

"I'm just saying. Always leave them satisfied. How long has it been for you, anyway?"

Brandon took one of his few remaining drags. "Years."

"Let me guess. Marianne? Senior year?"

"Yeah. My one and only."

"I'm not going to ask you to get over that one."

"But . . . ?"

"But nothing."

Brandon exhaled. He took solace in the fact that, for as much as he resented his friend's sexual charisma, under an elusive heart and epicurean tastes, his friend accepted him as much as he wouldn't accept himself. No more than any of these would-be friends and groups of the past.

The chaos of his thoughts drifted as he finished his cigarette and grinned. Something had occurred to him.

"I don't have to be part of a club to do . . . something, right? There are certainly enough . . . hungry and homeless folks in the Four-County Region to help in my own way, I guess."

"That's what I'm saying. Home, James. Four-County and for all. For the world, but not worldly. You don't need to be friends with the world. Just do the right thing."

"Right on."

Germy squeezed the last embers of his cigarette onto the sidewalk then went back into the apartment.

Brandon took a moment to let his thoughts settle. His one true friend's impetuous suggestion was a good one. He had accepted himself enough to have the self-control to move forward. It was a good decision. It was a good promise.

But he couldn't keep it.

***

" . . . *LOOK FORWARD TO MEETING YOU, Sarah. Warm regards, Brandon Marcel."*

26

Brandon finished his email then sat back. After a second read-through, he hovered the cursor over "Send" for a moment then clicked it.

He heard a few sounds outside and figured that most of the town had left for Thanksgiving break on this dark, wet Wednesday evening.

As usual, he was hoping to receive an email back shortly, despite his rational side telling him to wait until next week. So, he sat, and he listened, wondering if he should have caught a ride with Germy a few hours ago instead of stranding himself in the empty college town.

The fear of the quiet started to grow, and the ear whirling changed from imagined to real. Knowing the weight of anxiety was keeping him away from his guitar, he searched his mp3 library for the symphonic metal band, Lacrimosa. As the light arpeggios started, he looked outside for remaining leaves in the wind.

Marianne. He hadn't heard from his ex-girlfriend in a year. Given her serial monogamy after graduating high school and moving to outside Tampa, chances were that she had found another boyfriend a few days after breaking up with her last one. It was about time for the regular romantic turnaround.

Even though she rarely made contact with him, she was sweet when she did. Her gentle face and voice veiled a rougher lifestyle of bluntness, tattoos, heavy metal, and sweaty gym shirts, all of which he found attractive and endearing. She was too elusive, or perhaps too smart, to have a Gold Pavilion profile, but she could be reached by phone. And perhaps reaching out would pull his mind away from his latest attempt at social normalcy.

A half hour later, Brandon was pacing around the apartment balcony with a cigarette in one hand and a comfortably sensuous voice in the other.

"You know what I should do? I should be clingy with this guy,"

Marianne said. "I should call him ten times a day and ask him where he is, if there are girls there, if they're prettier than me, and . . . yeah, I totally should. This dude is going to be a mess when I get done."

"Right, right," Brandon replied. "Your schemes are always foiled by your conscience."

"I guess you know me better than that. Chad left his brains at the gym, anyway."

"That's what it sounds like. Maybe you should find a more worthy opponent."

"You mean, like you? There aren't many."

Brandon grinned. "Thank goodness, right?"

"No, really, you're smart, not too bad-looking for someone who needs to work out more, and . . . you're caring, you play guitar, do your own thing. You're . . . you're just you. Then you've got your best friend, the Germ himself. I don't get it. I never did, you know. Don't get me wrong, he's a great guy and all, but why is Contagious Kuhn the ladies' man of you two?"

Brandon laughed. "I actually think people don't like me for some of those same reasons. Hey, you dumped me for being too innocent, remember?"

"Yeah . . ." she said with a guilty stretch of voice.

Squeezing the burning tobacco out of his day's last cigarette, Brandon lowered his voice a pitch. "It's not just romance. I mean, to my professors, my boss, even my parents . . . I'm a prude without a cause. I'm the sharply carved piece that doesn't fit anywhere. It's like, sometime around eighteen, all of a sudden the rules changed. The great maxims of our youth are suddenly trite, and we're expected to either screw around, be successful, or both. As I've done neither, my value to others is pretty damn cheap."

"A prude, huh?" asked Marianne. "I definitely know you better than that."

He smiled.

"But I hear you," Marianne continued. "I might even agree. But we disagree on one thing."

"What? You think I'm going to be successful?"

"Probably not, to be honest. But you're still valuable."

***

PLUGGING HIS CELL PHONE INTO a charger, Brandon tried to make sense of the mélange of emotions presented by the anxiety around his email and elusive sense of contentment from his conversation with Marianne. He sat on the edge of the bed and stared at his band posters.

Tomorrow is Thanksgiving, he thought, which made him almost wish he had asked for a ride to see his parents for the holiday. But he also knew there were other ways to show that he was thankful.

He felt that something about this evening was a blessing. *A blessing that should be returned in some way. But how? By a club . . . or by himself?*

The whirling in his ear fell to a less noticeable hum as he crawled into the covers.

***

BRANDON SUDDENLY SAT UP FROM the passenger seat and rubbed his eyes. He couldn't recall how he had gotten there, but it felt oddly normal, like any other late-night trip home with Germy.

Windshield wipers swept on the slowest setting as a few raindrops fell. Leaning slightly to the left then slightly to the right, the old Accord made its way east through the Blue Ridge foothills. It didn't seem like there were any other cars on the road. The dim headlights provided enough light to see the bare road before them.

Brandon wondered why Germy wasn't talking.

Removing a pack of Camels from his pocket, he rolled the

29

window down enough to ash his cigarette. The car lighter popped out.

After he lit the cigarette with a puff, he turned his head to his left. "How long was I out?"

"Not long," said a voice sounding even deeper than Germy's usually did. "A little while."

Brandon took another drag. "It feels like I haven't slept in ages."

"I know the feeling."

Another trail of smoke rolled out into the night. "Did you want me to drive?"

"No."

The wipers made a slow swipe.

"Do-Gooder Brandon."

"Yes, Germy?"

"I've been meaning to ask you something. Where do you think all your talk of doing good . . . ends?"

Brandon sat back in his seat, the weight of sleep pulling him down and distorting his perception. The wipers made another round. As the rain slowed to a speckle on the windshield, it seemed as though the clouds were about to part. He took another drag.

"I don't know. I need a livelihood and . . . well, a life. I guess that's all any of us are trying to accomplish."

The driver smiled. "Yes, that's true."

"But I've been thinking lately. Too much, as you know. It seems like . . . with college ending, I might soon have a real chance at . . . doing something with my life. Finding meaning."

"Identity and existential crises. Happens to everyone, Brandon, especially at this age. You're still no different. Just as good."

"Well . . . no, I don't think so. Right now, it just seems like everyone wants this or that, whether it's something material or . . . more often, emotional. Social stature and pride. Thus all the career prep and social events. It's kind of limiting. I want . . . like a spiritual progression or . . . I don't know. But I know I'm different, maybe for better and for worse. Because I don't celebrate my differences; I mourn them. And that's what being truly different means, I think."

The clouds started to break enough for the sky to open, but there was little starlight.

"You don't have to be different," the driver responded. "It's a choice. You can take comfort in being a friend, being a family member, being a lover for someone." He paused for a moment. "But if you choose to be different, you really don't have to suffer. There's much greatness in being unique, being special, being above it. Think of it—rising to the top of some nonprofit, being successful and seen as virtuous. Either way, you know I'm on your side."

"Yeah." Brandon sat quietly for a moment, puffing his cigarette and mulling being special. "I guess the thing about that is . . . it's that comfort, emotional security," he continued. "The pride, the idea that I'm good no matter what I really think or really do, not having to face my con . . . science. That's the appeal of relativism. At least until you're left with all that insecurity, thus selectively applying morality to position yourself as beyond meaningful reproach." He looked back to the left. "Emotional security, it's a golden calf for the twenty-first century, for believers and nonbelievers alike. That's the popular pitfall I'm trying to avoid."

Aside from the dull hum of the engine, the empty road remained quiet.

Brandon finished his cigarette then pressed it into the full ashtray hanging out of the console. "You know, Germy?" He stopped for a moment, and then he kept tapping the end of his cigarette against the ashtray. "I . . . I might have to be different to get around that pitfall. Not because I want to be . . . but because I *have* to be. And there's nothing great about that. It's not virtuous. I'm a human being like any other, like you said. I need to accept myself and others as-is and find a way to make a real difference. Being different to make a difference. Not for pride, but conscience."

The driver sighed. "Do-gooder." He faced Brandon for a cold second then turned back toward the open highway. "It's always the same with people like you."

Brandon winced. "What do you mean?"

He smirked, his voice deeper and louder. "All you understand is pain and fear."

"Germy, what are you talking—"

"I'm going to say this because your unconscious mind will remember it while your conscious mind will not. Stop your little bullshit crusade. Just stop. You can keep telling yourself whatever you want to keep going, but you're all alone. Alone and unloved with no home. No attempts in your personal or professional life will change this. And I will ruin you physically, mentally, and emotionally if you come too close to putting right what I put wrong."

Brandon couldn't move. His eyes looked to the left, but they were afraid to see.

"There are many things I can do for you, but it appears that you only appreciate them when you're buried in pain and fear and will do anything to get out."

Brandon finally turned to see the driver, who also turned to look right back at him. Instead of Jeremy's eyes, he only saw two empty holes in a rotting face.

"And you will."

Brandon woke up screaming. He couldn't remember why.

***

IN THE OVERCAST AFTERNOON, HE worked up

the nerve to walk down to the High Country Pantry. He paced around the sidewalk for a few minutes, having a cigarette and mindlessly playing with his cell phone. As five p.m. approached, he watched the door as a few people walked out, only to watch it close and get locked. He watched as an elderly woman with glasses and sandy hair ambled across the street. Then he wondered why he didn't feel anything.

After walking back home, Brandon took out his cell phone with intent. He thought about calling his parents to wish them a happy Thanksgiving. He paced around again, wondering if they would answer or call him back later.

His phone sat illuminated in his hand. Seeing the label "Parents," Brandon felt a slight pinch of pressure in his chest and snapped his phone shut.

Sitting on his bed, Brandon looked at his Martin acoustic sitting on the guitar stand and realized he hadn't played in a week. Perhaps he could work on the song in A minor that he had been meaning to write. He had also been meaning to play along with B.B. King to work on his bends and phrasing. It reminded him of his impetuous attempt to play at Open Mic Night at the 11th Street Espresso House in his junior year of high school. He had stopped after his fourth song because he realized no one was paying attention. *Play for yourself,* he had heard from one of his friends. *Play for yourself.* But that wasn't a sufficient cause.

He stood up and went to his computer. He sat down and clicked open a browser.

Click, click. There were no new messages in his email.

Click, click. He checked his Gold Pavilion social media profile and looked at everyone's happy pictures from Oktoberfest, Halloween, and now Thanksgiving.

Scroll. Click, click. Refresh. Scroll. Click.

December

"HEY, BRANDON, IT'S GREAT TO have you here. Just fill out this sheet really quick, and we'll take it up after the meeting. Thanks!" Sarah Shea-Trivette handed him a clipboard then moved to shake hands with the next newcomer.

Brandon tried to not think about how her hands gesticulated or the mole in front of her right ear. Her blue T-shirt with "CAMPUS PROGRESSIVES," emblazoned in white ink above a heart containing a peace symbol, and nondescript jeans complemented her flowing strawberry blonde hair and composite natural elegance. She wasn't the kind of girl whom he ordinarily found beautiful because she was, in fact, ordinary. No tattoos like Marianne. No purple highlights in her hair like Katie. Ordinary and not elusive. Extraordinary in her ordinariness. But this fact itself was beautiful to him. The overcoming of his own preconception of preconceptions was beautiful. Even being there was beautiful.

To him.

And she was lovely, indeed. Swift and sweet to seemingly everyone. Of course, he tried not to think too much about it, but that was a regular promise to himself that he never seemed to keep. He thought she looked somewhat like *Aisling*.

With more than two dozen people present, the windowless and blank, gray room in the student union was almost full. Brandon looked to one side and saw two well-dressed women talking to a sheepish freshman with glasses, and then he looked to the other and saw a bearded man talking quietly to an older professor. The group was stereotypically collegiate, not only in their appearances but also in their impressionable and idealistic demeanors. Brandon understood this. He also understood that he fit this very stereotype, given the conversation he'd had with his mother at the dinner table a month ago.

Stepping up to the short podium, Sarah prepared to speak impromptu. "Thanks, everyone. Great to see you all. And I especially want to welcome all the new people here, thanks to all of our hard work recruiting.

"Let me start by saying that, even though the midterm election was not quite what we wanted"—a few people chuckled, and a few more groaned—"I think we've found great momentum. We have it nationally and we have it right here on this campus. We've stood up to say that we will not tolerate ignorance and greed. The other side can have their hate marches, and we'll just march farther—"

The group applauded.

"—because the stakes are still high, everyone.

"Why, in the twenty-first century, do we still have to tell people that college and healthcare are basic rights? We've come far, but the opposition won't stop pushing. They, the selfish rich and religious fundamentalists, won't stop until we move back. Way back. And you know what? We're not going back!"

A sharp "Woot!" started another round of applause.

"Thank you, guys, thank you. No, we believe in compassion. Yeah." There was an upward inflection in the middle of the syllable. "We believe in understanding. We believe in helping. This is the difference between us and them. It separates us from hate groups like the College Conservatives who disregard anyone who's not like them. I know, right? They won't stop until all women and people of color are subjugated. And then there are the Young Capitalists who believe in profit over people. Well, unfortunately for them, we're not afraid to speak up for compassion. We're not gonna let them cut one dime of public funding for corporate tax breaks."

More claps and cheers rang out.

Brandon's heart skipped a beat, and he felt a nervous excitement. The room was fired up.

"So, whether you're here because you want to fight corporate greed, or because you don't want some preacher trying to control your body, or you really care about people and want to help them . . . welcome. Let's make a difference together." She paused for a final round of applause. "Thanks. Get signed up for some of our holiday drives and the committee for next semester's events. We've got some great petitions and campaigns still going on in town, so get in touch."

The meeting broke into individual conversations; some brainstormed how to expand the availability of a documentary on social justice activism, while others discussed protesting corporations at the business school. A group of three debated whether or not to use their positions in the student government to issue a statement on the election. One thought that it would be a way to continue growing the club, while another thought that student government was merely a method of padding résumés.

Feeling unease in approaching these groups and trying to shrug off more than one source of hesitation, Brandon ambled through the crowd toward Sarah. He tried not to look at the mole. "Great speech. I'm on board," he said with a forced laugh.

"Aw, thanks!" She blinked and looked with a sense of familiarity at the gold print on the green T-shirt under his open peacoat. "Whoa. Did you go to Saint Monica's, down there in the Triad?"

"Oh, yeah," he answered. "Elementary to high school. Are you, um . . . from the Triad?"

"Nah. I just remember seeing those shirts at the track tournament. I grew up in the Triangle and went to OLF for the full twelve years. Yeah, my family was super involved at our parish."

"Oh, wow. How about that parochial education?" Brandon looked up and back down. Something spurned within him. It felt like hope. It terrified him yet continuously won him over with its allure. "If you don't mind me asking, do you still practice?"

Sarah nodded. "Absolutely. Well, I accept people of any faith, of course. But, personally, yeah, I'm still Catholic. Cradle Catholic, I guess. I really love the parish life, you know? There's nothing like it. Our youth group has a bunch of fun. I'm an officer in that group, too."

"Oh, that's so cool," he said.

"Yeah." She looked over his shoulder for someone else. "We had two great 5K runs last year. I wanted a marathon, but hey, that's how it goes. At least we got cool T-shirts from the corporate sponsors."

"Yeah. That's cool." He felt a phantom wince and shook it off into a grin. "It's good to get involved. For me, like . . . I think we learned some good values in those schools, you know, like compassion and understanding, right? And forgiveness. It's good . . . you know, when it inspires people to do stuff like this."

She narrowed her eyes and looked away. "Yeah. The Church's social teaching inspired me to study nonprofit management so I can run a social service organization after I graduate."

Brandon's smile lit up his face, and he listened through his cautious thoughts. *Extraordinary. Is this her?* So many others didn't believe in much of anything, and now it seemed that there was someone who did. *And she not only believes,* he thought, *but she's inspired to act. To become the change.* It was apparent to him that she was inspired to do benevolent things not for herself but for others. And thus a partner of his dreams. *We could do good together,* he thought. *This might be her.* He didn't want to think it, but he did anyway. *Ais—*

"It's pretty obvious that Jesus was a progressive liberal. I mean, come on, caring about the poor, acceptance, compassion, sharing? Pretty obvious. What a socialist hippie, right?"

"Ha, yeah," Brandon said. "I mean . . . yeah, that's pretty much it. Questioning authority and the power structure, too. And the whole . . . well, compassionate love is about helping your neighbor. Pretty hard to do that without social programs and a progressive tax code, right?"

Sarah wrinkled her nose. "Well, you need social justice and equality most of all."

"Right, right." He started to feel nervous again. "It's about society moving forward and . . . you know, doing good." Hope sparked. There was some scrap of typical romance there, but there was also something much more prominent and much more important—a sense of purpose.

Imaginative possibilities shimmered. A flash of pending weekend volunteerism and eventual professional meaning came out of a thought of friendship and basic human connection. A connection so mocked and ignored in an infotainment generation made of cynicism. The idealistic words of goodness he had longed to hear from another had finally been heard.

"And . . . love, yeah, you know."

She smiled. "Yeah. You're in the right place!"

Brandon grinned wider. "You know, I haven't really been active in the parish life since school. I'm interested in doing good stuff, maybe a service or . . . spiritual growth stuff. Are there meetings, or . . . is there some way I can help out a food drive or . . . ?"

"Check out the website. They have all sorts of stuff. You should really come out."

He didn't notice his face tightening up again. "What do you and your friends do?"

"Yeah, check the website. They have plenty of options. And we do stuff here sometimes. We're doing MLK Day again this year. You should check it out. We get shirts for that, too!"

"Oh, cool."

Sarah turned back toward the group around them. "You need to mingle! We've got some great people here. Maybe you can help with the petitions. You seem like an outgoing guy."

Brandon forced a laugh. "I'm not sure about that, but I can certainly find a way to help out with some . . . you know, get things together."

"Great, thanks." Sarah picked up a clipboard. "Good to meet you, Brandon!" She shook his hand fast and warmly then walked away.

Standing quietly for a moment, away from the bustling room, Brandon replayed the conversation in his head. As it faded into a static, he tried to remember his thoughts coming into the meeting. He questioned his own intentions.

One minute of ambling passed, and then another. He slowly paced a few feet over then back. Before his thoughts found coherency, he looked to his right and noticed a club member disassembling a folding table display by himself.

"Here, let me get that." Brandon grabbed the edge of the table before it hit the floor.

"Oh, thanks, man," the member responded, picking up the other end. They both turned it over and folded the legs in together.

"Do you need a hand with those boxes or pamphlets or

anything?"

"No, I think I've got it. But thanks, man." He grabbed the two small boxes underarm then picked up the table with the other before shuffling toward the door.

Looking back at the dispersing group, Brandon tried to remember his thoughts from a few minutes ago. He was now yearning hard to be a regular member of this group. To be accepted. Noticing his vanity, he tried to turn his thoughts toward how he could help between now and the next meeting.

From the corner of his eye, he saw Sarah chatting with two other students. A moment passed. He noticed her, but she did not notice him.

Anxiety welled up as he tried to be casual in his goodbye. "See you, Sarah!"

***

BRANDON'S UNCLE HAD A WRY smile as he threw back a swig of microbrew. "I always figured you were a bleeding heart."

A few flurries blew across the hazy gray sky, but it was not a white Christmas. Bing Crosby sang soft baritone on the stereo. The Marcels, Olsens, and Whiteners ambled around the candlelit kitchen island, sat by the fire in the living room, and chatted in the foyer. Three teenaged cousins argued about football by the wreathed door to the garage.

"I'm just saying, I think there's something to be said for a living wage," Brandon responded. "I mean, I know all the models of how the market is supposed to work, but it doesn't. A living wage sets a standard so that people can buy necessities and not have to live in squalor while working." He adjusted his grip on the Waterford glass in his right hand, but he didn't take a sip.

"No, no, I agree. I just hope you haven't broken this to

your mom yet." The middle-aged man laughed. "Or, if you have, I just hope you didn't implicate me, ha. I can wear a sweater-vest and talk sports, but my environmental science gig and Widespread albums kind of give me away."

"Well, maybe we should talk about it. Change begins at home, right? I mean, there's—"

"Oh, come on." The lanky middle-aged man tilted his scruffy face back. "It's the holidays; your dad would be pissed, too. Go start the revolution on your campus."

Brandon looked down. "It should be okay to talk about critical issues, especially among family members."

"True to your stripes, huh? I was pretty fired-up in those days, too." He took another gulp of his beer. "Yeah, good times. Enjoy it while it lasts. You have your whole life ahead of you."

The young man looked back up with a little incredulity. "That's what they say, too. I want to do some good. I don't think these supposed best years of my life have been conducive to that end."

"But kid, you're getting all that knowledge thrown at you. That's what you're going to use, you know? That's why you're there. Sure, get all serious and follow your deep thoughts if you want, but you're not going to be all Lao Tzu or whatever, spitting Taoist verses at forty-one. Ha!"

Brandon exhaled and tried not to think about his palpitations. "You're using the future tense. It's like it's always preparation. Preparation for preparation. Preparation for what?"

"That's what being young is all about. That's why you have to enjoy it. Seriously, forget about good this and that and finding Ms. Right. Have a drink and find Ms. Right Now. Don't worry about principles and differences. You're already changing things, right? Just indirectly."

Brandon looked at him again, this time with a touch of defiance. "Yeah, it's always indirect. Preparing for change in the future and indirectly changing things now. And advice like not actually working in social services, just work corporate and donate. It's always an arm's length distance. Just like friendships. Just like family."

His uncle rolled his eyes and took a hard swig. "Okay, whatever. If you're gonna get upset over this—"

"I'm not trying to—"

"Change . . . whatever," his uncle said. "You'll get over it by the time you're my age; trust me. Worry about being direct when you have kids and a gut." He turned back toward the lively festivities.

Looking over his uncle's shoulder, Brandon saw that his mother was laughing with one of his older cousins. He opted to not join their conversation about the hotel mix-up during the family trip to Myrtle Beach the previous summer.

After the failed attempt at discussing the living wage with his family, he made other plans. Opening the door to the garage, he edged himself between the luxury SUV and mounted bicycles to the backyard and carefully positioned himself behind a steep hedge.

He lit a cigarette and placed the lighter back in his left pocket. As his hand brushed past his cell phone, he just had to check it. Nothing. No texts, despite his eight sent texts of Christmas tidings. He tried to ignore the palpitations with thoughts of Marianne.

***

THE SOFT BLUE GLOW OF the laptop provided little lighting to the cold upstairs room. Having two days left before the New Year and a week before having to face his last semester, Brandon felt urgency. Urgency to express his thoughts, and urgency to hear those of others. Urgency to have a semblance of purpose and human connection while he was still young and ostensibly free. Thus, with little thought and much abandon, he made the anxious decision to take his intellectual pursuits to the latest frontier and last refuge of public discourse: internet forums.

Having been thoroughly flamed on roughly every previous attempt, he knew the likely consequences all too well. He also recognized his own naivety in the belief that this pinnacle of communication technology could be a place in which substantive discourse happened. The very fact of elevating the pool of discussion from his disengaged family, at school, work, coffee shops, and every other venue to exponent upon exponent to billions around the globe was still inspiring.

Alas, the global pool of discourse had no chlorine.

Clicking through the GeeNews-posted blogs, Brandon found AlterProgress, "Progressive Online Activism for Today and Tomorrow." Tabs across the top of the page featured sections on daily news, social justice, civil liberties, reproductive rights, and the environment. The headline article was: "The Party of Privilege is Blocking Us Again." The young Marcel quickly created a login account with the name MannaGainst. Then he sat back, checked his cell phone one last time, and then looked up and clicked on the "Comments" button.

Scrolling through thousands of comments, he found a few that resonated.

"*We need new legislation,*" wrote FedXTC1913 in a new thread. "*If we had a living wage, the companies would have higher employee productivity. Eventually, some of the greedy bosses would come around. But the neo-confederate nullifiers will never come around.*"

A dozen comments followed.

OlpheliasDress stated in the next thread, "*Compassion begins here. How can we preach foreign aid if we still make workers starve in our own cities? It's judgmental hypocrisy. I've got a link to that new Urban Institute study on income distribution. I'll find it and post later."*

Brandon smiled. He felt the tinge in his heart of connecting to those who shared his passion for making a difference in the exact ways in which he wanted to make a difference. They demonstrated informed opinions and had no qualms expressing these opinions to the like-minded. His apprehension for any interaction began to melt as he read the responses.

"That's the thing they don't get," stated Manna4all in the first response. *"They go ad hominem and say we're just lazy and want handouts, but WE are the WORKERS. We're the productive ones. Capitalism is theft!"*

Adding a modicum of comfort to his bourgeoning sense of belonging, Brandon saw this as the point to join the fray. *"Well-said indeed,"* he started. *"It's not about handouts; it's about social justice and equality. Prosperity should flow from the ability of all to the needs of all."* He hit the "Post" button then sat back with the smallest sense of satisfaction. A tinge of nervousness came over him, but the feeling in his chest did not pull. His ears did not ring.

Yet.

It didn't take long for a response to come. However, it was not as expected. Brandon's epinephrine and cortisol jumped as his all-too-brief feeling of belonging collapsed.

"Hey, MannaGainst, you got imitation being the most sincere form of flattery down to a science," wrote Manna4all. *"First my username, and then you misquote Marx. Wow, dude, if you want to talk with the big kids, come back with your high school diploma."*

Brandon's hands shook too much to type. He stepped out of his chair and paced around the cold room. He scratched the side of his head. After a moment, he spoke aloud to himself. "I'm trying to . . . This doesn't make sense. It's not rational.

Why would my own side argue against me? Why is this happening?" He gathered his thoughts and sat down to type his response.

"*Manna4all, I wasn't trying to be imitative. I just thought it was a good, succinct statement to affirm your views. I also campaign for a living wage. I'm an activist with the Campus Progressives. Could you let me know what you think is the most practical way to pass meaningful legislation?*"

A few fast minutes passed before the Manna4all responded with, "*Well, I don't need your self-important "affirmation," as you say. Campus, huh? Let me guess, you go to a southern pseudo-college and just read Marx for the first time, right? You're making us look bad. Stop.*"

While the room inverted in Brandon's panicked mind, FedXTC1913 also responded. "*Either that or more rich white kids with rich white kid guilt. Rich white kid's burden, yeah? There's a bunch of those in the south. I think you called it, Manna.*"

Rubbing his temples until his thoughts regained coherency, Brandon began to form his next response. "*I don't know why you're assuming my race, region, and socioeconomic status, but this isn't about me. You each have expressed supporting legislation to advance the living wage. We shouldn't argue style or semantics with each other, but argue against those who believe the myth that the minimum wage raises unemployment. We should refine our views among ourselves by discussing things like labor pricing, the means of production, and monopsony of employment.*"

Brandon tore himself away from the keyboard, grabbed his coat, and then ran out of the room, down the pitch dark staircase and threw open the back door. He lit his cigarette before the door slammed shut behind him.

Standing on the porch and looking over the well-lit houses of his parents' neighborhood, he took a hard drag. He tried not to think of the ad hominem yet accurate assumptions of his background while surrounded by McMansions. To no avail. There seemed to be a faint scent of feces in the air. It could have been a neighbor's terrier after a late walk or his mind's assessment of life in the here and now.

It occurred to him that his parents might have heard the door slam and come downstairs, but at the moment, he didn't care if they caught him.

A cloud of smoke drifted from his open lips, held for a second, and then ran with the winter breeze.

Why?

He knew he shouldn't be surprised at how the conversation had gone, but it didn't lessen his profound disappointment. A hundred course credits and a high grade point average spoke to his formal education, which he had thought might guard his ego against the derision of the anonymous hordes. But, at that moment, he knew more than ever that, no matter how many A's he earned or years he waited for a meeting of well-intentioned and well-educated minds, the faceless world wide web was no more interested in discourse than the faces of his minuscule corner of that world. And yet, this did nothing to subdue his next series of fruitless attempts.

Sitting back down at the computer with renewed smoke stench, Brandon found a new response.

"*It looks like MannaGainst isn't just another fake intellectual,*" OlpheliasDress wrote. "*He's a fake economist, too. Did you study supply and demand, Manisshit? We're supplied with real intellect here, so we demand that you babble somewhere else. Like with batshit twats of the reichwing, so you can annoy them for us but feel right at home with fake intellect, Manisshit.*"

Brandon took a deep breath then typed, "*Per your earlier comment, you support compassion and do not support being judgmental. How are your personal insults and judgments congruent with that comment? Do we want to be witty sciolists or wise scholars?*"

Not even a minute later, OlpheliasDress posted an even more incendiary response. "*You don't know a damn thing about compassion or scholarship, rich white boy. The oversensitivity is a dead giveaway. You're an embarrassment to whatever little fake school your parents pay for. And YOUR comment demonstrates how judgmental YOU are, Manisshit. Here's your New Year's Resolution: shut the fuck up. Just STOP."*

Brandon's already elevated blood pressure rose higher as his sympathetic nervous system instantly brewed another consciousness-racking and lifespan-threatening concoction. He sat back up again, paced around again, and rubbed his temples again. The thoughts wouldn't stop. No longer could he focus on theories and practices of price, social policy, or wage laws. He could only focus on his own deficiencies and his final failure to connect on his driving passion.

His fingers began to type . . . then stopped. His chest weighed heavily and the tinnitus had begun. Placing his face in his hands, he wished he had brought his old acoustic guitar on the trip. As it stood, he was completely alone.

Then the corner of the laptop screen changed a few pixels. It was a private message alert. *Great*, he thought. *Now it's even more personal.*

He inhaled sharply then let out an audible sigh. *Click.*

"You're right, and you're wrong. They should be focusing on the issues, but they're not, and you can't change that. You can only change yourself. The State doesn't understand this. In fact, the State doesn't understand anything. It's just people. People with all the same faults as all other people, but with an added conceit wrapped in power. Private business seeks profit, as we all do in our own lives, but the State seeks power. Business and State are especially destructive in collusion. The State is force, nothing more and nothing less, and with no guarantees of efficiency or goodwill. Certainly no guarantee of rights in my lifetime. If it is not limited to guarding the only natural rights—life, liberty, and property—for all people, it becomes destructive to these rights. I don't want my rights protected because I'm gay; I want them protected because I am an individual who happens to be gay. Question your assumptions. Put down the Marx and Keynes and pick up the Bastiat and Mises.

"But don't question your intellect; you have it. It's just that, like so many outlets for discussion, this forum is a den of wolves. A pack of collectivist wolves. Whatever our generation says about intellect, here or elsewhere, you should know this: to truly think for yourself means being prepared to be by yourself. The individual is supreme over the State and the horde. But, despite our different beliefs, as long as we care for each other, individual to individual, even as strangers . . . we are never alone.

"From one to another, take care – Batshitreichwing."

The reflex was to roll his eyes, but Brandon didn't. He realized that his heart rate had slowed and his breathing was back to normal. His adversarial desire to argue had been replaced with a sense of gratitude, though the temptation to argue still lingered. Instead, Brandon shut his laptop and looked away.

Thoughts were turning. Paradigms were shifting. More important than his political sentiments was his faith in human nature, which seemed to be cautiously rejuvenated.

He looked up, scratched his unshaven chin, and then turned back around toward his laptop and opened it. Putting his earbuds in place, he opened his mp3 player and clicked on Liszt's "Nuages Gris" piano solo to give voice to the grave uncertainty and haunting conflict topped with uneasy optimism. He anticipated that the coming year would be different than so many of the previous ones. That it would be *tomorrow* instead of just tomorrow. That somehow, through the daily delicate wreckage of the postmodern human heart, there would be a connection.

That there would be love.

January

"SARAH, GOOD TO SEE YOU! How did the holidays treat you?"

Sarah Shea-Trivette raised an eyebrow at Brandon as she walked with folded arms along the sidewalk in front of the Convocation Center. They were both clad in black, wool coats, multi-colored scarves, and full backpacks, feeling warm enough under wisps of winter clouds and low daylight. "Hey, guy. It was pretty good. Midnight Mass and family time. How about you?"

"Pretty much the same. My parents had both sides of the family over. I tried to get my progressive uncle all excited about some of the stuff we're doing, but he didn't want to talk politics on the holidays, you know?"

"Yeah."

"So, I did some digging online and found a few resources. There's a great study on the living wage from the Urban Institute that I think we could reference in our materials. Small but solid findings. Promising, you know? There's another one that's even more convincing about how corporations could actually benefit from enhanced regulations."

Sarah gave him a quizzical look. "Who did that study again?"

"The Urban Institute."

"I haven't heard of them. I don't think we need to change our materials for an obscure source."

"Oh. Well, I think they've got a good reputation," Brandon

responded. "Could I send you the link? You've gotta see this study. The econometrics look pretty tight and . . . you know, we could . . . really make the case about fighting deregulation. It's ultimately about win-win scenarios."

"Well, I don't know about all that. I mean, sure, feel free to send it to me. But we're covered."

The couple approached the largest intersection on campus where several other students stood to wait.

As Sarah watched the traffic light, shifting impatiently for it to change, Brandon turned to look at her. And there it was. That one little mole, sitting just in front of her right ear. He smiled, and then he turned back toward the traffic light as it changed.

"Finally," she said.

"Where are you heading?"

"I'm going over to the student union to get my regular cappuccino and see if they've posted the new service opportunities for the semester. They usually have some good ones for MLK Day. I thought I'd check out the options and see if they fit our project."

"Oh, service opportunities? I've been hoping to do more of that," he said. "Do you mind if I come with you?"

Sarah paused for a second. "Oh, sure. You might have to wait a while at the coffee shop."

"No problem."

As the two strolled quietly through the central grove of campus, it occurred to Brandon that other people seeing them might think they were together. This also made him smile.

They walked up the steps to the student union, visible breaths disappearing around them. They waved to a fellow club member talking on his cell phone outside the door then entered, where Sarah headed straight for the coffee stand.

Brandon hardly noticed the thirteen minutes pass before Sarah rejoined him again with a steaming cup in hand. She took a sip as they walked side-by-side down a long, gray hallway to a glass case next to a large bulletin board outside of the Student Government office. The displays were filled with new posts for the semester.

"It looks like Beltway needs volunteers again," Sarah said as she skimmed the wall of posts. "They do some great work with the disabled."

"That's cool," Brandon responded. "What kind of volunteer duties?"

"Um . . . I can't remember. I did it one afternoon during my freshman year. We just, y'know, spent time with the disabled people."

"Oh, okay."

They continued to scan the different posts, side-by-side, boy and girl, careful and capricious, beast and beauty. Lost and found.

" 'Blue Ridge Footprints'," Brandon read aloud. " 'Regional Emergency Services.' That sounds like work we should be doing."

Sarah took a sip and gave him a look. "Well, if you think these services should be provided by privately-funded nonprofits. I think we need government oversight."

"Well, I mean, uh . . . whatever it takes, you know? Service and . . . volunteering, right?"

"Hmm," she said. "Yeah." She stopped for a moment and checked her watch. "Well, good luck. I have to head to class in a few minutes, so I'll catch you online. Hey, why don't you post that article on Gold Pavilion? That's more positive than your statuses about not finding someone to jam guitars, grumpy. You can't force people to play guitar with you, but you can promote social justice."

"Ha, yeah, good idea. I didn't realize anyone saw that. I . . . yeah." He looked back at the board. "So . . . are you thinking of, uh . . . volunteering at Beltway or . . ."

Sarah took another sip and looked at him with intent. "Why?"

"Uh, why—"

"Why do you want to know?"

Brandon blinked. "Oh, just curious. Looks like a good place, so I was thinking of going there."

Sarah rolled her eyes. "I think I know where this is going."

"What, you mean—"

"Oh, come on."

Brandon suddenly became flushed. A deep breath didn't quite suppress his nervous shaking, so he reflexively checked his cell phone, and then looked back up at the board.

"Just be honest, Brandon."

"Honest? Well . . . I'm honestly trying to find some good service opportunities. I'm not trying to—"

"Find a way to ask me out?"

"Yeah. Yeah, I—"

"Do you like me?"

Brandon looked away and took another breath. "Okay. Yes, I do, but what's more important right now is to—"

"Real smooth," she scoffed. "I mean, I've seen some creative ones, but I just think this whole act takes the cake."

"It's not an . . ." Reason and passion came together and stopped. It was as though his mind's eye was a frozen screen. With a quick gulp, he reset it as best he could. "Sarah, right now, I want to get more involved, and that's why I came to the meeting, and that's why—"

She shook her head. "Listen, guy, that's fine. That's fine. You're a nice guy. A little angsty, but nice enough. You're welcome any time. But just know that I'm not only about change and compassion, but also honesty. So be honest with me from now on, okay?"

Brandon's face fell. "Okay. I am. I just—"

"Then I'll see you next time," she said with an abrupt smile. "Making the world a better place is about happiness, right? So be happy—happy and honest. No more grump, okay? There's nothing to be grumpy about. Life is good. Be happy. Good vibes. You can do it, guy. We can do it! See ya."

"Oh, okay. Definitely."

***

FIRST, HE STRUMMED A MESSY A minor chord. Then a D. Then he strummed a tighter A minor.

Brandon sat on his computer chair in front of the music stand, thinking of many things, other than the notes before him. Thinking and dreaming, his mind was insatiable. He dreamed of a call or text on his cell phone. He dreamed of wearing a blue club T-shirt. He dreamed of little orange notification boxes appearing on his Gold Pavilion profile. He dreamed of a home. Above all, he dreamed of Aisling.

He strummed the A minor again when his cell phone lit up. Reaching for it felt like a dog snatching a tossed bone.

"Hey, Germy."

"Word," his friend greeted.

"How goes it?"

"Chillin' like Bob Dylan on penicillin. You?"

"The same. What's up?"

"We haven't hung out or whatever for, like, a month, so maybe we could get smashed and go burn a Barbie or something. Barbie-Q. Find us that musty-ass junkyard in the hills, because I've got some Pyrodex and a fifth of Smirnoff."

Brandon stuck his tongue in his cheek. "Wait a sec. Are you talking about a mysterious place?"

"No, I'm just talking about vodka."

"Vodka, vodka, vodka. Sure. Let me get my keys."

Germy cleared his throat. "We need to catch up on life crap. What's going on?"

Brandon rolled his eyes at himself. "Other than not connecting with family, not connecting with strangers on the internet, and not connecting with the new girl, not a whole lot."

"It's a beautiful day in the neighborhood."

"I know, Germ, I know. But hey, you actually caught me while I was playing guitar, so at least I've been doing something worthwhile."

"Yeah, that's good. I hope you're not bothering with all of that music theory crap. You don't need structure. You don't need order. You don't need anything. Just rock it to Russia."

"Well, some of us are mere mortals in the realms of creativity and still need maps. How is your photography project going?"

"I haven't done a damn thing."

"Figures. But yeah, it's not like I'm trying to make drama. As always, I'm trying to connect. Yeah, yeah, I don't *need* to connect, as you say, but there was this Maslow guy in psych class that had some different ideas about that."

Germy Kuhn scoffed. "That's perfectly fine. But tell me . . . are you really feeling more mentally healthy or anything? I don't think your endless puppy-dogging of your family, your new club, your new crush, or random people on the damn internet are going to pay dividends. They talk about dividends in your economics, right?"

"Uh, yeah."

"So, there you go. Solved your problem. I should start charging shrink fees for my pep talks. So, if you're not begging some guy walking down the street to hear your new political ideas, come on over and we'll crank out some explosions."

Brandon threw on his coat, threw open his apartment

door, and promptly torched the end of a cigarette. "Sounds like a plan." He inhaled. "So, what did you do for the holidays again?"

"Family junk; that's about it. My brother had his new girlfriend over."

Looking over the gray streets, Brandon exhaled and tapped his cigarette. "Yeah, my sister talked about her new promotion. And my dad talked about his new Mercedes. Important stuff." He took a deep drag. "It's not always like this. Under all the posturing, I think someone gets it. My mom, maybe."

"Gets what?"

"Wanting a point in all this. Like a house isn't a home unless there's actual love in the family."

Germy scoffed again. "Ha, family. A quaint notion."

The tiny embers of Brandon's squeezed cigarette butt fell onto the sidewalk. "Germy, you'd make a good family man if you believed in family. Just something to think about."

"Ha, beliefs. It's all structures." Germy sniffed then cleared his throat. "I think plenty."

***

THE GYMNASIUM WAS EMPTY EXCEPT for two basketball nets and ten folding tables when the nineteen volunteers entered for the Martin Luther King, Jr. Service Day. Under their winter jackets and scarves, each wore a yellow "Campus Progressive Service Day" T-shirt, emblazoned on the front with three stick figures jumping and with their hands held up high. The back of the shirt featured sixteen corporate sponsor logos, each of comparable size and evenly spaced.

When the students realized the volunteer director hadn't arrived, some chatted while others pulled out their cell phones.

A few minutes later, the two leaders arrived. Sarah Shea-Trivette strolled in casually, appearing feckless and elegant with her event T-shirt on top of her crisp, high-collar, white blouse with a green Prada bag on her arm. Pulling her phone out of her bag, she texted furiously then shoved it back into her bag and ran her fingers through the ends of her hair.

Conrad Evans, the volunteer director of a local emergency services agency, shuffled in through a back door and approached her. He was a gentle giant, nearing sixty, with thick glasses and a scraggly beard.

"Hey, Ms. Sarah," Conrad said.

"Hi. We're only here for so long," she said curtly.

"I'm sorry," Conrad responded. "Here, let me get everyone where they need to go, and then we can start sorting the clothes and toys right when the truck pulls up."

"Good. We maybe have two hours, so you and your people . . ." Sarah trailed off as she looked for one of her friends then whipped back around. "You all need to make sure that things run correctly. On your end, I mean." She turned back around. "There you are, Becca!"

Brandon walked in slowly and then held the door to prevent it from slamming shut. In his nervousness, he couldn't figure out the directions, so the extra ten minutes he gave himself to make the walk weren't enough. He had just missed the T-shirt handout, so the tattered G3 concert shirt under his jacket would be a constant reminder of his mistake to everyone.

"Hey, are we getting started?" he asked one of the volunteers who had arrived on time.

"I don't know what's going on," she replied. "I think we just sit tight until something happens, really."

Brandon walked through the crowd to a student whom he recognized from the Campus Progressives. "How's it going? I'm trying to figure out what we're doing now."

"Not sure," he answered. "Sarah talked to that big guy with the beard, so I'm going to catch up on texts until I hear something." He watched a girl walking past then turned back to Brandon. "Did you not get your shirt, man? You gotta get one of these. We're going on a pub crawl after this."

"No, I missed it," Brandon said. "Let me go ask that guy."

Conrad was cleaning his glasses when Brandon approached him. He put them on and blinked. "Oh, hey," he said.

"Hey. I was told you might know what's going on," Brandon asked.

"We're waiting for a truck to arrive with all the donations," Conrad responded. "We'll get everything set up on these tables and start sorting as soon as they arrive."

"Sounds great," Brandon said. "Can I help set them up?"

The grizzled gentleman had a baffled look. "Help? Oh, no, thanks. I think we're okay. A nice gal from the Young Capitalists brought over all the boxes earlier. I tell ya, I'm a pretty liberal guy myself, so I don't why . . . you know, right-wing folks would want to donate to help folks. But hey, whatever it takes to make a difference, right?"

"Uh . . . yeah. Absolutely!" Brandon said with a touch of confusion.

"Thanks for offering."

"Sure, yeah." Brandon was feeling hard cognitive dissonance around the notion that a Young Capitalist would want to donate to emergency services. Or any charitable cause. "So, why . . ."

Conrad looked up at Brandon with raised eyebrows under his thick glasses.

Brandon shook his head and refocused. "Sorry, spaced out. I didn't catch your name."

"Oh, it's Conrad," he replied. "Conrad Evans."

"Good to meet you. I'm Brandon. Thanks for getting all this going."

"Nice meeting you, Brandon. Sure thing."

Brandon walked back to the group, and Conrad smiled.

After fifteen minutes of volunteer socializing, the truck pulled up. One of the agency drivers opened the back door while the other gave instructions. The large trailer truck was filled to the top with moving boxes full of clothes and toys, all to be sorted for families in need.

As the volunteers began to gather, a particularly muscular volunteer pushed through to make sure he was the first to start. Another volunteer took pictures as the first box came down. The muscular volunteer pushed aside a rolling table and caught the first box and requested that two more be placed on top. After a few volunteers followed his challenge, Brandon pulled the rolling table around the other side and quickly stacked nine boxes on it. Several people jovially jeered him about cheating and being lazy, but he told himself to not take them seriously and to keep moving. The truck was soon empty and the boxes were then opened to be sorted.

Standing behind the folding table, Brandon took out his keys and cut open a box. There was a neat stack of four pairs of pants, a big bag of tube socks, a corner full of books, and several plastic packages of action figures. He picked up one of these packages and looked at it. "Super Wingman Fighter VII." It was an armored figurine colored olive green and bright yellow, placed next to a little plastic rifle and other futuristic combat accessories. Brandon placed the package back down and picked up a book. It was a large, glossy book seemingly meant for a young child, perhaps one who likes cats. *The Purple Kittens Meet New Friends*. The three cartoon kittens on the cover had lavender fur with darker purple stripes and big, wide eyes.

Time slowed down. Brandon took a few seconds to let his heart swell with what was happening before him. He placed the action figure neatly in the box at his feet then marked the sheet as he had been instructed. Picking up the book, he looked at it for a second then placed it gently in another small box and made the mark on the sheet.

His face weighed down under the burden of his eyes. He mentally told himself not to make a scene. Regaining his composure, he gently but quickly unloaded the larger boxes and sorted each item appropriately.

A few minutes passed. It seemed as though all the items were going to find their place eventually, perhaps within the next hour. Brandon let out a sigh of elusive contentment.

"How's it going on your side?" an African-American in her late-forties asked Brandon. He liked her voice.

"Oh, it's going just fine. How about you?"

"Much better now that people are moving!"

Brandon smiled. "Yeah, Conrad got us squared away."

"Yeah, he's a real asset for our organization. Seems sheepish, but just you wait to hear him on politics, ha. Oh, sorry, I work with him as the program manager. Name's Vicki. What's yours?"

"Hi, Vicki! I'm Brandon. I'm here with the Campus Progressives."

Vicki scratched the side of her head through her long, curly hair. "That's good. Although, I'm not seeing this year's shirt on you. But hey, thanks for coming. We need more progressive voices in our community getting out there and . . . creating systemic change, right? Make things happen."

"Yeah, definitely!"

"That's right. It's not real change if we just talk and not get the work done and done well."

From the corner of Brandon's eye, he saw a group of his fellow college student volunteers congregating around a large box. They opened it and found a collection of basketballs. With a spatter of shouts, a two-on-two game started up on the opposite end of the gymnasium. Brandon paused for a moment and watched them.

"So, when you're not bugging this kind lady, you're watchin' the guys play hoops, is that how this works?" Sarah asked as she approached the table.

"Oh, sorry," Brandon said, fumbling an empty box as he awkwardly arranged his work surface. "No, I was . . . yeah."

"Miss, he's no trouble at all," Vicki said. "He's already unpacked all those boxes there and marked them off as asked. A real trooper, this guy."

"Sorry, Sarah," Brandon said.

Sarah folded her arms and glared at Brandon. "You know, apologizing is a sign of weakness."

"Oh, sor . . . I . . . yes, I've heard that."

"You want to show that compassion, right? You really want to serve like we do, right?"

Brandon looked her in the eye. "Of course."

"Good!" Her expression was warm again. "So stay focused so we can get out of here." She turned back and faced the other side of the gym. "Okay, guys, next point wins. We got a pub crawl!"

There were a couple of responsive shouts as the ball bounced loud against the gym floor.

Brandon was trying to stop the compulsion to replay the conversation in his head, but he couldn't. He knew he should have been thinking about Vicki's efficiency and kind words or how all of the properly sorted collections at his feet would mean more help for more people, but he wouldn't. He just thought about how much he wanted Sarah to understand him.

And then the tinnitus started. It held for a moment, but no thoughts of an old Eagles' song could mitigate the shrill. This one was different. It got louder. And then it got louder still. His right ear felt as though it was pulsating, waiting to burst and send some kind of pressurized pulp onto the scuffed gym floor. He held his weight upon the table with a wobbling arm.

"Fella, are you feeling okay?" Vicki asked. "Rest easy, now. You're doing fine."

Brandon couldn't respond.

As he grabbed either side of his head, his mouth hung open in pain. He staggered behind the table until he simply . . . fell.

"Oh, dear!" Vicki crouched down and put her hand on his back. "What can I do for you? Oh, dear." She tried to get someone's attention. "Hey! Can you come here a sec?"

The Morning Star smiled.

***

AFTER AN HOUR AND A half, the doctor cracked open the door, reading his notepad as he stepped inside. His wrinkled hands tossed a few pages up, and then he adjusted his glasses. A moment later, he spoke. "Why exactly are you here today?"

"I've been having more trouble with the tinnitus," Brandon said. "It's getting really bad. It feels like . . . It feels like my head is going to explode. Maybe there's another issue. I was hoping you had some more ideas of things I can try."

"The medication's not helping?"

"No, it hasn't helped."

"Not at all?"

"No, not at all. No change."

The doctor sat down on the rolling stool and put the chart under his elbow. He rubbed his chin lightly. "Do you still think this is from meningitis?"

Brandon looked down. "I don't know, but that would —"

"It's not; I'll tell you that right now. That was a long time ago."

Brandon started to look back up but then looked back down again. "Okay. So there's no long-term impact or any—"

"Do you think you're some kind of special case? That makes

no sense. Now, I've seen some great improvements in depression and anxiety with serotonin reuptake inhibitors—"

"I don't think it's the depression, but the anxiety still—"

"Oh, I'm sorry, son. I was thinking I was the one with a medical degree and thirty years of practice."

"No, I . . ." Brandon looked away. Something burned within him that felt like assertiveness. "I think there may be another cause, or something we can do to—"

"There is something. There are more SSRIs we can try." He pulled out his prescription pad. "Let's get you started on some—"

"No."

The doctor sat back and looked straight at Brandon. "*No* what?"

Brandon looked straight back. "I'm not going to keep taking these things forever. I've been on five medications, and all the latest one does is make me gag over the toilet every once in a while. And . . . you know, it just doesn't feel right. I feel like I'm just going through all the motions, you know? I still feel all the bad emotions. I don't get quite as upset, I guess. It's slightly better. But then I can't really feel the good emotions, either. And it . . . um, keeps me from . . . you know, finishing."

"Uh-huh, right. If you're having sexual trouble, we have to—"

"No, no, I'm just not interested."

"Oh, of course, son. But I think your girl—"

"There is no girl. It's just that I . . ."

The doctor dropped the clipboard down hard on the table. He stood up from the stool and kicked it out of the way. "If you don't want to try anything, I don't know why we're talking."

Within Brandon, there was welcomed defiance. "Because I paid the forty dollar copay."

The doctor opened the door. "Make sure to check out before you leave. Down the hall, second door on the right."

***

CLICK.

The sounds of the keyboard and the mouse joined the hum of the electric heater in providing the dissonant sonata of Brandon's apartment on a dark evening in late January. Every few minutes, he heard a car drive past. One of them shook the walls with its subwoofer bass. A few minutes later, he heard the girls from across the parking lot step outside—one of them was on her cell phone. A few minutes later, it was quiet again.

Click.

He knew he wouldn't get ahold of Germy. They had already seen each other a few weeks ago, and having two visits in a month was a rarity. Perhaps Kim would respond to a text. It hadn't worked the last three times, but the four-letter word sprung eternal. Matt usually did respond to his texts; that is, if a single word counted as a response. Shelly preferred instant messaging to texts. Even though she was always online, her frequency of response was roughly every other night. Tonight was an off-night. And Marianne wasn't answering her phone.

Brandon tried to remember what he wanted to discuss with . . . anyone. A reason was always helpful when resorting to calling his sister. In fact, she would probably be upset because she needed a quiet night before going into work the next day.

The cell phone snapped shut and he returned it to his pocket. The heater shut off.

He sat back in his desk chair with unusually proper posture, placing his hands neatly into his lap. He listened.

The winter wind blew through the stubby trees planted in front of the apartment. Two cars passed by, and then another. He tried to think about something other than the lack of responses and the

Sunday evening of cramming he would need to do for a test. Then his downstairs neighbor turned on his always-loud party playlist. This usually bothered him enough to make him resent his own lack of assertiveness. But on this night, he was actually grateful for the noise, because it would drown out the sounds of his upstairs neighbors having sex more than his earbuds could.

Leaning forward, he rubbed his right temple and tried to think of what he could do to prevent the billowing veil of anxiety from slowly covering him over the course of the evening. While the panic and tinnitus hadn't yet driven him to pick up his guitar, the notion of playing for enjoyment led to dreams of proficiency, which would, in turn, lead back to anxiety.

I am not proficient. I am not accepted. I am not good. I am Brandon. I am whatever. While he rationally knew that this notion, pervasive across all endeavors, could not always be true, it never stopped him from thinking it. Dreams were the things of children, the boon of the few greats and the curse of the many failures. Brandon had suspected for many years that he was the latter. Now he aspired for inadequacy.

Click.

Reaching for his pack of Camels with his left hand, Brandon fumbled with his lighter in his right, dropping it. He picked it up, grabbed his peacoat off the back of his computer chair, and went for the door. A few flurries blew into his apartment as he stepped outside and lit the cigarette. He exhaled forcefully and tapped his cigarette.

Looking over his small college town as he heard the war between the party playlist and foreplay, Brandon's perpetual introspection restarted. His privileged life. His prosaic life. He contemplated Sarah and his sent texts. The thought of

Marianne came as light as the flurries, harmonized by four faint chords of Lou Reed's classic "Satellite of Love," and then passed by again promptly. He worried about final due dates and monthly bills. He thought about net present value and networking with job contacts. He thought. And thought. And thought. He tapped his cigarette. The pressure and the ringing started again. Contemplation. Worry. Thought.

Aisling.

He took a deep breath. Then, forgoing the final drag, he squeezed the last embers onto the parking lot below and pinched the cigarette butt between two cold fingers.

Returning inside, he removed his coat and returned to the computer chair. Instead of checking the *6stringmartin89* email account, new AlterProgress postings, or the elusive but all-powerful little orange notification boxes on Gold Pavilion, he searched for old photographs.

"Snow, rustic house Blue Ridge." He found a really nice one from Newland. It even had a maple tree.

Aisling.

He closed the laptop lid and took another deep breath. Then he stood up and unbuttoned his shirt. Most likely, he wouldn't actually fall asleep for a few hours, so it was good to go to bed before midnight.

When he pulled the comforter over his shoulders, he closed his eyes and nuzzled his head against the pillow, imagining an embrace.

Flurries fell. He slowly inhaled through his nose, held it for a moment, and then exhaled just as slowly through his mouth. The thought of cover letters came but quickly dissipated as he thought about what kind of porch he could maintain on a small cabin off of an old highway in Watauga County. It could work. He could make enough managing a food pantry to keep up with a little cabin. But, most prominent of this dream was the empty vessel of who would join him on that porch.

Slowly, inhale through the nose, exhale through the mouth. Thoughts. Gentle thoughts. Peace.

Aisling.

***

WALKING FRANTICALLY ALONG THE CROWDED walkways, Brandon shuffled past designer label-clad underclassmen and texting juniors. He hadn't had time to grab his backpack on the way out of the apartment, so he had secured his collection of cover letters in a waterproof folder, as to guard against the distinct possibility of being knocked from his hand and into one of the piles of slush throughout the campus.

As he snatched his phone from his pocket to check the time, he had a fleeting thought: out of the twenty or so times he had pulled out his phone that day, this was the first time he actually had something to check.

One fifty-seven p.m. This meant he had less than three minutes to arrive on the third floor of the career center, which was located atop the steepest hill on campus, of course.

Starting out the climb, Brandon tried to think more about watching for ice patches and less about the futility of this meeting. His ears were numb, and the pressure in his chest pulled hard. Two and a half minutes later, flushed and quietly panting, he shook hands with a different counselor than the one that he had seen in the autumn. He didn't recognize the logo on this man's Polo shirt, either.

"Did you ever follow up with those contacts?"

"Most of them," Brandon replied. "Most of them."

"So, how many interviews did you get?"

Brandon inhaled. "None yet."

"You haven't? We're a few days away from February.

Time's a-wasting if you want a real job. You had a good internship, so what's the holdup?"

Brandon took a deep breath, remembering how he had spent the summer after his sophomore year as an unpaid accounting intern in one of the largest firms in the Triangle. By all accounts, other than his own, it had been a great opportunity. But, for all the lessons in advanced spreadsheet formulas and double-checking of paystubs in his fifty-hour workweek, the best financial lesson that he had learned that summer was that the institution of unpaid internships led inevitably to his first credit card debt. It had hit three thousand in as many months.

"Well, I . . ." Brandon sat up. "I've been trying to find some kind of job at a nonprofit."

"Nonprofit jobs? You're not going to be making much money doing that."

He exhaled and looked down. "I understand. But I think part of the reason I'm not having much luck with these other positions is that's just not where my heart is."

The counselor laughed. "Well, is your heart's in having a decent car and house, you're gonna have to make real money for those. Unless you like being in debt."

Brandon looked up. "Other than these student loans, the only time I've had debt was wasting my summer productivity on that unpaid internship for some great opportunity that never came."

"Okay, okay, chill. Why don't you work with that? That's how you get a real job, you know." He scratched his neck under the collar of his Polo shirt. "Get a real job, then you can donate to whatever charity you want."

"Yeah, I've heard that, but nonprofits need educated managers like anyone else, so that's . . ." Brandon trailed off, lost in his own reasoning.

"You want to be productive, you said? Then you want a real

job. Work a multinational. Don't waste your time with some charity. Even small businesses are better. I mean, I know this is college and you're young and idealistic and all that, but eventually, you have to grow . . . I mean, you know, think realistic, not idealistic."

Brandon tried to not roll his eyes. "I do want to be productive; that's the point. I want to make a real difference, not play some elaborate game for the promise of money."

The counselor tossed the file across the desk then leaned back in his chair. "Okay, okay, I get it. You don't want to be working for the man, right? Yeah, I saw Campus Progressives on your profile. Okay, fine. You still have options to make that degree worth something. And you might be able to do charity stuff, too."

Brandon leaned forward. "Yeah, that's the idea. Thanks for hearing me out. So . . . you said there are options?"

"Yeah, with your interests, I think you can look closer into working for the feds."

"Work for the government?"

"Yeah. Working at the federal level can be good money. Not as much as a company, but good job security and benefits. They can use economics people in all sorts of ways. Work for the Federal Reserve. You can't get much closer to the money than that."

Brandon shifted in his seat. "Now, how about social services in the government?"

"Sure, if you're in Social Security or something. There are all sorts of social programs to save the world. Maybe you could do AmeriCorps to pay off your loans."

"AmeriCorps?"

"Yeah, it's like all sorts of service things and helping people."

68

"So . . . are these projects that the nonprofits . . . can't do; is that how this works?"

The counselor tilted his head up, and his eyes followed. "Ah . . . well, no, I think it's like . . . to do the stuff that people . . . aren't doing, you know? Because . . . that's what the government does, right? Like, social service, because that's . . . that's what charity is. You work for the government. That's what you're all about, public service and charity stuff, right?"

"I, well . . . I want to just do good."

"Okay, good. Let's see if we can write some more of those cover letters, then. Find some contacts with some federal government service agencies. Your friends over at the Campus Progressives can probably help you, too. It's all about networking."

"My friends?" Brandon smiled and adjusted his grip on his folder. "Yeah. They're helpful."

"Nice to have a crew, right? Yeah. It's all about networking. GPA, skills, and all of that don't matter much in the real world. It's all about networking. Be outgoing."

"I'll try. I'll send these letters out, and then talk to my friends and see if I can learn about the different government agencies. I'll get on it tonight."

"Good. Find some contacts, network, and be outgoing. That's all there is."

"Yeah." Brandon collected a few of his cover letters sitting before him, put them back into his folder, and shut it. "Whew, making progress. Yeah. Thanks!"

***

STARING ONCE AGAIN AT THE blue glow of his laptop screen, the accidentally intrepid job searcher's eyes glazed over a taskbar full of links to the United States Agency for International Development, the White House Office of Faith-Based and Neighborhood Partnerships, and the United States Department of

Labor Employee Benefits Security Administration. Each of these pages had tabs. And tabs within tabs. There were plenty of sections and subsections and sidebars, as well. There were also pop-up windows for additional logins, security protocols, and PIN numbers. Oh, the redundancy of PIN numbers.

Logging back into the expired Social Security page, it felt as though finding the employment page was a Sisyphean task. Postings were frequently listed but had no geographic pattern. He could start in a community coordinator position in Palm Springs or at an entry-level position in Duluth. He could even find an entry-level position in beautiful Meridian, Mississippi. If he were to make such a geographic leap, he would then have to convince the interviewer that he really could see himself settling in Anywhere, U.S.A., despite how slow starting over would be for a not-so-outgoing professional. And, even then, he'd still have to find a way to acquire the position-required security clearances that he knew would be problematic, given his long, detailed mental health history. And after that miracle, somehow be selected. And after that miracle, convincing himself that this was indeed the greatest good he could do.

But it all began with another fury of typing and clicking and printing and mailing and calling and waiting and looking for yet another employment webpage.

The webpage. All the webpages. All the text. All the information contextualizing other information for more information and more text. The text. The webpage. It all meant something. It was power. It was a way to do something. It was force. A means. It meant something. It meant his possible future. It meant his impossible past.

Brandon rubbed his eyes, grabbed a stack of papers off the printer, and then tossed them on top of his leather case. He checked his cell phone. The highlight stopped on a blank text from someone named James at four forty p.m. that day. He turned back toward the monitor.

The pixels. The text. The webpages. The logins. The passwords. The acronyms. The colors. The frames. The lines. The power. The power. The power. The power.

"I just . . ." He rubbed his eyes. "I just want to do good."

He put his face back in his hands. It felt peaceful for a moment. The world seemed to sit back and wait for his thoughts on what to do. On where to start. He took a breath and tried not to think.

There was a slight flutter in his chest. His right ear started to hum.

Taking a deep breath with the night, Brandon looked back at the soft glow of his computer screen. With a few taps of alt+F4, it all collapsed. Then, clicking on the internet browser, he found his way back to AlterProgress and typed in his password. One click, then another, and then he found himself looking back at the one comfort from a month ago—the email from his ideological adversary.

"*Whatever our generation says about intellect, here or elsewhere, you should know this: to truly think for yourself means being prepared to be by yourself. The individual is supreme over the State and the horde. But despite our different beliefs, as long as we care for each other, individual to individual, even as strangers . . . we are never alone. From one to another, take care – Batshitreichwing.*"

Brandon extended his fingers to type but stopped. He still couldn't decide if he wanted to argue the supremacy of the collective over the individual with Star Trek references or to express gratitude. Aside from the fact that this argument was one of the few remaining following his subconscious tectonic shift in his sociopolitical paradigm, he was just appreciative. It was simple kindness amid the soulless screen.

While such kindness could be found from someone in almost any ideology, Brandon almost missed the irony that his ideological friends had shunned him while his ideological foe had welcomed him. This realization formed his response.

"Thank you."

After hitting the "Send" button, Brandon sat back in his chair. He didn't notice, but his heart had slowed and his ears were clear.

Drumming his fingers on his knee to Black Sabbath's "Children of the Grave" in his head, a song befitting his generation and the murk of winter outside, he thought about the stranger's words and doing public good.

Everyone has rights, Brandon thought. *This is why we do good. The greatest good for the greatest number. Is that . . . utilitarianism absolute? Damn philosophers, obtuse like Germy. Either way, good is sovereign. This is why we must be progressive in our tax policy and for our entitlement services. Well, that and . . . when supply meets demand, efficiency is achieved. But the market is inefficient. These inefficiencies must be corrected by government intervention.* He stopped drumming his fingers. *But . . . is the government more efficient?*

He thought of a Government Accountability Office study from his contracting class and market data from his public-private partnership seminar. The research findings had been as conflicted as his thoughts.

He shifted his focus. *It's not even about efficiency. It's about motivation. People in the private sector are motivated by greed and power, and the government is motivated by service, by . . .* Looking away from his desk and back again, Brandon felt a sting but couldn't stop the thought. *Power. Institutions and law . . . can't account for either virtue or vice.*

Closing the laptop, he unbuttoned his shirt and began to shake off his shoes. It was best to rest on these thoughts of rights, motivations, econometrics, and most of all, determining his professional purpose. His mind would keep turning for another hour, but his rest that night would at least start peacefully. Because, even if he did not know his purpose, somewhere under his dissonant and doubt-filled brain, he was inclined to believe that he had one.

Brandon got into bed, turned into the fetal position, and held his other pillow. He filled his mind with his most inspiring thought and his most heartfelt wish—the woman of his dreams held incorporeally in his arms.

That sense of peace did not come without resistance.

***

"BRANDOOOOOOON! COME ON! YOUR FATHER is going to be late for work, your sister is ready. Get your shoes on now; the new ones I bought you! Appearances matter."

"I knooow, Mom!" A ten-year-old Brandon finished buttoning his uniform shirt over his frail frame.

His mother grabbed his brown lunch bag, handed it to him, and smiled. "It's just that you're such a handsome young guy. You're growing up so fast! Well, up, anyway. You could put some meat on those bones. Fifth grade already?"

No.

"You'll be fine, sweetie. It's just another year. Pretty soon, you'll be done with middle school, and then high school, and then college, and then you'll go out there and do great things. Great things!"

Her son smiled as he laced up his brown school shoes. "Not fast enough, Mom."

The proud mother stood up to walk out of the room, and then she turned back around in the doorway. "You can't change the world quite yet. There's so much to learn." She started to turn then looked back again. "And make some friends, okay? You need more friends than your cat. You'll need some social skills to make a difference. I know you like bikes more than baseball, but teamwork is important!"

Brandon stood up and grabbed his backpack. "I know, Mom. I'll try." He started to walk out, but his mom held him back.

"My son . . ." She looked at him straight in the eye then kissed his forehead. "My son."

"Love you, Mom."

Okay, stop. Stop now. Stop.

But it wouldn't.

Ten-year-old Brandon ambled down the hallway and skipped down the steps to the garage. His father started the car as his sister sat down in the front seat. The garage door opened noisily to a cloudy morning in late summer. There was a second of silence. Then the engine started. Brandon climbed into the back seat.

"You want to stop here, don't you?" the Morning Star asked.

Please.

"Let's see what happens."

Please.

"Remember this. Remember what I can do."

Please.

"Get on your knees."

***

THE BAR WAS DARK, LOUD, and crowded. Simple rhythms over the loudspeakers drowned the conversation from one dim corner to the other. Brandon might have been able to concentrate on what the petite girl in an impeccable clubbing blouse and tight jeans was saying if he could clearly hear her, but he couldn't, so he just kept nodding whenever he heard two or three words in sequence. She said something about working out. He told himself to take a quick swig of his glass of the happy hour draft.

He hated beer.

When a different but equally simple rhythm began thumping even louder than the previous, he leaned closer to the girl. She suddenly stopped speaking, sat back up, and turned to another girl, giving Brandon an uneasy look before turning back. Picking up her High County Honey Wheat Ale, she took a gulp then turned back to Brandon. She seemed suspicious of him, but he knew it wouldn't be socially appropriate to inform her that the only girl he had checked out in the last hour was the girl in the tattered sweatshirt sitting in a booth across the room with two thinner friends.

He thought about a classmate's mockery of his "frumpy" clothing preferences, which came just before a comment about his obsolete cell phone and a question about how he could be so "boring" in his tastes in clothing and technology. Brandon shrugged off the thought and took a fast sip of his beer.

He hated beer.

Compulsively taking out his newer but still obsolete cell phone, Brandon began texting Germy. He figured requesting the presence of his only friend in town was worth trying on a night like this, as unlikely as it was. For as nocturnally active as Germy was known to be, he wasn't sociable. Each weekend night, his wiry frame would delicately slink across the town like creeping sex, only touching down when finding a willing partner. And yet, even though Germy was licentious, he was caring. He held a soft glow in his heart for each of them, just as Brandon held a soft glow for each person who rejected him. The respective fiery hopes of this Apollonian and Dionysian were matched only by their frigidly rational assessment of human nature. Their own personal and professional efforts had reflected this very assessment, one built since their moribund, suburban childhoods and now complete in these first few adult years. What is a human being? Potential squandered.

Fifteen minutes later, there was still no answer, nor would there be.

Brandon folded his phone then leaned over to put it in his left pant pocket. The petite clubbing queen to his side had quit turning back toward him, so he figured the time for manners had passed. His blank expression was illuminated by a neon sign for a cheap pilsner.

As he watched the girl in the tattered sweatshirt walk out with her two friends, Brandon felt even cheaper. He knew the coming hour or so of hitting refresh on his browser and checking his phone would be the only thing resembling recreation in this typical weekend. He thought about this and took one last sip.

He hated beer.

***

AFTER HITTING SNOOZE FOUR TIMES, Brandon sat up and rubbed his eyes. He grabbed his phone off the nightstand but stopped short of opening it. He blinked and peeked through the slits of his blinds. The gray morning was quiet.

The thoughts of the previous night and the research papers that he needed to write found him frozen. The unknown fears burned deep below and flickered all around. He felt like a feckless alloy welded to an iron bed. There wasn't a reason to get up. Not yet.

But, when he realized he needed to check out a book from the library for one of those papers, he remembered fingertips. The fingertips of the woman in the library, lightly touching her three small earrings. It had been about two years ago now. He had seen her from behind and across from his study nook. It had been her fingertips; the tips of her dark olive fingers on her ear. They ran through her long, black hair then softly touched her three earrings as she read.

His smile came and went. Connection or not, a moment of beauty mattered. But, for the many socially constructed assumptions of family and friends that he had supposedly established in the supposedly "best years of his life," he was still inexorably alone.

That was at least one—the individual. Where choice began and ended.

Light snow started to fall outside. In Brandon's mind, the light guitar intro to Metallica's "Nothing Else Matters" started to play. Open strings closed on thoughts of a paradoxical reason to get up— faith. He took a breath then threw the covers off.

February

GERMY KUHN SLAMMED ON THE brakes a second before his old Accord would have crashed into the ivy-draped brick wall at the end of his parents' driveway. He turned off the blasting Cradle of Filth song and shut his ashtray.

Opening the car door to the cool haze of the first Saturday morning of the month, Germy stepped out and stretched. He shut the car door with a needed wiggle for the lever to catch. The walk up the well-sealed wood porch ended at the foreboding kitchen door. He turned the knob with obvious hesitation.

"Hi, Mom. Hi, Dad."

Mr. and Mrs. Kuhn casually leaned over their kitchen island as they finished up the morning newspapers. The hum of the large refrigerator cut off, and the automatic mood lighting shifted for a second. The faux-antique grandfather clock ticked.

"Hello, Jeremy." The balding man in pleated khakis glanced up with a cold yet pensive expression on his unseasonably tanned face.

A disheveled Germy, shrugging off his tattered jacket, put his camera bag down against the kitchen table in the breakfast nook. "What's going on?"

His mother's face was buried under foundation and accents, though she still wearing her florescent orange tracksuit from her morning workout. "Glad you decided to show up . . . finally."

"I was just here at Christmas, Mom."

"Jeremy, be honest. You're avoiding your chores."

"Did you hear about Grayson?" his father asked.

Germy leaned gently on an ornate mahogany kitchen chair. "Yeah, he got into Chapel Hill. I saw it on his Gold Pavilion status."

"How about that? Your own twin is going to get his MBA at Chapel Hill."

Germy shifted his weight off the chair. "Pretty cool."

"Did you comment to congratulate him?"

"Yeah."

"Good." Germy's father folded the Weekend Style section and tossed it on the marble countertop. "You could do something like that."

"My GPA's two point four."

"I mean if you tried."

Germy folded his arms. "I'm graduating in December with a philosophy degree."

His middle-aged father leaned over the counter and glared. "No, you listen. That's my point. I mean, *really* try. Piddle-dinking around doesn't cut it. You need to get your act together. I don't give a damn if it's your grades or your job or whatever. You need to quit piddling around. Your mother and I are sick of supporting you."

Mrs. Kuhn looked up and nodded hard. Then she reached across the counter for her Home & Garden Monthly.

"You don't . . . really support me," Germy said. "I've been working and paying all—"

"Really? The hell we do," his father replied. "Who paid for the alternator in that piece of crap again?"

"I thought that was for Christmas. Grayson got a whole jet ski."

"No, no, little man. It's a Sea-Doo, and it's for the family. He just keeps it at his condo. Just because you sat on the dock all last summer while the family had fun doesn't mean you can start twisting facts about it. You wouldn't even take off your T-shirt at the lake. Maybe if you got off your ass and lifted something, you might have half the build he does."

Germy stood silently.

"So, what's it going to be? Put up or shut up, skinny boy? Maybe work out and get a girl? Do you even like girls? Maybe get a real degree? Or at least become a manager in that little restaurant you work for a measly thirty hours a week. Your mother and I worked our way up from nothing. You really need to cut that greasy mop on your head and start dressing like an adult. Those black T-shirts. Don't you want to drive a real car and live in a place like this?"

"Not particularly."

"Well, if you want to be a loser, I guess that's your choice."

"I'm also going to school fifteen hours a week, and Grayson only works during summers, and . . . Grandpa-pa was a doctor."

His father's tanned face went flush. "You little . . . He was a pediatrician, *goddammit!*" He slammed his fist into the marble surface as Germy's mother lifted her magazine. "They make squat! No, we did *not* have it easy like you, you lazy-ass liar!"

Germy's worn-stoic face almost fell. "I'm—"

"They really don't make much for doctors," his mother added with nonchalance. "I'd be making that much at corporate if I wasn't stuck being a branch manager."

"It's good to see you, too, Mom." Germy took a deep breath. "So . . . with all those suggestions, what do you two really want me to do? Like, what's the prior—"

"Oh, so we need to give the smart-ass all the answers?" his father responded. "You can't figure this out on your own?

Your brother just got into one of the best business schools in the country, and you come in here and pull this?"

"I'm not trying to pull anything. Mom, do you—"

"Don't bring your mother into this. You have no excuses."

"Oh," his mother interjected, "Jeremy, remind me to talk to you about fixing the siding again. The workers didn't do a good job this time. That's what I need you to do."

"Sure thing," Germy said with just enough of a sigh to be heard.

Her blank expression turned into a bitter frown. "Now you're getting an attitude with *me*?"

"I'm not trying to, Mom."

"Well, you and that tone. What a piece of work you are. You just wanted to come home and sit around for the weekend, is that it?"

"No, I—"

"Get out of my face," she said as she gritted her teeth. "Your father and I have had enough of you already. Get out of my face. GET OUT!"

Germy picked up his camera bag then walked quietly toward the staircase. He didn't stop as his father spoke.

"You're nothing like Grayson, you little shit with that attitude. You hear me? YOU HEAR ME?"

***

CAREENING DOWN MEMORIAL HIGHWAY, WELL above the speed limit, Marianne Silas tapped her cigarette ash out of the window crack then pulled back her billowing brown hair with a tattooed thumb. Her left hand found its way back to the steering wheel as she typed a text message with her right.

Tossing the phone into the back seat, she hit the gas, passed a car, and turned up Rob Zombie on her stereo. The sunroof was open, and she could smell the saltwater.

Spotting the exit, she flew across two lanes of traffic and threw her foot down on the brake pedal. The old Mustang stopped sharply behind a Buick occupied by a retired couple.

Marianne pushed her oversized sunglasses higher on her face then reached for a pack of cigarettes in the cluttered passenger seat. *Damn*, she thought, *I left my bowl at work*. She turned the stereo up a notch louder and sat back in the seat.

Coming down the exit ramp, the Buick inched into the left lane. Marianne flew past it, made a tight right turn, and then soared down a street lined with strip malls and palm trees. Flying across two lanes on the left, she made a quick left turn into the parking lot of her apartment and swerved into an open spot. She cut the ignition then threw her keys, cigarettes, phone, and a small, pink and white box into her purse.

As the door shut behind her, Marianne heard the familiar Katy Perry tone and pulled her phone back out of her purse. *Brandon's lonely again*, she thought.

She was used to only checking the name of the sender for most of her text messages and not the messages themselves. The inbox was almost always full.

Silencing the ringer, she tossed the phone on the couch. Then she pulled her sunglasses off her face and dropped them on the coffee table. The stone silence made it clear that her roommate wasn't home.

Marianne glanced back at her phone, and then at the coffee table. A copy of Ethoz Art Journal and pages from an unpaid power bill sat across a paperback of C.S. Lewis's *The Screwtape Letters*, a hardcover collection of Salvador Dalí's works, and the New American Standard Bible.

She thought about a worry. She never "worried," per se, other than about losing her bowl and a certain present one.

Holding her purse with a nervous pull, she walked down the hall and into the bathroom, shutting the door behind her.

A moment passed. The toilet flushed, and the sink water ran. A few seconds later, the door creaked open, but the light stayed on.

Marianne walked gracefully down the hall to the couch and picked up her phone. She scrolled through her contacts, past H NICHOLS, MARK OWEN, and JOHN PIERSON. She stopped and scrolled back up. The blue highlight stopped on BRANDON MARCEL. She thought about his voice. She thought about his kiss. She smiled.

After a slow stretch, she put the phone on the coffee table and let out a deep exhale. With her smile still lingering, she looked over the coastal neighborhood outside the window and took another slow, deep breath. Then she turned and walked back to the bathroom.

She picked up a white plastic strip, looked at it closely, and blinked twice. She grabbed the small pink and white box and looked back at the strip. Her pupils dilated, and her mouth fell open.

"Oh, fuck." Her curse echoed in the bathroom.

***

UP IN THE HIGHLAND COLLEGE town, Brandon Marcel sat quietly at his laptop. He felt a tinge of ill-fated excitement when he saw the orange notification appear in the corner of the screen. It was a comment response to a thread in which he posted, but it was to another user. There were no responses to his comment comparing union membership figures between regions to make a point about countering stagnant wages.

There would be no responses; he knew this. And knowing made it worse.

Whether he held to his faith or not, this was not a night for miracles.

He clicked "Refresh."

He sighed.

***

FAR OUT ACROSS THE BARREN Rockies, bursage, and saguaro of the Sonoran Desert, the dreams were hidden. The yellow lights of the Valley of the Sun filled the snowless night of late winter. Endless neighborhoods of closely packed houses, one after the other, populated this heat metropolis between the mountains. Through settlement, growth, irrigation, and state-of-the-art air conditioning, the caustic environment became a comfortable sanctuary of commerce, a dust land of lights, and an arid home to millions.

Home as it was, woman does not live by psychrometrics alone.

Janelle Leora sat quietly at her laptop, hunched over her desk, her sad eyes and the round face that she had inherited from her Navajo great-grandmother were filled with blue light. She cleared her throat.

A streaming video she wasn't even watching ended. The cursor sat still then blinked again. There should have been an orange box, but there wasn't. There were no notifications of any kind.

She clicked "Refresh."

After two and a half hours, she stopped waiting for her new friend from Linguistics 3040 to log on.

There wasn't even a friend from high school to beseech her healing words through one young adult dilemma or another. She was alone again.

The annoyance passed through anger into regret, and so she closed the browser and shut her laptop. Turning in her chair to the large bookcase behind her, Janelle looked for a friend. Spotting it instantly, she stood and walked to the oversized bookcase.

Tucked nicely away among the many paperbacks was a tattered and frayed copy of a Wally Lamb novel. She reached out as though it were her firstborn, and then laid both index fingers and thumbs upon it and lifted. The pulpy edges and scotch tape were frail in her hands.

She turned the book upward and looked at the cover that hung by scraps. It was white and blue, and the all-too-familiar face on the cover stared back at her. The corner of her lips curled a little. She held it for a minute. She held on so that her heart would not fall out of her chest.

It helped her to stop thinking about how her institutionalized mother wouldn't show up for visiting hours and all she had of her father was his short build and a meager inheritance. It was harder to stop thinking about her big brother Chris on his third tour in Afghanistan. Meanwhile, her best male friend and would-be lover just got engaged and no longer returned her texts. Indeed, after a week of mandatory social circles at college and prohibited socializing at her part-time data entry cube, the only company she could keep on a Friday night was rectangular, of paper and pixel.

As Janelle didn't want to wear the book down by gently tearing through it yet again, she set the kind pile of pages back on the shelf then turned back to her other friend, the laptop mp3 player.

She sat down and put on her Sennheiser headphones. Thousands of albums were waiting to be a friend on another empty night. She first thought about Jeff Buckley, but then the highlight stopped on one of her all-time favorites, "Life on Mars?" from David Bowie. As the first notes started, she didn't realize her right hand was playing air piano.

As she closed her eyes, she felt contentment. Contentment and a wondrous connection. She let herself marvel. But, opening her eyes again, she found herself back on her most fair-weather but addictive friend--the screen.

She clicked "Refresh."

She sighed.

Clicking through the tabs on all her Gold Pavilion profiles and all their communities, she swiftly assessed that there were no new posts. No replies. The Criminology page featured glib discussion. The Debate Club . . . didn't. Reading Room had become Gaming Room. The Newman Center's Singles Group had a policy that they didn't want to exclude anyone, even if it rendered it a de facto Couples Group. Her Dead Can Dance page didn't have any new activity. Abnormal Psych was all but deleted at this point.

Checking her cell phone again, Janelle scrolled through old texts. She looked again at one from her friend-of-a-friend.

"Your sweet. Good talkin after class. Your good girl."

Closing her phone, her sad eyes looked away, remembering the one site that she hadn't checked in the last hour. The thought alone was enough to twist her already gnarled heart once more.

She was the timeless voice of care for both family and friends, but if there was one institution that calcified her newfound appreciation for sitting home alone, it was dating. Her heart-shaped lips had only been kissed twice, and long ago. She felt no temptation to respond to the ever-present messages of the men who were truthfully only after the proverbial one thing. Unfortunately, months of sending without receiving had revealed to her that these were the only men listening.

Across the desert metropolis, the wind was still and the skies were clear, as usual.

Janelle sat hunched over her laptop and picked her top lip. There were no notifications.

She thought she heard the bell chime of her phone from one of her high school friends, but she hadn't. It was only a matter of time before someone would want her ear for a rant or lamentation. She was good at data entry, but she was excellent at counseling. While they were both part-time activities, the former was steady and paid, and the latter was neither. So, no bell.

At that moment, she heard only the faint hum of the laptop cooling fan and her house's air conditioning unit starting. She flicked a piece of skin off her finger then reached back for the mouse.

She clicked "Refresh."

She thought about the little orange plastic bottle that she hadn't touched since a classmate had told her that the only thing she really needed was a gym.

The Morning Star watched.

March

THERE WERE A FEW SMALL piles of dark gray snow left on north-facing hills and strip mall landscaping. Light gray ashes scattered in the wind from the red-orange glow of Brandon's last cigarette of the pack. Dodging a bike rack, he forced himself just another block to the Matthew Office of Financial Aid. The small clock out front read 10:16 in bloodred digits.

Trudging and dodging, trying to move and trying to not be in the way, one foot in front of the other. The weight of his chest was less bearable than usual on this bright and cold Friday morning.

Climbing the steps to the entrance, he tossed his cigarette butt into the trash tray, opened the door, and then pulled himself up a flight of stairs into the labyrinthine administrative offices and passed desks full of federal forms until he found room 2221.

Around a few corners was a wall-mounted ticket dispenser. Grabbing the arrow-shaped paper tab, he then sat down in a chair close to the counter and tried to think about music as he waited for thirteen minutes. Florescent bulbs muted the sunlight coming in through the high row of windows. He had almost forgotten what he was doing when his number was called.

The heavy-set, middle-aged woman wore a low-cut blouse

and heavy makeup. Her elongated vowels were typical of Southern Appalachia. "So, what did you need today, son?"

"Yeah, I . . . I'm having trouble understanding this whole repayment plan thing. See, I don't have a job lined up yet, so I think—"

"All that's on the website, son."

Brandon sat up in the chair. "Yeah, I was trying to find my way through it, but I couldn't really . . . figure it out, you know?"

"Well, that happens. It's all through the feds, though. We can give you their contact info and all, but this office is if you need . . . Here, let me getcha something." The woman turned around in her office chair and plucked a strip of paper out of a series of neat stacks. "Here it is. You can get all your FAFSA and Stafford Loan stuff here."

Brandon swallowed. "So . . . I can't work out my repayment here, then?"

"Gotta talk with the feds."

He looked down then looked back up again. "I guess because they're the ones that give out the loans." He thought about the colossal mess that his multiple applications for government jobs had become.

In that split-second, he thought he could physically feel a thought turn over in his tinnitus-racked head. It was a moment of brief clarity that was not common in an increasingly complex society. It was a new idea.

"Well, son, we can help you with questions related to—"

"Actually, I think I can figure out what I need now." It wasn't true, but he didn't want to lose the moment. "Thank you so much."

Passing by the flanks of administrative office doors, Brandon refocused. This last foray into bureaucratic wonderment led to a flood of considerations. *Why is financial aid such a monster? Tuition prices keep rising over the years, even adjusting for inflation, which guarantees anybody taking the loans will be paying that much more into the future. Why does it keep rising? It didn't use to be like this. Even with more people in college, this can't be consistent with demand. It doesn't add up. Where is this market manipulation coming from?*

As he stepped outside and reached for his cigarettes, he remembered he didn't have any left. Exhaling in frustration, he lifted his hands as if to gesture as he mentally conversed with himself. *It's like healthcare. Even after our long fight against corporate greed, we finally get the legislation to control the costs and expand access, and then the costs . . .* He looked away for a moment. The weight in his chest was coming back, but his mind could not be deterred. The ideas were simultaneously uncomfortable and exciting. *". . . rise anyway."*

Brandon found himself standing motionless on the brick sidewalk. The sun fell behind a few clouds then came back again. *If the publicly available metrics are accurate, most nonprofit colleges and hospitals used to provide these services at lower costs and have more opportunities for those whose parents didn't pay for them. What happened? Why are they so stingy and greedy now?*

He thought about bumming a cigarette off a fellow student. However, after the packs jumped in price after the last round of legislation, the unspoken sentiment among smokers was a lower inclination to share because of the higher prices and regulatory control.

I guess there's something about the incentive structure, but it's more about the constraints of . . . well, no. We need government intervention to stop the greed. Wait, isn't that trying to legislate morality? And what the Right-Wingers say about regulatory constraint, compliance costs, and litigation risk might be . . .

Feeling too excited to not rely upon his notorious habit, Brandon found a student puffing away.

"Hey, man," Brandon started, "can I get a smoke from

you?"

"Sure. Hold on." The wiry guy with aviator sunglasses seemed reluctant, but he grabbed a pack from his coat pocket and pulled out a cigarette.

"Thanks," Brandon said as he went to light it.

"Don't mention it. You know what the Scouts say, right? Do a good turn daily."

"Ha, yeah. I do know that."

Taking the magnificent first drag, Brandon exhaled and returned to his thoughts about the consistent theme of rising prices. *You have inflation under the increase of monetary supply by the Federal Reserve buying up the treasury bonds and hoping like hell that banks lend more and this economy gets better, and then you have market inefficiencies. The free market fails; therefore, it needs to be controlled. So, the government intervenes, and then*—he exhaled—*prices rise.*

"Dude, don't make a habit out of it," the wiry student who let him have a cigarette interrupted his thought. "I'm happy to do a good turn, but you also know what they say about good intentions."

"Yep. The road to hell is paved with them," Brandon said with a smile. "But I've always wondered if the intentions were really good if you have enough foresight to see the gates ahead."

"Hey, that's a good one! Right on."

This notion led Brandon right back to his thoughts about government intervention. *All these departments and programs were created and designed specifically to help people. Help people get an education, help people get health care, help people get the basic necessities. Are we just not taxing the rich enough? Income taxes aren't enough—it keeps amassing at the top. But then . . . the rich also don't control the costs alone. They get regulatory help! The lobbyists write the bills! It's the entire market and all its manipulations that lead to this status quo. Manipulations. Inefficiency. Rent-seeking. Deadweight loss. Bureaucracy. Power.*

Just then, the individuals at whom he directed his frustration were no longer monolithic wealthy people, but Presidents Woodrow Wilson and Lyndon Johnson. To his dismay, he recognized these men as commonly revered heroes of his own adopted ideology of ostensible compassion known as progressivism. This was surely an uncomfortable line of thought.

Corporations are to blame. They are protected against regulatory reforms by lobbying for economic rent, and then being empowered by bailouts, privatizing profit, and socializing losses, and all backroom legislative deals, all of which are—Brandon realized that his cigarette was just hanging in his hand, untouched—*government intervention. So, by definition, we . . . do not have a free market. Or there hasn't been one, at least, since the Federal Reserve and the income tax in 1913. The Progressive Era! What the hell?! That makes no sense. Yet we have . . . corporate and government power . . . corporatism.* He took another drag and blinked. It was becoming uncomfortable to think. He was still ignoring the pull in his chest.

But people are selfish, greedy, and abusive! ABUSIVE! That's why we can't have a free market. That's why we need regulations. That's why we need to consolidate power in a central government. We need to consolidate power into . . . other people? No. Germy is wrong. It's a question of definitions. Someone who doesn't trust the private sector is a liberal. Someone who doesn't trust the public sector is a conservative. So . . . what if we really can't trust either? This corporatism, this collusion between centralized government and business, is the status quo.

Brandon tilted his head back as more implications flowed into the cracking ice of his mind. His most prized ideals of compassion and understanding, the very core of his beliefs and, indeed, his best understanding of his own purpose were as susceptible to paradigm subversion as anything else. It was as luminous as it was terrifying. It was as if the rock had been removed from his intellectual cave. The cigarette sat in his fingers.

So . . . Johnson's historic War on Poverty and welfare programs . . . did they just subsidize poverty? But we have to help! Only a federal government has the power . . . and is also the most removed.

Do some programs really create dependencies instead of opportunities? Systems on top of systems? Progressivism . . . progress . . . to what? The individual must give up primacy to the greater good of . . . government power and authority. Conformity. No, no. An unrestrained free market is too dangerous. Competitors come in, and we can't control prices, so it's more efficient. Wait—more? No. The market fails, and the government must correct it, so long as the correction truly does work. Like . . . patents that keep out competitors. Well, if it doesn't work, could there be greater prosperity? Even so, the greedy rich would just take the wealth. They wouldn't help those who were still struggling with private charity. Regulate greed? But you can't legislate morality! He reminded himself to breathe.

What if . . . government power is mechanical, but human interaction is organic? Why do we confuse the two? Even if human nature is self-destructive, can mechanizing it necessarily lead to a greater good? It does give a sense of certainty. The certainty of doing good! Is it . . . a false sense of certainty? Control can destroy. And we need to expand access, not dictates! We need opportunities, not dependencies! Sustainable system improvement, like improving the conditions of poverty, is meticulous. The closer to the work, the better. From the federal government, state, and local to . . . individuals. And trade . . . helps.

Brandon's mind continued to evolve. He also realized he was doing exactly what Germy had always advised him not to do—obsess over something he couldn't individually change.

His student loans would have to be paid regardless of who or what was responsible for the rising costs. But this thought lent itself to considering what he could individually change—his career. All these thoughts acceded to his mental undertow of realizing that, if progressivism was not what it previously seemed to be, the implications on his attempted social circle and networking opportunities would not have the desired result of making a real difference. He figured that his family and his career counselor would advise networking no matter what. The voice of his conscience, this time being the combined effort of Shakespeare and Germy, advised being honest with himself.

He finished the cigarette before attempting to cross the main intersection. His hesitance against buying another pack reminded him again of the stranger's goodwill. But Brandon disagreed with the Scouts. Instead of just doing a good turn daily, he thought one should do as much good as could be reasonably done, the fullest realization of individual good.

Perhaps the maximum good that can be done is not best through centralized or collective power . . . or any power at all. Goodness is a choice, not a political structure . . . like Germy said. Damn. And like any choice, it begins and ends with the individual . . . like Batshitreichwing said. Damn.

As his life of solitude had continuously affirmed, the individual is ultimately the only one left to answer for itself at its end.

Both schools of thought—good turns and good living— necessitated going a step further. A step further this day. A step further this year. A step further this life. A step further *now.*

Looking down the sidewalk, Brandon saw a middle-aged woman with frazzled hair pacing around a car, looking around frantically and cursing under her breath. The momentum of his conscience compelled him to temporarily suspend his introversion and speak.

"Hey, is there something I can help you find?"

The woman sighed. "Not unless you can miraculously find a parking spot on this damn campus. I'm trying to help my son with his account, but I'm illegally parked and need to find something called a Jett Building."

Brandon nodded. "Yeah, on-campus parking is an oxymoron, ha. But I have an idea." He pointed down the street. "See that three-story, brick building just behind the Convocation Center? Park in the number five spot. It's my friend Jeremy's, but he's out of town for the next two days. They don't check unless the renter complains."

"Wait—really? So, I just . . . okay. Great. That's so kind of you!" The woman started to turn away then turned back to Brandon. "Thank you! And thank your friend."

"Will do. Oh, and . . ." He turned and pointed down an adjacent street. "See those seven towers? The Jett Building is on the far left."

"Oh, good. Thank you so much! You're a lifesaver."

"You're welcome, ma'am. Take care!"

Brandon knew he could still catch the light to cross the street as the woman went on her way. The smile on his face was unfazed by the coming round of internet searches, clicks, refreshes, and neglecting to play his acoustic to drown out the ringing. It was also unfazed by a thought that altruism was perhaps a mere evolutionary feature to benefit the species and that goodness meant nothing. If there was anything that pulled him through his life of coping with the past, present, and future, it was the idea that there was good with and without scientific explanation. Goodness and truth were sovereign to human qualification and quantification. While on a very short list, this was something he knew, some way or another.

What he didn't know was that this casual spark of goodness and truth could initiate a causal firestorm in a way that no centralized power could, whether by Keynesian Multiplier or any such theory. Just as the wiry student with aviator sunglasses had taken his own experience of a needed hug from his roommate and subconsciously turned it into a gesture of goodwill for a fellow smoker, Brandon had turned *that* gesture into another. Instead of getting a parking ticket and having an argument with the desk clerk at the Jett Building, the frazzled woman would have a little more peace of mind. As would her son, as would his girlfriend, as would his girlfriend's classmate, as would the desk clerk at the Jett Building, *and on and on.*

Aisling smiled with him.

***

"WOO-HOO!"

The Polo shirts, blouses, and kitschy accouterments of the crowding patrons sported various shades of green. They filled McMurphy's with many loud expressions emanating from their socialization and alcohol consumption. It was billed as a Greek mixer for an Irish holiday, but few of the participants were actually of significant Greek or Irish ancestry.

Members of the campus fraternities and sororities mingled along with the campus academic and political groups. The room was loud and dark and green with wood and neon accents. There was little space between the packs of people and their drinks. In general, the Hellenics were more obnoxious, and the non-Hellenics were more pretentious.

"Don't they all look the same?" Brandon's Campus Progressive companion smirked and shook his head then took a swig of amber ale. "Not just the green shirts and shamrocks. They always look the same."

"We all kind of look the same," Brandon shouted over the raucous din. "You think?"

"Say what?"

"We, I . . . yeah."

The soon-to-be ex-Campus Progressive had meant this evening out to be one last time to be with them. It was very apparent to him now that, even if he didn't have second thoughts about the ideology, his belonging in this club would always be anything but. He had been in this situation several times in previous years, always leaving after a few months, and always with unapparent regret. He hated the social psychology of clubs, even as he admired the sense of belonging and individual people in them.

"I mean, would it kill them to crack a book? Maybe then they'd question their pampered, white, suburban lives, y'know? Seriously."

If it had been three months ago, Brandon would have unquestioningly concurred, but he found himself biting his lip. He was tempted to point out that the current membership survey of Campus Progressives indicated that they were all white and the majority came from upper-middle-class income homes, but he kept his demographic findings to himself.

"Republican trust fund babies, y'know? They're just in it for themselves." He took another swig of beer.

"So, what's your part-time job again?" Brandon asked.

"Part . . . what? Oh, job. State employment office. See, that . . . that's public service."

"You help people find employment?"

"Well, you know . . . I help with the claims." He took another swig of beer. "Help people."

"So . . . help them reach self-sufficiency, connect them with opportunities—"

"Man, people need their checks. Checks, I file them. Public service. And I get good pay. Better than those little job help nonprofits, anyway."

"Oh." Brandon thought about the economic efficiency of such services under government versus nonprofit organizations. "Yeah, I hear government pay is . . . better than nonprofits."

A slow minute later, Sarah Shea-Trivette entered the room with two tall and brawny club members, each with a beer in hand.

"Hey, guys!"

Brandon nodded, feeling a twinge. It just occurred to him that his feelings about her had changed with his sociopolitical paradigms.

He was surprised to find that, through these new differences, he actually felt more endeared to her now. He figured that, even if their public policy assumptions were different, their expressed mutual commitment to compassion, understanding, and openness was, in light of these differences, a thing of beauty.

And she was all the more stunning in her white button-down and green plaid skirt.

"How've you been, Brandon?"

"Just fine, Sarah. Yourself?"

She put her beer on the table and sat down next to him. "Great, great. Seize the day, you know? Erin go Bragh!"

"Erin go braless, WOO!" a passing shirtless man shouted.

She laughed, took a drink, and then turned toward one of her friends.

It felt as though some fifteen minutes had passed, but when Brandon checked his cell phone, it had only been four. The bar had grown louder and darker since his last attempt at conversation.

Looking toward the window, it hit him fast and hard that he had a better place to be.

He let another two minutes pass before he addressed the table.

"Hey, everyone, I have to turn in for the night."

Sarah turned to look at him and nodded, but he wasn't sure if she or anyone was listening.

"So, yeah, I might not be around for a while, because . . . I'll catch you guys online."

One of the men turned, nodded, and then turned back around.

"Be safe, everyone. Take care, Sarah."

***

THE SEAT OF THE COMPUTER chair was becoming too warm. Brandon had been home from the bar for three hours but still couldn't calm down enough to go to bed. Instead, he opened browsers like he was getting a fix each time.

He had considered joining another online community or starting his own blog, but he couldn't think of what he had to offer the world beyond his mess of new ideas and runny personal sentiments on music and love. That pathological pathos was a paradoxical mix of myopic optimism for connection and impulsive pessimistic need for expression.

The internet had provided an ever-tempting captive audience for introverted losers everywhere, and Brandon Marcel was no exception. He had issues with being exceptional.

The last Gold Pavilion status posting about rejecting the liquidity trap had garnered some interest from his second cousin and a random classmate from high school, but the five other economics majors on his profile hadn't responded. He had become used to the Campus Progressives not responding, even when his posts were highly congruent with their platform.

His sputtering sense of belonging was drifting further still. And knowing made it worse.

Watching the cursor blink, Brandon figured it would be better to find other web pages rather than to keep refreshing the same ones. Therefore, he first checked the weather then checked the GeeNews site. Even the world seemed bored this early morning after Saint Patrick's Day.

There was a brief temptation to check AlterProgress, but Brandon feared that his anxious passion and newfound commitment to questioning economic assumptions in human services would guarantee a pile-on flame war even worse than the last one. Instead, he found a button that led to websites at random and considered throwing all thoughts and feelings into the void.

Aisling.

The cursor blinked. Brandon leaned back slowly as if being lowered onto a bed of nails. He waited, and then he clicked on the link. If there would be no signal in everyone's noise, either in-person or online, he could at least absorb the noise for all it was worth in hopes of creating his own signal.

The website that loaded featured a collection of antiques from Brown County, Indiana. As he clicked through the site, nothing caught his attention until he saw a picture of an old classical guitar, looking as neglected as his own acoustic.

On a curious whim, he hit the back button and went to click the random website link again when his chest twisted hard and heavy like falling rocks. It was as if his own body and mind suddenly fought for each nanosecond of attention. In this fright, he just wanted to shake it all off and quit trying to break on through.

He took a breath then went to close the browser. His finger weighed upon the mouse when the heart beyond his heart spoke to him in a tongue beyond tongues.

Aisling!

He moved the cursor back to the link and clicked.

"How I Found My Favorite Band." It was an interesting page title, and the topic arrested him with immediate intrigue. It had to be personally hosted. Other than an advertising banner, the plain white page featured only two lines of purple text in Times New Roman. It invited him to a universe beyond his own.

"I found my favorite band by searching and listening and waiting.
Searching and listening and waiting for you. It is all I can do. – JNL"

Who? he thought. *Who is this? Who was the band?* he asked himself. *Who is this?*

Brandon reached out as though to respond but realized there was nothing else on the page, let alone contact information. He could check the page source or try to find host information, but he figured that perhaps it was something in which the time was not quite right.

He sat back in his chair. *Does this happen?*

No answers came. The questions would have to wait.

He opened the digital mp3 player and clicked on the Leonard Cohen album *I'm Your Man.*

As the day broke, light rain fell into a gentle haze of the coming spring air. His ears cleared. There was nothing left to do.

April

"REMIND ME, GERMY. ARE YOU a free will guy or a determinism guy?"

"I'm freewheeling all over this mofo. Fast and effing furious like Judas Priest."

"I'm serious."

"Yeah, that's the problem."

They sat with their legs hanging over the stone wall at the campus entrance, slowly smoking clove cigarettes. The weather of April was just as overcast as March. It didn't seem to change aside from increasing allergens. Occasional warm days made the prevailing cold days less tolerable. It could have been late in Lent or Lent could be over, but Brandon couldn't remember. He was going to miss Easter Mass either way.

"I guess I'm just wondering if . . . something changed," he said. "Or if I did."

"It doesn't really matter," Germy replied.

"You would say that."

"Evidently."

Brandon coughed. "Of course."

"Really, though, I mean, you're still worried about all the same old crap, right?"

"We did just have midterms."

"Yeah, your last midterms, and you're still obsessing. Getting all those A's when jobs are, like they always say, about who you know and not what you know. And you're trying to get friends for the sake of having friends. And you have enough medical quirks to make a hypochondriac feel healthy. Then there's your petrified freak-out at the idea of driving."

"Yeah, that about covers it, Germ."

"You obsess until you abscess. I mean, how many times a day do you check your email? And you're always on those social networking sites that would give Baudrillard, McLuhan, and Postman a field day. Looking for notifications, right? Hitting refresh over and over again? And the phone, damn. Always with the phone."

Brandon compulsively pulled out his phone. "Tell me about it." He held the flat, black device in his hand and just looked at it. "I don't even know most of what this thing does—apps, media, games, and all of that. Map functions? 'Mapp App?' I mean, what the hell am I going to need that for? I take public transportation."

"You take Germy transportation."

"That, too."

"And you obsess until you abscess."

"Hm . . . You know, you've always been the one to help me find new ways to think about things, Mr. Kuhn." He flicked his clove cigarette and took another drag. "Our demolition derby discourses often remind me that developing knowledge isn't linear."

"Oh, if only you were speaking literally."

"You'd be arrested for vehicular assault?"

Germy laughed. "Nah. I was gonna say that the logical positivists would learn something." He tossed his head back and his long, damp hair went with it. "But yeah, there are also some pretension-bashing pretentious hipsters and indie bands I'd like to make go kablooey."

"I knew it." Brandon smiled. "So, are you down for some jamming tonight?"

"Downtown with the clown sound."

"Come on; it's been ages."

"You know how we do. Nah, I think I'm going to watch that old Kurosawa flick *Ikiru*."

"Fine. At least you're bailing on me for a good movie."

Brandon flicked ash over the side of the wall then turned around. He tried to focus on the moment, but his mind kept reverting into his intellectual and emotional stew of worries made of his ringing ears, his employment prospects, and his life. He wondered how Marianne was doing. There hadn't been a text in his inbox from her in months. He also thought back to that morning after Saint Patrick's Day, and his tinnitus rang louder then faded.

"I don't know, Germy. It feels like life has changed keys. And it's not just the music and the message, but all of that Austrian School stuff I've been reading. Free markets, individual liberty. I think you'd like it."

Germy sat back. "Eh. Sounds better than that club, but I don't like organizations. A small business, at most. Remember that all your intellectual explorations may be good for you, but that doesn't mean the world's going to notice. It's not good at noticing. It's fucky like that."

"I suppose. I just feel like something, whatever it is . . . something has changed."

Germy scoffed. "You may feel that way, but do you think there's anything to it? You know I'm not into the Bible, but Ecclesiastes is right that there's nothing new under the sun."

"Yeah. I just . . . sooner or later, something has to give."

"Has it occurred to you that, after so many attempts of trying to be accepted by this person or that group, you're who you are and the only one who needs to accept that is yourself? As that therapist I had once said, the only person you can change is yourself."

"I thought you're not into therapists, either."

"Yeah, not into most therapists. They're out of their league with my brand of crazy. Maybe therapists and Bibles stumble on truths. Things like expecting anything of the world, especially a world like this one, is expecting too much." Germy gently flicked his cigarette.

"Mr. Happy-Go-Lucky." Brandon laughed.

Germy didn't.

***

SITTING BEFORE THE ALMIGHTY LIGHT blue glow of the laptop screen, Brandon felt as much as ever that he needed to do something. In spite of Germy's objections to all things organized and social, his statement that nothing had really changed led Brandon on the search for new social networks.

Graduation was only a month away, and Brandon expected his personal and professional development to undergo some kind of solidification at that point. He also didn't want to tell his parents that he had developed a fundamental philosophic disagreement with his one and only active extracurricular club. Between his mounting impetus for connection with his peers and this fear of rejection from the most formative group of all, he knew he had to act.

The natural course of action seemed to be finding a comparable group that would reflect his new ways of thinking. There had to be a group that thought the most good could be achieved through a combination of maximum prosperity through economic efficiency and the free choice to turn compassion into effective private philanthropy. And one that valued neither centralized corporate power nor centralized government, but the individual.

Certainly not the Republicans, Brandon thought. *Their worldview is a watered-down version of the Democrats combined with theocracy, and theocracy serves neither "theo" nor the "cracy;" it makes for false faith and prejudicial laws. Intransigence is not principle and sexual orientation is not equivalent to sexual morality.*

As his bleeding heart considered people of different sexual orientations and identities as well as those yet born, he conjured another objection. *They all have their issues with respecting individual liberty.* The obvious choice seemed to be the Objectivists, but what the Objectivities lacked in political efficacy was almost admirable compared to their supposed virtue of selfishness, which was anathema to him.

Capitalism. He couldn't believe he was actually considering what was a dirty word just a month or two ago. *I should join the Young Capitalists. How do I do good with this degree that I'm about to get for the community, the country, and the world? Advocate for a free market. Be efficient in my own work. Maximize efficiency and prosperity in macroeconomics. Advocate for profits to be willingly donated to social services. Subsidiarity! Revolutionize the more nimble and effective private philanthropy. Assure liberty for each individual to do good. Be free to be good.*

With a mind full of personal doubts being temporarily overruled by passion for reason, it was as good a mantra as any. Yet, the threat of theory without practice remained, and so he resolved to first take a concrete step to connect, and then to take a concrete step to remake his life according to the dictates of his conscience.

Shifting his weight from side to side, he leaned into his desk, grabbed the mouse, and browsed the Young Capitalist homepage. He thought his next evolution of turning theoretical good into practical good had begun.

Reality would set in soon enough.

The Morning Star waited.

***

WALKING OUT OF THE STUDENT union with a folder of Young Capitalist paperwork, Brandon saw Sarah walking up the steps. She was wrapping her earbuds around her mp3 player, her hair blowing in the bright spring breeze.

"Hey, Sarah, how's it going?"

"Hey." Even though she looked down, her body language seemed to smirk. "I didn't see you at the meeting."

"Yeah, I wanted to talk to you about . . ."

She looked up at him. "I saw your political identification on your Gold Pavilion page."

"Really?" The unexpected attention made him tense. "I—"

"It's okay. You're fine. You have to live your own life and make up your own ideas, right?"

"Yeah, definitely."

"It's okay, Brandon. Just don't post an angsty status if I don't always agree with you."

"Nah, I wouldn't . . . Nah." He leaned from one foot to another. "You know, one of the things that inspired me to get involved at all was your involvement. And, you know, despite these new ideas in my crazy head . . ."

She raised an eyebrow.

". . . it's still the case. We might kinda disagree on the how, like, how to do good—you know, helping people through government or private charity and philanthropy—but we still agree on the what and the why—making the world a better place. We both believe in compassion, understanding, and forgiveness."

"Compassion, understanding, and forgiveness," she repeated with a faint grin.

"Exactly. So, even if we try different ways to get there, that's what really matters, right?"

"Hmm." Her expression was growing with skepticism.

"You know, Sarah, we're getting ready to graduate here in a few weeks and try to find jobs. What if I get a management job in a national nonprofit, and you get a management job in a government agency, maybe we'll meet in the middle and really . . . you know, be the change we want to see in the world. Like that Gandhi quote, you know?"

She laughed. "Sure, Brandon, you can be just like Gandhi." She turned and started to walk away.

Brandon lifted a smile full of belief. "No, really, this . . . It's really a beautiful thing, I think."

Her saunter stopped, and she turned back around. "Wait—what is?"

"This. Us. It's, you know . . . we see beauty in the diverse, you know? People of different political or social viewpoints coming together for core values and to get things done. It's beautiful."

Sarah recoiled. "No, no, no. I like real diversity—social justice and equality. That's . . . No, we're totally different now. I support policies that ensure people of different races, colors, and creeds will come together. No, I support real diversity." She folded her arms.

"I . . ." Brandon waited a second. He looked down then back up again. "I think we want to achieve the same thing; it's just that our thoughts on how to do that go in different directions. As you said, you think it is best done through government intervention policies, whereas I think the government should just protect individual liberty, so greater economic prosperity can help alleviate the conditions of poverty, and then we come together as a free society through our organizations, nonprofits . . . those things we both support."

She smirked. "I heard you the first time. A little unrealistic, but okay. What's your point?"

"Sarah, these are great endeavors. We just disagree on the means but agree on the ends. But we can use our professional lives in our own ways to achieve them. To make a difference."

"Hmm." She turned around again.

Brandon shifted his weight and ignored his chest. "I really think it's a beautiful thing—all diversity. Just voluntarily, as long as life and liberty for all people is sacrosanct."

"Sure. I believe in real diversity and really making a difference. What's wrong with that?"

"I . . . think we . . . Okay. Yeah." He shook his head and turned around. "See you."

***

FLIPPING THROUGH A COPY OF Ethoz Art Journal, Marianne had difficulty sitting still. She shifted in her gym shorts.

The waiting room was as unfeeling as any other waiting room. The periodicals were as outdated as any other waiting room. She glanced at the little blue plastic wastebasket just inside the front door.

"Ms. Silas?" the thin, redheaded nurse said as she leaned around the open doorway.

"Yeah." Marianne tossed the magazine on the table then picked up her purse. Her stroll down the hallway was in turns easy and burdened.

"On the right," the nurse said. "Just put your things on the counter, and I'll grab a gown. The doctor shouldn't be very long."

Marianne shifted her weight on the stool. "Okay."

"Did you have any questions, Ms. Silas?"

"No, thanks."

The nurse smiled. "First appointment nervousness is common, Ms. Silas. Just relax. You have nothing to feel guilty about."

Marianne faked a smile in response as the nurse walked out, and then she slouched on the stool. She thought about reaching for her phone but decided to stay seated.

While she shifted nervously, she preferred to cope with the empty air rather than quasi-encouraging texts from Chad. Weathered, tattooed hands swayed in her lap. What she wanted most of all was to smoke a bowl. No kind words, pats on the shoulder, or a dozen good reasons for one course of action or another would be sufficient. Even a cigarette would be wonderful.

The thoughts started to bleed again. Like the coming spring storm off the gulf, it started with a sprinkle, and then a deluge. Arranging the work schedule, paying the annual gym membership fee, finishing school somehow, dealing with the boy, and this month's bills.

It was mostly dealing with the boy. A woman like Marianne would always make ends meet, whether it was pretty or not. In her mind, each man was always subject to short-term concerns, but rarely long-term concerns. Chad was cool enough, fun enough, and confident enough. He could keep a job better than the rest. And he was fit. He wasn't the most intelligent boyfriend that she had ever had, but he was funny. *Cool, fun, confident, reliable, fit, funny.*

Typical.

It was a trait that encompassed so many of the ones before him and the likely ones to come.

The hottest guys, like the hottest gals, were so immutably typical. They felt so great in the immediate moment, only to feel so small with time.

There was no way Marianne could have this man's child. Even if he could keep a simple job, his financial responsibility had not been nearly as thoroughly tested as a father's would. But, most of all, it was because he was a man in all ways but the ones that mattered most.

Unlike . . .

Marianne had once referred to her longest-standing relationship as the only one in which she was treated as a person instead of as a girlfriend. That boyfriend actually wanted to know about her sketches, her Yeats interpretations, and her dreams. For him, she was beautiful in spite of her exceptionally thin figure, clubbing tops, and designer accessories, not because of them. He demanded a connection of hearts and minds. The superficial was never enough, which felt to her like work and intrigue. It felt like meaning even if it was not meant to be.

She got up and grabbed her purse, rifling through the plastic makeup cases until she pulled her phone out. Scrolling through all the unread texts in her inbox, she had reached nearly a week back before she stopped on the most recent one from him.

"Hey dear, hope you're well. We should catch up sometime. All the best, love . . ."

It was simple and good when their lives were anything but. The wrong way on a one-way street. A fleeting sense of a long gone time.

Don't think of the past. This is about the future. No way at all. No way. NONE.

She clicked off the cell phone and held its dark pink hull in her weathered, tattooed hands. Her index finger adjusted as though it was another hand to hold. She smiled.

Love.

Thundering back into the present, Marianne suddenly realized the internal gravitational constant that had been waiting to be discovered and pull her away from this place. She tossed her cell phone back into her purse then zipped it and slung it over her shoulder. The nurse appeared with a gown right before Marianne made it out of the door.

"Here, just slip into this, and I'll—"

"I'm done here."

The nurse smiled less sincerely than before. "Ms. Silas, again, it's common to feel—"

"That's great, but I'm canceling. Pardon me, ma'am, but fuck this."

"Oh no, I understand. It is your choice. If you'd like, we can—"

"There is no choice other than fuck this." Marianne nudged past the nurse and then walked down the hallway.

She opened her purse, felt around for her pack of cigarettes, and then snatched them out. As she crossed the waiting room, she found herself stopped just before the front door. She then turned and looked at the only woman waiting, one in her mid-thirties, sporting short blonde hair and a business suit. Her professional appearance was a sharp contrast to Marianne's sweaty gym look.

The woman looked up from the same Ethoz Art Journal that Marianne had been reading a few minutes earlier.

"Excuse me," Marianne started. "I . . ."

Holding the page with two shaking fingers, the otherwise poised professional stared back at her in silence. It was uncertain who was answering to whom and why.

". . . I can't do something this devoid of love. Can you?"

Marianne threw her pack of cigarettes into the little blue plastic wastebasket then walked out before she could see the woman's reaction or hear her answer. She had figured that this was all she could do.

She had figured well.

***

THE MORNING LIGHT WAS BREAKING as Brandon walked toward it upon the flat surface of the giant rock hanging from the mountain. He remembered that his last hike was one that he had taken alone during his sophomore year.

His boots hitting the ground didn't make any sound. He looked down at them as though they were broken. As he came closer to the edge, he then looked ahead and saw a distorted but familiar silhouette standing by it, looking over the vast Carolina hills below.

"Oh, it's you." Brandon couldn't think of his name.

"Yes, it's me."

Brandon walked closer until he was just a few feet behind him, not feeling comfortable enough to walk closer. He turned his head to the right and lifted his hand to his shoulder, but there was no pack to take off his back. There was no water bottle from which to sip. There was also no cell phone to compulsively check, but he didn't feel that compulsion at the moment. He felt nothing but a faint curiosity.

"Brandon, you are making this interesting."

The weight on his feet shifted. "How so?"

"Hmm, hmm." Leaning to one side and back, the figure made something of a squint as he looked out toward the rays of the newly rising sun. He almost seemed to smile, but Brandon couldn't see the front of his face. "You're doing well. I thought you would give in as you have in the past. You're actually doing well this time."

"It seems like it matters this time." Brandon didn't quite understand the meaning of his own words, but he spoke them with atypical confidence. "This time, something is at stake."

The man seemed to smile wider. "Hmm. I actually like that, you know—a little fight. And you're right on one thing. Something is at stake. But *matter* is a matter of opinion."

Brandon paced in a slow arc, away from the figure but toward the edge. He looked out toward the sun, opened his eyes wider, and then sat down, letting his legs hang over the edge. They watched for a moment.

It was quiet.

It wasn't peaceful.

"How is it going to go this time?" Brandon asked confidently but still slightly surprised at the hidden knowledge from his subconscious coming through his mouth.

The figure looked at him then turned back toward the sun. "You see that light ahead?"

"Yes."

"It's very far away, isn't it?"

"Of course."

"It's even farther than you think. It's impossible to reach, and you know it." He looked up as his mouth turned into a wide grin. "It's beautiful, isn't it?"

"Yes." Brandon felt that the truth he heard mask a deep lie. "A light of lights. But I know . . ." His thoughts inverted, and he couldn't finish speaking. "I know—"

"You know what? You don't know anything except that you can't control anything. Except how much pain I inflict on you. Just think of your terror behind the wheel when you try to follow your thoughts to their conclusion. You can try anyway, but you'll fail anyway. For all the great pains of body and mind, there's nothing quite like futility." He crossed his legs and leaned back. "Although tragedy . . . tragedy is really something. Rejected *love*, it's my favorite tragedy." He laughed. "It's really something, especially in layers with futility."

"It's nothing I haven't faced before."

"You're not over it. You're not over any of it. You and I both know that you don't get over anything. It just builds until you break. I'm trying to make this easier on you, Brandon. You don't believe me, but that's fine. You will when you realize you can't make it to the light."

"I can make it. If I can find . . . a sense of home, of shared love, I . . ." His words parsed in pensiveness as he watched sunlight fill the horizon. But pending horror struck him as he realized there was a darkness swarming beneath his feet.

He threw himself back, trying frantically to get away from

a void that swallowed everything around it. It seemed like the rock that he stood upon tilted toward it like magnetism atop of gravity. A sense of final rejection ached within the nothingness, coming closer and closer beneath him. An undoing beyond death.

"I can . . ." He lost his words.

"Look. Right down there. You never see what's right before you, right in the moment, but you'd better. You see that?" The gaping void grew wider and deeper and darker. "That's real. It's all you have. You know it. So, enjoy all the maple trees and songs and whatever little things you force yourself to think about to get through the day. Because, at the end of the day, you're just alone in a chasm, a voice in a hole. You sit there and squirm. Do you understand?"

Brandon couldn't speak even if he wanted to do so. His ethereal sense of curiosity and peace withered away, slowly at first, and then swiftly.

"It's fun to watch," the figure said. "You don't know about all the do-gooders before you. Special snowflakes, right? They all fell to the earth and melted. They die down there. Did you know that? Little loveless losers, just like you, sitting in their holes, trying and failing. And for nothing. You can be the same way if you want. Or, you can go in a different direction."

Brandon nodded and thought about alternatives.

The dizziness and darkness paused.

"I've found, after all this time, that no matter how rich or poor, educated or not, religious or not . . . most people have garden-variety desires." The man laughed, sending a deep pitch into the rock beneath them. "Oh, but not you. You're different. You don't want fame and fortune, do you? Big houses, big cars, big muscles, big egos, big drugs; six-figure salaries, trophy wife under one arm, and a hot lover under the other. Anything?" He turned toward Brandon's silence then away again. "Nope. We both know that no one gets everything they want, but you don't even want the regular stuff. Not even good ol' smug self-righteousness to stroke the ego, huh? Hmm . . . close." He nodded. "That one's close. Do-gooder seeming and being are the closest enemies."

After an empty moment, he tilted his head. "But you can have something, right? You have a simple dream. Well, good. That means you have a chance at real happiness. Here, how about . . . a normal life. How does that sound? Racing at the mud run with your own group of friends, playing guitar in a real local band, a good job just to pay the bills, work at a little charity; how about that? A wife. A wife! Yes. A nice, plain, slightly overweight wife who's smart, driven, kind, and wears your old camp T-shirt to bed. Simple, easy, and fully obtainable for most people who aren't you. You see people everywhere who don't appreciate their normal lives nearly as much as you would, right? The meaning of *their* lives is to live, not to love. They're easy. They want success and ego-stroking, while you just want contentment. Well, you're wiser yet somehow more naïve. This is all why it's so fun for me."

Brandon sat on the notion and tried to ignore the horizon.

"You could always get over your hang-ups with medication and take something to make that hole below disappear altogether. There may be side effects that blur the light and leave you here, but that's just a disclaimer. Even with nasty side effects, it's still preferable; you'll see."

Within Brandon's mind, the possibilities came and went, each receiving a node of consideration to be left aside.

"It's your call. I'm just asking you to be more open-minded. You're the open-minded one, right? Oh, you also have your so-called principles. That really makes things interesting.

"So, go ahead, run for that morning light. It's beautiful. I would know. Just don't feel so damn sorry for yourself when the inevitable happens. You'll have a moment here or there on the way, so good for you. It may not be easier, but it keeps things interesting for me."

From the corner of Brandon's eye, he seemed to stand ever higher and even into the sky, ripping into it.

The formidable presence looked down upon him and spoke plainly and deeply, the words shaking the rock beneath them.

"You have a choice. Think it over."

May

THE SEA OF BODIES ROLLED over the always hot cement of campus and through the dry desert air. Most of the women were dangerously tanned under the small cover of stringy tops and tight jeans. Bright highlights seared through their hair. Some wore backpacks, but most preferred to carry handbags and not bother with books. Men wore jeans made to look as though they had years of wear, paired with T-shirts sporting faux graphics designed to look extreme and tough. Cell phones were always close at hand as texts, apps, and calls were accessed between classes.

Janelle walked with a hunch under a full backpack. She didn't look up very often. When she did, she felt as though she had that much more reason to look back down.

After crossing a courtyard, she ambled up a staircase and into a classroom. She settled into a desk near the window and quickly checked her phone. Students gradually drifted into the classroom even after the bell rang. It was the last week of classes before finals but there was a sense of composure and regularity.

"Heuristics," the professor began. He was young and had completed his doctorate only two semesters ago, and yet he spoke with gentle confidence. "Heuristics are an important part of human psychology. At their best, they work as a practical assessment when a thorough investigation isn't feasible, often through limited experience and knowledge constraints, factoring intuitive or . . . tacit knowledge. Short-cuts, at their worst, introduce cognitive biases that manifest themselves in mass errors of judgment, and even to great prejudices that hinder true understanding in the hard sciences as well as the soft sciences."

Janelle went to pick her lip and stopped as she remembered that she was in public.

"But, whether they are used to our detriment or not," the professor continued, "one thing's for sure: we use heuristics constantly, especially in our personal lives." He paused for a moment then grinned.

"Speaking of anecdotal evidence, think back to high school. You had cliques, right? Well, the higher rationality afforded to humans has less of a role in these associations than you might think. It's somewhat rare for the logic and reasoning centers of the prefrontal cortex to be used for these purposes." He laughed. "You reserved it for algebra, right? So, we use baser instincts and selective experiential reasoning to make immediate judgments in our interactions, even for associations with profound emotional impact. Go alphas! We love 'em in high school and the workplace, right? They get things done, right? They defend us and help us, maybe? Unfortunately, as any heartbroken friend can tell you, the time-cost savings of such judgments aren't worth the quality of friendship. In fact, neurological studies of social hierarchies in East African baboon troops have demonstrated that removal of the domineering, stress-inducing alphas of the group can make societies in which there is less stress, greater longevity, and more productivity. Counterintuitive, right? Granted, given that the scenarios were anomalies, the samples are limited. But there's something to be said for the sensitive ones in advancing society. Betas, right? They're just not our first picks, huh?"

The professor stopped his hands mid-gesture and tilted his head downward. "The point is that heuristics can be another way in which our minds can trick us into not acting in our own self-interest." His smile faded. "Or in the interest of anyone else, for that matter. Evolution's tricky. I wish I could say it gets better, but . . . well, despite the maturity of the prefrontal cortex by the twenties, the dynamics of adult relationships aren't really that different. In this age, at least."

With her hand resting underneath her chin, Janelle thought about her own limited number of friends from over the years and the frequency with which they called her for company and catharsis, a concept that her professor had dismissed in a class earlier in the semester. She wasn't sure if she agreed with him on that topic, but this one today had resonated, though she didn't know why.

"By the way, make sure to add the evolutionary psychology definitions to your study guide," the professor said. "I'll have it up on the web-board tomorrow. And remember I have office hours Thursday. Now, I think there were two other topics to cover today . . ."

After class ended, Janelle found herself thinking about the relative level of rationality and true empathy among her strained friendships as she shuffled across campus and the scorched blacktop parking lot. Sunshine was everywhere.

When she settled into her old Civic, she pulled out her phone again and checked for texts or calls. She had one from Emily.

"Thanx sooo much for the chat other night. Things better w/ guy. Sweetheart! Luv."

A smile came and went. Janelle's personal counseling to her family and few friends was something of a labor of love. It was obvious to all that her perpetual care for the problems and relationships of others was at least somewhat attributable to her not having such an active life or love for herself. She would drive from home to school, work, and errands. On the rare occasion of going to social functions, she still found herself in the supporting function for others, and forever seen as "just" a friend. It was a labor and it was a sacrifice, but it was love. Her love for herself would have to come through her appointed best friends, who could never quite find the time to call her back or come over to check in on her.

She knew her friend Emily would use her advice to work out the latest disagreement with Evan. What she didn't know was that her support would assure that Emily and Evan would have just the wisdom and emotional fortitude to get married and have a loving family, one that would not have been possible otherwise. The alternative was for Emily to remain alone and not finish her degree as Evan had encouraged, and for Evan to go from one divorce to another. The infinite possibilities boiled down to this unknown certainty: without the critical component of one person freely choosing to overcome her jaded cynicism each time she responded to yet another texted request to be there for her friend when her help was truly needed, there was a love that would not have been.

Janelle turned on the ignition then turned up "Perfect" from her The Smashing Pumpkins' playlist. She lip-synched to the first verse as she turned out of the parking lot. Her special outing this afternoon would be to the doctor about her thyroid.

She pushed down the sun visor and cracked the window. With her left hand, she steered, as she turned up the air conditioning with her right.

***

THE APARTMENT DOOR SLAMMED BEHIND Brandon as he tossed his cap with a yellow tassel on the couch then tore off his pile of honors cords and black gown as though they were spiderwebs. He went for the top drawer of his desk and pulled out a pack of Camel Lights and his lighter. Holding a fresh smoke between his fingers, he peeked through the blinds to make sure his parents had pulled out of the parking lot. Then he stepped onto the balcony and finally lit his cigarette, savoring the first drag as he reached for his cell phone to text a call request to Germy.

After three pensive drags, Brandon became impatient and pulled out his cell phone again. He scrolled to Germy's number and pressed the "Call" button. Four rings later, his friend picked up.

"What the dilly?"

"I think you know."

"I got your texts. Are you freaking out again?"

"Germy, you of all people should understand the terror of being alone with your family for big social events, trying to say and do all the proper things. I still don't know why you couldn't have shown up, at least for the end."

"I just got off work. Besides, you know how much I love big social events and traditions and formalities and—"

"Structures and organizations, yeah, I know." Brandon sighed.

"Well, congraduation. Here's a portmanteau. Should I send you a folded piece of cardstock with my name on it?"

"Oh, no, I would never want you to have to commit to any traditions."

Germy laughed, adjusting his grip on the phone. "You know how we do. So . . . why'd you call me again?"

Brandon exhaled and leaned against the wood balcony. "Well, since you won't give me a clear answer on free will and determinism, let's shift our personal analyses to the topic of purpose. Specifically, the purpose of my life."

"Or the purpose of your strife?"

"That, too."

"So, you *are* freaking out. Okay. Um . . . I think we're going to have a dishwasher position open up in a few weeks."

"Germ, I'm not sure that I could—"

"Oh, you're too good for that now, right?"

Brandon groaned. "Give me a break. It's not like bagging groceries and being a security guard were too good for me then or now. It's just practical, okay? I have to find a way to pay these student loans off."

"Don't they defer if you're unemployed?"

"I still don't understand how that works. Besides, I need to feed and house myself, and I don't like the prospect of living off my parents."

Germy paused, adjusting his grip on the phone again. "Yeah, living with parents is not my idea of fun." He cleared his throat.

"After finally making all those calls to the consulting firms last month, per the career guy's advice, and sending résumés all over the place, I've got a grand total of zero responses. What the hell am I supposed to do at this point?"

Germy laughed. "I know we're friends and all, but I'm the last guy you should consult for career advice."

Brandon took another quick drag. "I'd argue that you're the first guy. My parents think I should get an MBA, and everyone seems to think I should sell out to the same government that shackled me to these loans. Loans I wouldn't have had to take if not for that very market distortion of guaranteed loans driving up prices. Anyway, I actually think a consulting firm is a better choice overall, but sixty-hour weeks won't be good when I . . . you know, have a family . . . someday."

"Hmm . . ." Germy pondered. "Hey, how about that soup kitchen idea? Ever go there? And I bet you could run one of those food pantries. That's a way to get involved as you talk about."

"I'm not sure they pay enough," Brandon responded. "I mean, I'd probably just be scraping by. My parents and Sarah wouldn't think much of that. The consensus on how to help people is to make a good salary and just donate back."

Germy scoffed. "And how far has listening to other people got you?"

"You're other people, too, you know."

"Fair enough. But think about it. People can donate money, and that's perfectly fine, but where's it going? There has to be people doing the actual work of the organization, correct? I think it might as well be one of the smarter people around who is prone to caring too much rather than caring too little."

Brandon raised an eyebrow. "Thanks, I think."

"That's what I'm saying."

"But I also want people around me to be proud of me."

"There's your problem. Isn't pride one of those deadly sins in your beliefs?"

"I guess. Well, I'm going to write up a few more cover letters this week. Oh, and I'm also going to see about getting a different club membership."

"What? Another club?" Germy was genuinely incredulous. "You didn't learn your lesson with the last one?"

"I think you'd like this one more. It's the Young Capitalists. They basically promote free markets, less government regulation—"

"I thought they're the ones who support big corporations and all of that crap. I hate big anything."

"No, that's the thing," Brandon implored. "It's not pro-big business; it's just anti-government for the sake of free enterprise. You're an anti-government anarchist, yeah?"

"Eh. I like Henry David Thoreau. Screw the government, screw the businesses, the environment rocks, chuck it all, and live simply."

"*Live simply* and live sordidly?"

Germy laughed. "Sure. That's the natural order of things,

you know. Live simply and sordidly."

"And blow stuff up?"

"And blow stuff up. Naturally." Germy cleared his throat. "For real, though, why bother trying another one of these clubs? I think the only organizations worth your time are the small, local ones in touch with what's really going on."

"We'll see. I'm just going to submit this next round of job crap and check out what the club's all about. I don't know what else to do. My lease runs out at the end of the month, and I don't think my parents want me to move back in any more than I do."

"You'll find something."

"Doubt it," Brandon said with a sigh. "I do all the showy crap my father says, detail all my data analysis skills, hit those applications with style and substance, and I still don't hear anything except the occasional stock rejection. And yet, after dozens of these, I keep trying. Anyway, what are you up to this week?"

"Chillin'," Germy said. "Killin'. My second shift crew is going to go paintballing. If I don't score literally and figuratively, I'm certainly going to blow something up."

Brandon rolled his eyes. "Well, make sure to use protection. Literally and figuratively."

***

WHEN THE LAST CARDBOARD BOX fell to the floor of the Advil bedroom, Brandon smirked to himself. All had proceeded precisely as he figured it would. He truly hated being right.

"We think you're a great candidate. We found another who more aligns with where we are."

"You're doing all the right things. Keep it up, and you will find something!"

"It's on the website. If we have anything, it's on the website. You'll have to keep an eye on the website. Make sure to check the website."

And the most honest: "By the time the post is up, the position has already been filled. We're just required to have a posting for it."

Brandon didn't know the exact number over the past four months of attempts, but the truth was that he had made thirty-seven calls and had sent sixty-six pairs of cover letters and résumés. At that same time, he had made seventeen calls to Germy's voicemail and had sent thirteen text messages to five different friends to complain about the job search. He had received five calls in return from Germy and four texts of consolation from others.

When he considered the possibility of either living off his parents or the government, Brandon felt deep shame. His studies of economics and his most recent intellectual pursuits into free-market thought had reminded him of one important fact about himself: he didn't want a handout, but an opportunity.

I only need a chance, he thought.

Then again, as Brandon now saw it, this was not an economy built for opportunities. It was built for crony capitalism, which struck him as inefficient and nothing resembling fairness. It wasn't even unfair. It was something else. In a matter of decades, "who you know, not what you know" had transformed from a professional idiom into a de facto religion across sectors.

In a superpower sustained by bailing out any large corporation that was too big to fail and providing economic rent to election donors, mediocrity reigns and merit is for fools. Generation Me had ushered in Generation Need with an economy built for handouts and a reigning moral hazard. And the moral hazard provided a perverse incentive.

It would be better if I didn't care. If I traded substance for style. Yes, style, not substance. Substance is pretentious anyway. He shuddered for a moment, feeling as though his thoughts were being influenced, but unsure how. *It's all about now, not later. Wit, not wisdom. Seeming, not being. Yes, like all those standard pieces of advice. Fake it 'till you make it. Look the part. That's what I need. Then I would have a chance. A chance to be liked.*

A chance to be normal.

Sarah's last text described him as "nice but needy and dependent," which had hurt enough for him to seek solace from personal pursuits in professional pursuits.

Her own friends and ex-lovers have many relationships and other friends, which provide constant affirmation and support. And yet . . . she holds them up as standards of strength. Yet seemingly untested.

Brandon tried to remind himself not to impose reason on an inherently unreasonable world, but it didn't help. *It's not fair. It's not unfair. Style over substance. No good deed goes unpunished. It's anti-fair.*

His cell phone rang.

"Hi, Mom."

"How's the unpacking?"

"I just brought up the last box. How was work?"

"It was fine, just fine. Make yourself at home. I'm going to drop something off with Barb, and I'll be home around dinner. Could you get the table set up?"

"Sure thing, Mom."

"Thanks." There was a pause. "So, did you call all the temp agencies like I asked you to?"

"Yes, Mom. Well, most of them. It just kept ringing for two of them."

"Brandon . . ." She grit her teeth. "Brandon, I asked you to call all of them."

"I did call them all, but two of them wouldn't answer the phone." He heard a car honk on the other end of the line.

"Don't lie to me. Why would a business not answer the

127

phone?"

"I . . ." Brandon's face went flush. "I'm just saying what happened. Feel free to try them."

"It's your responsibility."

He heard the engine rev through the phone.

"I'm trying to help you. You couldn't get even one interview, and now this is where you are. You're going to have to deal with it, beat the streets, pound the pavement. Do you want to be jobless? Call. Now."

"Mom, I'm sorry. I—"

"Don't start with the apologizing. You need to start following your father's example. Or your sister's, for that matter. You know she had her job lined up a year before she graduated?"

Brandon took a deep breath, reached for his pack of six cigarettes, and pulled them all out together. "Okay, I'll call again and . . . somehow get them on the phone."

"We're not going to support you forever. We were self-made. You can be self-made."

"I wouldn't want you to, anyway. I just need a roof and food until—"

"I need to run by Thruway. I'll see you at home." She hung up.

Brandon pulled the phone away from his ear and looked at it in his right hand. By now, his face had turned from a pink to a solid red. He could almost hear the palpitations. The tinnitus was deafening, and no mp3 player, laptop, or guitar was available to fight it. The chemical concoction pulsing between his mind and body had reached maximum chaos.

The six cigarettes crumbled in his left fist and fell to the floor. He held his cell phone with delicacy for a moment then flung it against the side of the oak dresser. First a pop, then a shatter. His blind wrath sent a cardboard box across the room. Piles of compact disc cases crashed against the wall. He kicked a hole in a box. And a second. And a third. His face boiled. He screamed and aimlessly staggered around the room, thrashing against his belongings.

"I just want . . ." he huffed. "Why can't I just . . .?" He tried to catch his breath as the panic raged. "I don't need . . ." With his hands, he covered his ever-red face and tears slipped between his fingers. He felt the need to drop to his knees, but he remained standing, standing then staggering.

Somewhere in the emotional flood, there were pieces of reason trying to calm him and make sense of the near future and perpetual past. *There are still organizations I can call. Professors might have contacts.*

Germy, Marianne, and my family still love me. Don't they? Somewhat? I guess. Well . . . I can do this. He could make ends meet. He would not want or need the cars, houses, clothes, games, or status that fed the avarice of his peers, whether they had jobs lined up or not. A functioning, albeit outdated laptop and a lower-model Martin acoustic was enough for him. Almost. *I may be loved. Maybe. I still want to be liked.*

His rage seized on the last thought and manifested in another dumped box, leaving the floor covered in his Econometric Modeling notes.

There was a burning realization that wouldn't be smothered by any line of reasoning. Brandon knew that, no matter how simple he chose to live or the ideal simplicity of free individual choice, these were all potentials and dreams. They weren't real.

The reality was that his life and all lives in this society were buried under the constraints of increasing complexity and uncertainty, internally and externally. Brandon was no exception. He couldn't convince a few potential employers to make an exception to their regulations and policies for the sake of anyone's potential any more than he could force himself to become the gleaming model of social pleasantries and technical proficiency that so many other potential employers had sought. Nor could he be the chrome-alloyed model of confidence so many potential friends had sought. That so many potential lovers had sought. *STYLE OVER SUBSTANCE!* his inner voice shouted at himself. *Thinking for yourself is trite and pretentious!*

Everything was stuck. In life and love, most everyone wanted a sure thing, as false of a promise as it was. Like millions of players sitting at the card table of livelihood by day and the card table of love by night, the increasing uncertainty of the next deal and the game itself drove decisions into irrationality, consistently favoring short-term gains, even if they meant long-term losses. Thus, preparing for the long-term, as Brandon and so many of his generation had, was a losing strategy.

We missed the writing on the wall. Nixon said decades ago that we're all Keynesians now, and Keynes said the long run was misleading because, in the long run, we're all dead.

In a civilization where unreality was the reality, the constraints of complexity and the irrational desire for immediate power rendered simple kindness as elusive as reason itself. He was stuck with an irrevocable impetus for the desire of desires: the timeless bound in the dirt of the moment. It would take a miracle to break.

Dishwasher.

His body felt limp, but he didn't fall. He stepped across the torn binders, tapes, and scattered white pages and found a place to step. Then he walked to his father's office.

What good is college? Especially if you're an introvert without many technical skills? I thought organizations wanted data analysis and personnel management.

Opening a browser, he found a local job website and

clicked on its restaurant tab. He clicked on "Apply Online: Position: Dishwasher." *I am inherently objectionable.*

Through Brandon's dark cognitive mess came a soft memory. He was sitting alone on a brick wall after Statistics in his second semester when he was approached by his classmate from Tanzania. The tall, lithe African had told him not to look down. *There is no Swahili word for loneliness.* Several came close, but there wasn't anything that quite captured something so sick and empty and typical of Brandon's homeland. *No true loneliness.* Something always breaks through.

June

"ONE DAY, YOUR PRINCE WILL come," the classmate said. "That's what they say. I'm for real, Jan; you're like the ultimate girl next door. But yeah . . . it's . . . We're such good friends and all. I don't want to ruin it, for real. Know what I mean?" He threw back the last of his Bud Light then held the can at his side.

"Yeah." Janelle considered this one progress. The last "good friend" rejection made her cry, but this time, she forced a friendly smile. "Good friends."

"Now, come on; we don't want to spend the whole night out here on the stoop," he said. "I'll let you know how our jam goes. You were right about that whole 'make sure everyone in the band has the same goal' and all, so yeah . . . thanks." He crushed the can. "For real, you're so smart and so sweet . . . and you have great taste in music! Know what I mean?"

She held the smile. "And remember not to turn up your amp so loud. I know how you are in the car."

"Yeah, yeah," he said with a head shake. "Let's see what everyone else is up to."

It was well past midnight and the party had started to die down. A dozen people were left in the dark house. The stereo didn't thump as loudly, and people were no longer grinding to it. The ones who weren't drunk or having sex were getting lost in conversation.

There was a breeze over the desert as she passed through the frame of the sliding glass door. She breathed in the dry air and sighed. Something seemed right in the world at this moment. Despite her latest and perhaps most predictable rejection, Janelle felt a sense of calm. The best she could tell was that this rejection was a kind of confirmation, a gesture to stop moving in that direction and make her own.

"Actually, I think I'll take off," she said to her male companion after she shut the door behind her.

"Nah, Jan, don't let me being a jackass ruin your—"

"No." She grinned. "I just think it's a good time to take off, seriously. Are you okay to drive?"

"Yeah, I . . ." He blinked with vacant eyes. "Yeah, let me get my roommate to drive."

"Good." Janelle gave her supposed good friend a hug, dug through her well-stitched canvas bag for her keys, and then walked out the door and past a row of cars. After she opened the door to her Civic, Janelle stopped short of turning the ignition when she saw her favorite CD sitting on the floor of the passenger seat. There was a sudden impulse to check her cell phone, stronger and more random than usual. Pulling it out of her canvas bag, she slid the top open.

Nothing. No texts and no notifications. Her mouth curled. She clicked on the icon for her email. No new messages.

She dropped her phone and looked straight ahead out the windshield. Her chest hurt hard for a second, and she thought about the orange plastic bottle. She considered packing her phone and starting the car and heading home, but she didn't.

Over the lonely years, through social conventions online and off, she had reached out for friends and she had reached out for boyfriends. She had cast herself to their wind. And yet, she could still feel her own wall shutting something away that could hurt her .

. . or heal her.

She had cast herself to their wind, but now, somehow, her wall was no longer necessary. She would now cast herself to her wind.

"I found my favorite band by searching and listening and waiting. Searching and listening and waiting for you. It is all I can do – JNL"

Her thumbs sat above the phone for a few seconds. The browser glowed blue on Janelle's face. She looked up at the empty road ahead of her then looked back at the phone. She typed her email address into an HTML box and clicked on the save key.

***

THE MELODY FADED INTO SILENCE as the cursor drifted from one group of pixels to another. Scrolling and scrolling hundreds of songs, each inspirational in some way at some time, all seeming insignificant at that moment. One little adjustment on this or that side of the equalizer wouldn't make much of a difference. Recorded music, the interface of the moment being captured for the eternal, still had one great limitation—it can only play what has already been heard by someone.

Brandon rubbed a bloodshot eye and clicked on the upper-right hand corner of the music player. None of his playlists would do it. He wanted to listen to a certain song, but that song had yet to be written.

He considered getting up and digging through the closet to find his acoustic guitar, but the instrument had become too intimidating to hold. He couldn't control it because he couldn't control himself. His knowledge of theory was spotty and picking technique was improper.

The tinnitus buzzed but not quite loud enough. The palpitations beat but not quite hard enough. His head and his heart felt as worn as ever, and the massive quantity of music on his computer and the diminutive quantity of happy memories from his recently completed college experience could not alleviate these forever typical and nonetheless vexing symptoms any more than the Advil walls surrounding him.

The cursor waited.

The clock on the lower right corner of the screen passed another minute.

The cursor blinked.

Brandon rubbed his eye again then put his hands back on the keyboard. The constant compulsion to check his email for non-existing messages rivaled his constant compulsion to check his cell phone for non-existing calls or texts. A brief temptation to join another current events forum came and went. He knew better than to return to AlterProgress or any of its clones. Getting into another video game would probably just drain time and money. Like music, nothing seemed to work. He wasn't sure if billions of webpages not being enough was a statement about him or the internet.

He sighed and clicked on his list of bookmarks, beginning to scroll down the hundreds of entries. The text rolled for a moment before a snap.

The tinnitus and palpitations returned hard and loud. He felt his heart racing beyond the point of a panic attack and the warm dampening of sweat along his hairline. He compulsively tugged at his gray T-shirt.

The mouse fell to the desk as he stood up and aimlessly paced, trying to think away the thinking before the terror could tear him apart. The mass pulled harder until he forgot about killing away the noise in his ears. Multiple deep breaths had no effect. He knew the fear and his heart and his pain could not be stopped, neither naturally nor artificially.

Deep within his mind, the rage of his body hit something else.

A moment of desperation. Desperation of that degree almost always sent him to play a speed metal song while reaching for a cigarette, but at that moment, he didn't. He wouldn't. At that moment, it felt truly wrong. What was right was to sit right back down and open just one of those webpages near the bottom of his bookmarks in a new tab. It felt forced . . . and right. *Click.*

"I found my favorite band by searching and listening and waiting.
Searching and listening and waiting for you. It is all I can do – JNL

Something was different now. Obviously something was different with the page, because now the initials hyperlinked to an email address. But something was also different with JNL. Something was different with him. Something was different for them.

Brandon's innards pulled hard as he clicked on the link. A box popped up, and then he typed, still forced . . . and right. He thought he heard a deep voice when he clicked "Send."

"Hello JNL, I'm Brandon Marcel, just another web denizen. Who is your favorite band? I still haven't found mine. Pleased to find you. :)"

***

THE MIDNIGHT SOFTENED AS THE day began. The subtle kiss of Janelle Leora had spread far yet unnoticed. Each word of comfort in a call or text, each video post of her favorite songs, each pause as she waited to hear what was going on for everyone that she knew before she said anything for herself. The world's back was turned to her fire, feeding off the warmth while always watching the darkness in anticipation of another light.

The light passed to her friend from high school when she posted a *hug* to his Gold Pavilion profile when he got rejected from graduate school. After he saw this post on his phone in the checkout line, he passed the light to a store clerk with a broad smile. After he arrived home, he then also passed the light to his sister by taking her out to dinner to keep her from starting to smoke cigarettes again over her boyfriend's outbursts. She passed it to this boyfriend when he finally lost his job at the print shop. The boyfriend passed it to three more people. They passed it to another ten. The light was good, as it was sovereign and perpetual.

And now one would finally turn toward her.

***

"HELLO?"

"Hi."

"Whoa, I can hear your voice."

"I can hear yours, too!"

"We've established that neither one of us is deaf."

"Aha, yes. You know, your oh-so-cool profile with all your esoteric macroeconomics and acoustic tonewood talk doesn't have any dorky jokes."

Brandon laughed. "Well, as my best friend Jeremy would say, you know how we do."

"Apparently, Mr. Serious!"

He couldn't stop smiling. "So, uh . . . what do you like, Ms. Janelle?"

Janelle couldn't stop smiling, either. "You know, you don't have to be nervous. I'm the one who should be nervous."

"Sure. So, uh . . . what do you like to set on fire?"

"Fire? I don't want to set anything on fire. This world's enough of a fire zone already."

"Then you would never fit in with our group . . . of . . . two people."

"I don't want to fit into your stupid group!"

"I feel that way sometimes."

"Stop complaining."

"I'm not complaining!"

"Yes, you are!"

137

Brandon laughed again. "So . . . how's the weather across the country?"

"It's warm." She mocked a scoff.

"No kidding."

"What do you want, jackass? The easiest job in the world is being a meteorologist in Phoenix. 'What's the weather like today, Tom?' 'Hot and sunny, Bob!' 'No shit, Tom.'"

"At least you only have to deal with a literal desert, not a metaphoric—"

"What did I say about complaining?"

"Dammit!"

She heard the smile in his voice join her own as she settled into the recliner under the large canopy above her back porch. There was something ethereal in the searing atmosphere that afternoon in mid-June. Two weeks of exciting daily emails had led to this call. But, for Brandon and Janelle, the time was an instant flying by and a timeless age interwoven.

"So, what do we do now?" he asked.

"I'm sure we'll thinking of something."

"Yeah." He kept smiling as he exhaled a whimsical smoke over the walkway behind the house. The humidity of the day had just begun to ease. The two planted trees in the backyard stood wet and quiet over the crickets. He knew his parents would be home soon, but he didn't care for once. The blessed stillness of this day dared any concerns of Middle America to fall upon his mind. Somewhere in his heart, the bassline from Ben E. King's "Stand By Me" started.

"Maybe we should go for a walk," she said.

"What? Right now?"

"Uh, yeah? We're living in this super-futuristic space age where people can walk around with their phones. It's pretty cool."

"Okay."

"I mean, we've got a few thousand miles between us; there's not much else we can do together. I have the Cactus Wren Park directly across the street from me, and I know you have your deciduous trees everywhere, so let's be like Xzibit memes and explore while we explore."

"We do have nice trees." Brandon cleared his throat. "You know, I used to ride my bike out every day after I got home from school. All weekend, too. The sunlight through the trees, smelling barbeque over the wooded hills, kids playing in the distance . . ."

"We played bikes before and after the summer," Janelle said. "Good times back then."

"Yeah, the neighborhood seemed so much . . . bigger back then, you know? Each street, each grove of trees. It was like its own new country or frontier. And the creek—my creek—it went on forever."

"I know what you mean." Her smile widened. "When we lived near Mesa, we had the mountains nearby. On the weekends, Dad was out gambling and Mom just stayed at home and told us not to go too far, but of course that just egged us on. My brother and I would hike up some dirt path and look over town, then go out farther into the dust land and just listen. It was quiet up there, but epic, you know?"

"Yeah, sounds like it."

"Chris would take me out to see if we could spot coyotes. It was like this stealthy hunt in broad daylight. He'd pick me up and hoist me on his shoulders to look around. And when I was looking closely, all focused on his whispered commands, he'd suddenly drop me and toss me around, laughing. Strong guy, huge hands, but gentle, you know? Out in the desert." She took a breath. "It was good. Now he's hunting people in a desert on the other side of the world."

"Wow," Brandon responded. "Your brother's in the service?"

"Army Rangers."

"Whoa, that's pretty intense. I . . . yeah. My granddad was Screaming Eagles in the Bulge."

"Oh, cool!" Janelle took another breath then curled the side of her mouth. She looked up, thought about hope and thought about family. And then thought about the jump in her chest and tried to stop thinking. "Did you ever think about joining up or anything?"

"Yeah . . . after high school. I actually started college a term late." Brandon took a drag and scratched at the ridges on his upper left arm. He tried not to think too much about exactly why he was turned away at the military entrance processing station. His mind was a whirlpool of faith and fear. "My, uh . . . health, well . . . exercise-induced asthma wouldn't make it past processing."

"Oh, really? I think your smoking-induced asthma wouldn't make it past processing."

Brandon laughed. "Yeah, that, too. I don't know, maybe I'm too, uh . . . emo for the service?"

"You're too emo for many things, aren't you? I thought I was the lonely virgin here. Cheer up, dammit!"

"I am cheered! And you learn fast. I am a little emo, but I'm also very . . . inteo."

Janelle jeered. "*Inteo?*"

"I invented inteo," Brandon replied. "Necessity is the . . . redheaded stepchild of invention or something, so I took the liberty."

"Right. Well, I invented pants. Virgins need them, because we're not taking liberties."

He squeezed his cigarette's last embers onto the sidewalk. "I invented the internet."

"I invented you."

"I am you!"

Janelle laughed. "You're something, all right." She held her smile. "You are something else, asshole."

Brandon laughed and kicked the glow out of the ashes. "Yeah, I wish. But you are kind to say so, Ms. Leora." He grinned. "You're . . . yeah, you're pretty cool."

"*Pretty cool* even?"

"Yeah. That's my final answer; how's that?"

"Hmm," she responded. "Okay, I'm game. So, it'd be great to hang out, but I'm afraid it's a little bit of a trek."

Brandon closed the door behind him then trotted up the steps. "It's only a couple thousand miles."

"That's fine," she said with a steady glow of hope in her shared acquiescence to the situation. "Just get in your car and start driving."

"Oh, sure," he said with a chuckle. "Logistics aside, I don't have a car."

"Really?"

"Yeah. I take the bus and bum rides."

"Really? Could you save up for one?"

Brandon's radiance faded a touch. "Well, maybe, but I . . . I'm actually . . . deathly afraid of driving."

"Wow, deathly even. I love driving. Windows down, blasting tunes down Thunderbird. Why's that?"

There was a cold touch on his chest. He felt haunted. "I just . . ." He hesitated, taking a breath. "I don't know. I don't like having that in my hands, I guess. I got my license and all, so I can borrow my dad's car if I absolutely have to run an errand or something. It just . . . kind of terrifies me."

"Oh, okay." Janelle curled her lip again. "I guess that's tough to get around."

"Yeah." The sinking had begun. "Literally! There's that dorky humor." He shuffled his feet. "It really is nice to hear your voice. It's been great."

"It has." She sat up in her chair as she felt the triple-digit sweat coming down. "We should do this more often."

"Of course. Hey, you know—"

"Hmm?"

"I know you're not cool with posting pictures and all, but . . . do you think I might have earned seeing you by now?"

"Oh." There was a cold touch on her chest. She felt haunted. "We'll see about that."

"*We'll see*? You've already seen all my crap."

She forced a chuckle. "I guess. Check your inbox in a little bit, m'kay, babe?"

"M'kay." His radiance returned.

"Talk again soon."

"All right. So long, Janelle!"

"Later, you sweet dork." She let her phone close softly and she stood up. More sweat fell, making the top of her tank top even wetter, but she didn't think about the ever-present heat. She was more than used to feeling this way on the outside. What she wasn't used to was the way she felt inside. There was a spring coming through her core and cascading down her short frame. She felt sustained. She felt reciprocated.

When Brandon shut his phone, he found that he couldn't stop smiling. His senses were worn in a good way. There was light. Bit by bit, it broke through. From the moment he opened her first email until this moment, he felt as though he would never have to look for light again. However, when he checked his email later that hour, he clicked through urgently, only to find his senses suddenly transfixed and locked. It was now a paradox.

Janelle was pretty, this was true. She had a soft, round face, with long, hazel eyes, a thicker bottom lip, and a dark ponytail.

Her expression was blank but potent, standing in front of her bookcase. There was goodness in her. She was pretty in a less glamorous, more earnest way. It was exactly the kind of beauty that he had always sought and cursed his contemporary social norms for not appreciating. It was indeed good, and she was indeed beautiful.

But she looked nothing like Aisling.

July

THE RACK OF DISHES CAME through the other side of the large steel Hobart, hot and wet, but Brandon noticed the faintest of spots on the lower edge of a dinner plate. He didn't want to risk losing his break again, so he frantically scrubbed the spot, scratched it with his fingernail, blew on it, and then picked the entire rack up and sent it back through the Hobart again.

Reaching into his pocket, he pulled out his cell phone, touched it lightly, and held it with the sides of grease-tipped fingers. It was just over half an hour until his break. He was looking forward to smoking and even more to texting his new best friend. Through the sweat, the steam, and the stink, he still smiled.

Once the minutes wore down and the last rack of boiling dishes came crashing through the conveyor belt, Brandon scrubbed his hands hard, smacked them against his apron and jeans, and then walked past the freezer to the stale, white break room.

Shelves full of giant cans of tomatoes and greens were positioned on either side of a plain linoleum floor with filthy corners. Brandon stood next to the small fan blowing out of an opening in the window and lit a cigarette. The wisps of smoke and the text on his phone made the pervasive smell of bleach bearable.

"Gotta chill," the new busboy said as he walked around the corner. His voice was intended to be urban, but everything else about him was suburban. "The man's hasslin' me about my tats. Like having flames is violent or some shit. Just gotta chill. Hook me up with a smoke."

"Sure thing," Brandon said, taking out his pack.

"Thanks, man." The rolled sleeves of the eighteen-year-old busboy's ruffled white button-down showed his toned and tattooed arms. He lit the cigarette and leaned against the wall, taking a drag. "Whew, all right. Brandon, my man, you goin' on the Hilton Head trip next weekend?"

"Oh yeah, the . . ." Brandon's thoughts turned over twice. Placing his pack back in his pocket, he brushed the thumb of his cigarette hand against his upper left arm. The prospect of being shirtless on the beach crossed his mind for less than a second. He might as well be completely naked.

"*The* what?"

"Sorry, yeah, I just . . . Nah, I don't think I'm going to make this one."

The busboy scoffed. "For real? You gonna skip on Hilton Head? Man, I don't know about you, but I don't get to go to the beach every weekend."

"Nah, me neither." He thought about his upper left arm. "I haven't been in years."

"For real? You gotta go at least once a year, man." The kid exhaled and flicked his cigarette.

"I'm not much of a beach person, really."

The busboy scoffed again. "What? You don't like half-naked girls all over you and gettin' hammered?"

Brandon raised an eyebrow. "No, not really."

"Man, I didn't realize you were playin' for the other team or some shit."

145

He tried to not roll his eyes. "I think there are other ways to meet and connect with people, I guess."

"You gotta meet people somehow." The kid flicked his cigarette again, and the ashes scattered in the fan. "You don't wanna check out bikini girls? Eye candy, man."

Brandon stood up straight. "I don't think the mere display of skin should imply sex any more than the mere display of flames should imply violence. It doesn't have to be so . . . basic."

"What?"

"Well . . ." He turned away then back. "It's a preference. My own attraction requires more, um . . . subtly, I guess." He let his eyes drift away. The thought of Janelle gave him a faint, fleeting smile.

"For real? Bikini girls, man. What's wrong with you? Whatever." The busboy flicked the butt out the window and shuffled back to his shift.

Brandon shook his head and tapped his cigarette. He tried to not think a mental picture of being shirtless around people. It gave him a hint of nausea. It wasn't that he was self-conscious. The true threat to his self-esteem was the knowledge that such recreation would be an apex of pleasure for his peers and an abyss for him. *All my peers.* All his *normal* peers, forced by social convention to be around him. Having an excuse to show off their bodies, as though that most simple expression was adequate connection. He didn't feel any pride or pretense that he didn't share their preferences; only shame for that fact. Always shame.

The thought of Janelle and the thought of *her* gave him a new mental image of being naked in her arms. The shrill stopped, and he felt a semblance of peace again. *Just some peace and quiet, outside of the darkness and the fire.*

There was goodness, and it was good indeed. Things would work out. Things would go. He would make it somehow. *Peace.* He just didn't know how.

Why does she not look like Aisling?

***

BRANDON HEARD THE DOOR TO the deli close softly behind him. It was a quarter before nine, and the sandwich maker was just starting to close down for the night.

The clerk was just over fifty. He was a similar build to Brandon, but with a noticeable gut. The hair under his black cap was fair, and his oval eyes had thick crow's feet. As he shuffled from the walk-in freezer to finishing up his last sweep, he looked up for a second then briskly turned back around to the large bread box. He flipped the warmer switch, closed the lid, and then turned toward Brandon.

"Hey there, guy. What can I do you for?" His voice had a bit of volume and depth, with just a hint of a Western Carolina accent.

"Hey. If it's not too late, could I get just a . . . half turkey with provolone, peppers, olives, and mustard?"

"Sure, it's not too late." The man had a kind grin.

"Good deal. Thank you."

"You got it."

Brandon paced slowly as his sandwich was being made. His gaze fell into blankness as his day and his life receded into the dark blue humidity of the July evening. He looked across the stucco wall then gradually turned back to the deli counter. The clerk was working diligently, and yet, every point of the labor seemed to Brandon as though it was constrained by another calling, a more fulfilling calling. The man emanated unrealized potential.

The clerk reached his plastic-gloved left hand inside a jar, took a small handful of olives, and then spread them across the white slice of cheese. Underneath the wrinkled plastic on the ring finger, Brandon saw a weathered wedding band. It struck him.

As the moment began, he felt very akin to this man yet very different from him. They were apparently both underemployed men who made the most of their own situation, but the difference was that the clerk had a contentment that Brandon did not have. *Is it because he's married? So that he could be at peace, no matter what consequences he endures under the cold inefficiencies of our broken division of labor?* Brandon didn't know but suspected that the fact was related yet incidental. Contextual.

As the moment ended, he felt that he had gained greater insight and greater uncertainty. This was the price of wisdom untainted by the elusive comfort and vulgarities of new prejudices: an exponentially increasing amount of uncertainty, binding him to the chaos of his mind. *Where does it end? Where did it begin?*

"Hey, did you want some cayenne sauce?"

Brandon blinked. "Cay . . . Oh, sure."

"Very good. I love this stuff. Spicy, you know? I've heard capsaicin is good for you."

"That's cool," Brandon said with a smile.

"Then again, you know you can't believe everything you hear."

"For sure."

The clerk quickly and neatly wrapped up the turkey sandwich in wax paper, dabbed a piece of tape across the top, and then removed his plastic gloves. He rang up the order, swiped Brandon's credit card, and then handed it back to him with the receipt.

As Brandon took his sandwich with quick thanks, he once again noticed the ring.

The mental image stayed with him until he reached the door, which he stopped short of opening. On the adjacent bulletin board, he saw a black and white flyer for High Country

Pantry. There was a particular picture on it with a dot-matrix printing of a food sack and a smiling mother and child. He was transfixed. Then he blinked, turned away, and pushed the door open. His gaze receded into his blank life and the dark blue humidity of the July evening.

***

"SO, HAVE YOU BEEN MAKING your phone calls?"

"Yes, Dad. I've got a new list for tomorrow morning."

The heat of the late Sunday afternoon was getting to both of them.

"Then how do you find the time to sit on that computer and mess with that phone all day long?"

"Dad, I'm sure you know there's more than one way to network."

Brandon's father only responded with a smirk.

"I do think it's important for me to have some kind of social life."

"That's why they have bars. You don't need to be sitting on that computer all day long unless you really want to be a dishwasher for the rest of your life."

"Dad, I—"

"You need to get over that driving phobia and get a car, but to do that, you're going to need to earn real money."

"Dad—"

"Real people, real money. Do it."

Brandon was relieved to hear the low bell ring of a new text message. He pulled out his phone and saw that it was from Janelle.

"See? Here we go."

"Dad—"

"Whatever."

The leather squeaked as Brandon sat up from the spotless designer couch and went for the staircase. He looked at his phone again and smiled.

The cicadas outside were getting louder as the sky dimmed over the hills. The house seemed noticeably darker than it was a few seconds prior.

Shutting his bedroom door, Brandon decided against continuing the text exchange and reached for the call button.

Just then, the phone rang, but it wasn't Janelle. It was an unknown caller.

Brandon flipped it open in a fumble. "Hello?"

"Hello, is this Brandon . . . Marcel?" The man's voice was brisk and confident.

"Yes, it is. Who is—"

"This is Randall Hunt, president of the Young Capitalists, Triad Chapter. Hey, ya got a minute?"

Brandon took a quick breath and tried to mentally adjust from relaxation to the welcomed stress of opportunity. "Sure, yes. What's going on?"

"Well, Brandon, I'm sorry I'm just getting back to you now. I know you emailed your résumé some time ago and left a few messages. Sorry about that."

"Hey, no problem." Brandon's pace couldn't outrun his nervous tone. "Thanks for dropping me a line."

"Sure. I see that you just graduated back in . . . May, you're an economics guy, and . . . you're interested in getting involved in our group here, maybe making some contacts for jobs. That sound about right?"

"Yes! I've really come to embrace the sort of free-market ideas of the Young Capitalists, market efficiency to maximize prosperity for all, sorta . . . make the world a better place. And I'm also currently looking for a position, as well, so there's the—"

"Yep, networking," Randall said. "Certainly. Well, we're

all about that. I think you'll find that our folks have some good connections to help get you a job. So, welcome!"

There was a relief. "Awesome, thanks! So, what kinds of events are there, or . . ."

"Yeah." Randall's voice trailed off. "Yeah, we have a few different events each year. We have our summer meeting coming up next month over at the Nepott Club downtown, seven o'clock on the . . . sixth, I think."

"Oh, sounds good! What all—"

"We're having three speakers come that night. We've got one of the Mises guys and, let me see . . . oh, hey, there's an economist from Hoover who will be in the area. I think he's originally from North Carolina or something. And . . . a consultant from Vazio & Leer."

"Vazio, really? My sister works over there."

"Oh, cool. Yeah, we usually start with speakers, have Q&A, and then chat over snacks after that. It's mostly college kids and young professionals, of course. Good networking. Oh, and our discussion topic for that night will be . . . 'Is the U.S. really a free market'?"

Brandon smiled. "Oh, there's a good one. I'd, uh . . ." He stuttered then continued, "I'd say it's a common misconception for the progressive crowd. We have constant policy intervention to support the welfare and warfare federal outlays, and people think we have a free market because of rent-seeking corporations and crony capitalism. Seems like it's all in name only. I mean, we haven't had a free market since at least before the Federal Reserve, right?"

Randall laughed. "Sounds about right. You really are a true believer, aren't you? Well, that's good. I think you'd enjoy our group." He paused. "So, Brandon, when you're not getting mad over the latest round of quantitative easing, what do you do for fun?"

Brandon was pleasantly surprised by the apparent invitation to connect as friends rather than only professional acquaintances.

"Well, I . . . I go hiking sometimes, and . . . I listen to a lot of music, and I . . . enjoy playing guitar."

"Guitar, really? What kinds of styles do you play?"

The optimism almost became hope, and the relief almost became comfort. "Oh, mostly rock, some blues, some classical. Do you play?"

"Yeah, I've been playing for a few years. A little prog and avant-garde rock and heavier genres. Djent and hardcore stuff."

"Oh, wow, right on. Real smart and heavy stuff." Brandon shifted his weight. "You live in the area, I take it? What do you do?"

Randall cleared his throat. "I'm an information systems guy."

"Hey, that's cool."

"Not really, but thanks!"

They both laughed.

A second passed, and then Randall's brisk voice thundered back. "Well, good to touch base with you, Brandon. Looking forward to meeting you in a few weeks. We'll get you signed up and ready to go. You have my email, so let me know if you have any questions."

"Excellent. Thank you so much, Randall! It's really good to talk with you. I can't wait for the first meeting."

"All right, then. I'll see you."

Brandon closed his phone and immediately started analyzing how he had responded throughout the conversation. Through his worries, he did have a sense of hope for his ever-elusive sense of belonging. At least there was a chance to connect professionally. More importantly, there might even be a chance for him to connect personally.

He thought about the new yet close friendship with Janelle from across the country, his in-turns present and absent best guy Germy, and his old flame Marianne. He wished each of his disparate friends would come together like a group. And even if it couldn't, they were, he dared to think, real friends. Perhaps Randall could be one, too. Given Randall's connections and legitimate career, he could be a friend of which even Brandon's father would approve.

The air was heavy and still, and the cicadas sang. In each nanosecond, the world stopped and started again. At least there was a chance.

August

THERE WAS LAUGHTER. SOMEWHERE IN the rapid-fire cultural references and ratcheting levels of teasing, Brandon and Janelle found themselves unable to sleep at three o'clock in the morning. Brandon was on his fourth cigarette and second lap through the streets of his parents' neighborhood, illuminated by closely spaced yellow-orange lights. Other than the presence of hills, natural grass, and the occasional deciduous tree instead of the occasional cactus, it didn't look that different from the neighborhood that Janelle saw from her front porch. Each house looked like a slight variation of the previous. Nonetheless, there were warm souls scattered from house to house, each trying to make the most out of their quasi-successful Middle American quasi-dreams. And on this night, the groaning of air-conditioning units was broken by this emanating warmth from within and laughter without.

"I'm pumped about the band's new flick."

Brandon exhaled a cloud of smoke through his smile-reddened expression. Within his mind, the sweet melodies and soaring electric guitar notes of Steve Vai's "I Know You're Here" played as he tried to focus on the words instead of the feeling. "Which band is that?"

"*The* band, jackass," Janelle said with a grin.

"But which band is that?"

"We've been over this. You never listen to me."

"Fine," he said as he took another drag. "You never accept me. You're just like all the other assholes growing up. You're just cuter."

She laughed. "Please. You and *acceptance*, as you call it. Have you ever felt accepted by anyone?"

"My cat."

"Exactly. You know I accept you just fine."

"Do you?" He wasn't sure if he was serious about his own question or not.

"Well, you would know if you've been listening to me these past two months."

"I'm listening to you right now!"

"No, you're still talking."

Brandon faked an indignant scoff. "I'm only talking right now to tell you that I'm listening."

"And that's the whole problem."

"Gah!"

"Ahaha! Oh, come on; you know I lo . . ."

The conversation stopped. While the warmth of the hearts remained the same, the air seemed to get warmer on both sides of the country.

Janelle awkwardly cleared her throat and stood up. Brandon lifted his cigarette hand then dropped it back to his side as if to gesture for an unknown statement.

In the momentary quiet, Janelle heard the crack of a distant monsoon storm, and Brandon heard the crickets around the neighborhood stream. The passing seconds felt like hours, and Janelle could only handle so many.

"Damn. Last time I checked my watch, it was eleven eleven. We've talked four hours, whew."

Brandon shifted his weight, his heart rate increasing again. "I think we've proven that we can talk for hours."

"No, the number four, jackass."

He chuckled. "I know."

She sighed. "So . . . about that."

"About . . .?" Brandon's heart beat faster as he hoped she wouldn't realize that he was playing dumb.

Janelle looked up and saw a flash across the western skies. "My little Freudian slip there."

He realized he couldn't play dumb for a moment longer. "I wouldn't quite call it Freudian, my dear."

"Well, you know I—"

"No, I . . ." He turned around and found himself walking in the opposite direction, back toward his parents' house. "I figured it was something we'd have to talk about sooner or later."

Janelle sighed again. "I'm reading your tone here, and . . . you know, it doesn't sound like you're quite feeling things the way I'm feeling things." After the saddening ten or more near-hits with would-be lovers, she didn't want to be right yet again. Not this time.

"Janelle, I . . ." Brandon felt as though his heart was turning inside out, and everything that was right was being made wrong, and it was all of his doing. "I . . . I can't tell you how much I care about you, dear. I can't tell you how much this means to me. I can't tell you how . . . full . . . you've made me feel since I heard your voice for the first time. I really can't tell you." She sniffed then spoke with a steady tone as she paced. "Brandon, I think what you really can't tell me is that you just don't like me."

"No, I—"

"It's okay. Say it. I'm pretty used to it by now, you know."

"I . . . I really . . ." Brandon felt his chest tearing within. He realized he was now being both typical and a heartbreaker—

two things he never really thought he would be. "It's not a matter of not liking; it's just that . . . right now, I'm just not . . . seeing you in that light, you could say."

"That light. Hm. Can you say it?"

Brandon took a drag, exhaled slowly, and shook his head. "I . . . don't think I can."

"All right." She let the seconds pass with comfort. "Why?"

"I just can't. I—"

"No, I mean, why don't you feel the way I do?"

His pace turned inward like a broken counter-clockwise jaunt. He scratched his head between drags. Sweat rolled out of both sides of his bent elbow. "I don't know."

"Hmm." Her heart was beating fast, but there was stillness in her tone. A dead stillness. "I think I might."

Brandon took a quick breath and ignored his chest. "Okay. Why do you th—"

"Remember what we were talking about this time the other night? The long talk?"

"Refresh me."

"I swear, you really don't listen."

Brandon let out a more aggressive sigh. "Okay, I know I didn't pick up on the band thing, but I do know we talked about—"

"Harm."

His feet, his hands, and his lungs stopped. "Harm."

Janelle cleared her throat and looked back across the distant skies for lightning but saw none. "Self-harm."

"Yes. What—"

"It's . . . uh, not the most fun topic in the world, but I think I speak for both of us when I say that things have been different over the past two months, right?" Time sat in the stillness of her voice.

"Uh . . . right," he responded. "Things have been different. Better."

"You know, one would think this all means we've both finally found what we're looking for and all's well and good in the world, but we know better. I know you know better."

"What do you mean?"

The desert heat was rolling away with the coming storm's winds.

She turned back toward the house. "Remember your comment there at the end?"

"Yeah." His voice quivered. "The blood?"

"Yes. I would like to hear more, if that's okay."

"Yeah, fifth grade." His chest pulled tight, and his ears began to ring. "So, I had, uh . . . yeah. It's like it just started that one day, and . . . I've never known why. My mom gives me a kiss, I get in the car, and . . ." His heart beats faster. The mess of emotions had sprung even harder than before. It still felt safe, so much safer than anyone before, but it was never pleasant. "It was . . . blinding. Like that day was like . . . a dark art house film with parts missing, you know? I get in the car, I go to school, I'm taking this test, and . . . I come home in the car, and next thing I know, it's late at night and I'm in bed and there's blood all over the sheets.

"I told my parents I threw them away because I spilled chocolate milk on them. Avoided being shirtless ever since." Brandon took a hard drag. He looked for the stars but found none. "And the gym nut teacher who married rich kept blaming me for things for the rest of the year. Shame as education. And no one believed me. They seemed to think my behavior and complaints were from the meningitis I had earlier that year. So the . . . cutting . . . stuck.

"And yes, my cat was there for me. I mean, what does this have to do—"

"Like I said the other night, I think there's courage in

you." The small sound and simple kindness of her voice was a solace. "But you had another comment about that first night. I've been thinking about it." The air died down. Her tone quieted. "You said you were comforted. You thought of loving someone, and you were comforted."

"Oh . . . yeah."

"You . . ."

Brandon puffed hard for the last bare flecks of tobacco. "That night, I had . . . just lay there for a while. There was this lack of energy, just empty, like everything had spilled out. I didn't feel anything at all, and it . . . it seemed like I was lying on the edge of something, about to fall off." He flicked his cigarette butt. "And then, just for a moment, there was this flash. I mean, I just imagined it, but I saw it and felt it. It . . ." Tensions and pretensions faded away. There was something holy in her. It scared him. It scared him because it smelt of trust and hope, but he continued anyway. "It was like this sorta . . . like being in someone's arms. And her face was kind. Like I . . . It was like I knew it was okay. It was going to be okay, because . . ."

"Yes"—her heart felt almost at ease—"I hear you."

"I mean, it was a daydream I had," he said dismissively. "Coping with puberty, most likely. I don't know if this was the point you had in mind or what." He looked up into the wet sky. "I don't think that mental image was some kind of premonition of a . . . dream girl or a twisted romantic ideal or anything." Contrary to accusations, he hardly ever lied. But when he was subconsciously terrified while consciously intrigued, the circumstances were ripe for it. "And to be honest, I still can't get over this thing with Sarah. To be honest, it's not over yet." That part was true.

"Hm . . ." Janelle maintained her soft composure while her insides were gently pulling apart. "Maybe it was an idea for the sake of an idea—coping with the present by yearning for the future. We all have some sort of ideals, you know? I've always imagined a handsome guy in jeans and an old band T-shirt who's simple on the outside but complex on the inside. A sensitive guy. A good guy. No signs of one yet, apparently." She mocked a throat clearing. "So, anyway, these ideals shape us in subtle ways. They make us who we are."

"Yes," Brandon said with guilt in his voice. "Definitely true."

"Things beneath nature and nurture, but inseparable from them." She leaned against her doorway and watched the dark clouds of night race overhead. "If I hadn't been rejected by every guy I liked in high school, I wouldn't be the fragile thing you're talking to right now."

"You're not fragile, dear."

Janelle scratched her nose. "Oh, but I am. And I always fall for it. Hope is a four-letter word, you know."

"Ha, that's for sure."

"It is." She glanced up then back down again. "After Mom went away and Chris had to manage Dad's money and manage me, I . . . you know, I ate. All the time. I didn't even think about it. I didn't even notice . . . until my peers did, of course. I didn't hear the end of it." She leaned against the doorframe and listened to the delicate roll of thunder. "Like you said, it was blinding. I didn't think about it at all. I kind of watched it happen. And the boys and the girls let me have it."

Brandon exhaled. He thought he wanted to be there for her entirely, but he just couldn't.

It was more like he just wouldn't.

"That's where the big, white medicine cabinet comes in," Janelle said. "Problem solver extraordinaire. Weight and weeping go bye-bye. Woo-hoo. The end."

Brandon stood still in the breeze of the dark morning and

heard a loud cricket. "Dear, you know . . . it isn't the end. I'm here, as much as I can be."

The other end of the phone was silent.

"And I know you. I've seen you. You're wonderful just the way you are. You are."

Her lips almost lifted into a smile, but then fell back again. The clouds still rolled, and the lightning was sparse.

"In fact, Janelle, I'm definitely weaker than you are. I mean, I was this little kid whose only worry was being pushed off the back of the couch by my sister. Both my parents are still around and well. And well-to-do. And then I had some kind of brain screw out of nowhere that made me cut myself to ribbons. That's pure crazy."

"Okay. So—"

"You have reasons for being the way you are. You have causes and pain. And you keep breaking through them every day. So . . . I mean, could you be any stronger?"

She smiled. "Thank you. But Brandon . . . obviously, my strength or compassion isn't what you really want. I think you're waiting for someone. I think you know nothing is going to work out with Sarah."

"Well, I still think Sarah wants . . ." Brandon shook his head. "Once she sees that I'm the kind of guy who cares, and that I *am* honest . . . anyway. Listen, whatever brain screw I made up to fight the brain screw, it's my imagination. That feminine apparition or whatever the hell it is, it's something to hold on to." As the conversation sailed further into inner warfare, he felt like a flaming wayward ship. Selfishness burned within him, and self-preservation moved up its flanks. His ears and chest hurt, but he continued to speak, damn the torpedoes. "Janelle, I hear her voice in yours."

She looked up, her eyebrow lifting. "But you don't see her face."

"I . . . don't know."

The night kept rolling and insisted upon not bringing her along. She was a girl standing by a door. The rocks in her yard sat lifelessly.

Like Brandon, she didn't want things. She wanted a family. She wanted love. She wanted the barest, simplest connection and a mind to share thoughts of the world and thoughts of books and albums and movies. It all rolled past. She now felt that the best chance for this was fading away. What she would have was another night by herself, physically and emotionally, and so many more. She would have nothing.

"Everyone leaves me," she said. "Everyone leaves, and no one comes. No one comes to me. I'm there for everyone, whether they're across the street or across the country. I support everyone. At the end of the day, it's just me and the desert." She rubbed her nose with her left hand. "Why won't . . .?" She stopped. "Why wouldn't you of all people—"

"Janelle, you're everything I've ever wanted," Brandon said with resolution. "And I'm never going to forgive myself for how I'm not feeling about it." His chest sank and didn't resurface. "I'm sorry. I wish I could be there for you in some way, but I can't. I'm really sorry, love. I . . . ."

She couldn't speak. The sky was black. And the wind had stopped.

"I'm sorry. I don't know what to do."

He had broken both their hearts.

The Morning Star smiled.

***

DRESSED IN A CHARCOAL SUIT jacket and carefully starched, French blue button-down, Brandon leaned over the balcony of the lavish art deco Nepott Club and watched the rays of the setting sun ascend the downtown skyline. He couldn't stop thinking about Janelle.

The previous day had ended with no call, text, email, or any updates on his Gold Pavilion profile; and a second day was coming to a close. He knew he had to make the most of this meeting; to make progress in his personal and professional networking. Germy would still be in school for a semester, and there wasn't anyone else who might actually want to talk to him about economics, society, or true love. With his cheap cigarette in one hand and expensive cabernet in the other, he had lost most of his composure and just wanted to hear that his faraway friend was okay.

"There you are," Randall said, closing the sliding door behind him. "Nice sunset."

"It is nice." Brandon took a drag. "Sorry. Had to grab a smoke break."

Randall smirked. "Usually, people take such breaks at work and parties, not at networking events where you're the only smoker."

Brandon exhaled. "Good point."

Randall, with his stocky build filling Perry Ellis clothes, leaned against the railing and scratched his goatee. "I liked your point about regulatory hypocrisy in the Tennessee Valley Authority ash spill case study. The feds were all 'do as we say, not as we do,' apparently. Way to protect the environment, right? You've got a way of finding elusive angles on an issue."

"Well, thank—"

"No, seriously. It's a real talent. Not just playing pleasantries. You see the root and how to get to it when most of us are grabbing at leaves and branches."

"Huh," Brandon said as he tilted his head back. "Still, thanks. I just . . . well, Randall, I guess someone can get a good look at the world from the gutter."

Randall laughed. "Now, that sounds like proletariat speak, comrade."

"Ha! Well, I was a Campus Progressive not too long ago."

Brandon shook his head. "But I mean that personally, not politically. I think we could make real progress on many issues if people would stop conflating the two. My life situates my views, not the other way around."

"Mr. Principle, huh?" Randall leaned back from the railing. "Principle is all well and good, but you've still got to think practically. Like guitar, right? There's music theory, and there's performing, you know? You want to play your Martin, not just think about it. So, you can keep ruminating out here or go make some contacts inside, all right? C'mon, work the room." He put his hand on Brandon's shoulder. "I mean, principles are great—they're our mainstay—but you've got to think about how to apply them."

Brandon nodded. "Fair enough. I mean, even if liberty guarantees the best chance of prosperity for all, there's still no sure consequence. There's no guarantee that people will think and act rationally." He took a drag from his cigarette and exhaled smoke into the thick, summer air. "We're only as good as we individually choose to be. Given the heavy constraints of our regulatory environment and a century of strong economic interventionism, even our fellow capitalists operate from fear and irrationality." He took a hard drag and looked down.

Randall raised an eyebrow. "There's more to your complaint than what you're saying."

"Okay, fine," Brandon said with a huff. "Every job contact tells me to check the postings, which I already do, so why network? After a few dozen people, I talk to a guy who says, by the time the posting is up, they've already picked someone. It's just a formality. No meritocracy. I mean, I know the consulting job went to a guy with a Sociology degree and no experience. It's all back to who you know, not what you know. I mean, why? This makes firms ultimately less productive. There's no rational self-interest. In fact, it's self-destructive."

Randall scratched his chin. "I hear you. In a market and a society dominated by the uncertainties of legislation, regulation, and litigation, people tend not to act rationally. That idea assumes a level of permanence that is, well . . . antiquated. You're a smart guy, Brandon, but I'm afraid you're a little naïve. Most of the time, employers—like dates, actually—have little faith in merit beyond basic qualifications. They go with their gut."

"That's not rational."

"Yeah, that's the point."

"Doesn't a philosophy of liberty hinge on rational self-interest?"

"Again, leave philosophy out of it and think practically. The world is the way it is. Deal!"

Squeezing the last burning tobacco out of his cigarette filter, Brandon turned back toward the building and walked as though he carried twice his own weight. He couldn't decide what was more disappointing: the truth behind Randall's words or the comfort with which the man had spoken them. He wasn't sure if they were meant as descriptive or normative statements.

Brandon tried to focus on the compliments, as few people would give him such credit. But a few negative thoughts seeped through the paper-thin attempt at confidence along with the stock idealism.

"I guess no one is really rational," Brandon said, as if to compromise. "But if we don't even try, if we just accept the status quo . . . capitalists thinkers like us won't have many principles left."

"We'll see." Randall's view glazed over, and his tone turned hard. "You still need a job. What exactly do you want to do?"

Brandon's chest twisted at the audible shift. "I, uh . . ." He tried to think. His mouth hung open until the brash quasi-professional words came. "I'm interested in data and market analysis, particularly in the philanthropic arms of business. You know, the company profile as a philanthropic leader in challenging economic times. You know . . . build up the profile, public relations. You know, to . . . make a difference."

Randall folded his arms and turned. "Public relations . . . and foundations. I can think of one guy to talk to." He wrinkled his nose. "There's not much money there, though."

"Yeah." Brandon tried to ignore the tightening in his chest. "That's fine. Don't let the one suit I own fool you, ha. I live pretty simply. I just want to do a good job and do good."

"Good, huh? Good luck with that. Hey, you could always break that Martin out and play some Kansas songs on open mic nights, right?" He laughed.

"Yeah, I . . ." Brandon tried not to sigh. "That's actually not a bad idea. There's a notion that starving artists out there just have to grow up and settle for a real job. After spending a year trying to get a real job, maybe I should settle with being a starving artist."

Randall laughed again. "Sure. You should still work the room before you set out your guitar case on Trade Street."

The last rays of light crept over the western horizon. The two professionals walked back inside. One thought of personal and professional connection while the other thought of unspoken rules and shedding professional deadweight. The sun set.

***

GERMY TAPPED ON HIS CLOVE cigarette and listened, holding the phone loosely against his ear. After flicking the filter across the parking lot, he brushed his free hand across the pocket of his faded black jeans. The contents were a cheap red lighter, a pack of condoms, and a wad of keys. He rolled his eyes.

"That's perfectly fine. Let that go. You don't need a relationship."

"Oh, sure," Brandon scoffed. "Says the guy who gets his groove on at least once a week. I'd like some semblance of a relationship, even if it's long-distance." He kept awkwardly shuffling down the street to the bus stop under another hazy day.

"Twice a week, but who's counting?" Germy reached into his right pocket for another clove. "It's irrelevant anyway. You said you're not feeling it, right? You're still after that activist girl who's so understanding or whatever, for some reason." He stuck the black cigarette into his mouth and flicked his lighter. "You don't need a relationship."

"I don't *need* anything."

"Yep, you got it."

Brandon scoffed again. "In any event, I think I should be feeling it this time."

"*Should* be?"

"I mean, Sarah's still playing it cool with me, and Janelle is . . . well, she's different."

A plume of clove smoke passed into the air. "Yeah, from the sound of it. So, appreciate her. Be there for her. That's all you really need to do. That's all there is to it. That's the only *should* here. You should be there for her."

"I should *be there* for someone I just met who lives across the country?"

"You'll find a way. It doesn't have to be literal."

"Hm."

Germy's insight disappeared into the malaise of Brandon's mind. A constant malaise of worry and a mounting sense of purposelessness and worthlessness. The gray matter warehouse shuffled an ever-increasing list of networking contacts, cover letters,

167

online accounts for every application, and thoughts of pending disapproval of parents, professors, and peers.

Then he thought about meaning. He thought about hope. He thought about home. It all led back to the heart and maybe Janelle, but it was really just Sarah. *Strawberry blonde hair and that mole. Jobs. Compassion. Dating. Understanding. Meaning. Acceptance.* Then he thought about home again.

And then the sky and the ground reversed. His palpitations and tinnitus started. Home was where the heart hits, and now the heart was hitting itself. Brandon's own arbitrary understanding of relationships confounded his arbitrary understanding of home. Janelle had a heart. It was a heart that Brandon couldn't touch or feel as his preconceptions were in the way. And so the goodness drifted away, and the sky sat beneath him, and the ground held above him.

At that same moment, Germy leaned against a brick wall and smoked his clove. The Christmas-scented smoke was a simple pleasure, and Germy knew that was all it was. It was fleeting. It was just a moment. He didn't worry about the eternal. He figured the eternal would be there for him when the moment was right. Unlike so many other philandering and substance-abusing Epicureans of another lost generation, the eternal would indeed be there for him. Because the eternal was always welcome in his simple thoughts and simple words and simple love. Jeremy Kuhn was a slut, but a slut who cared for his sexual partners and his friend.

Simple love worked. When perfected, it did cast out the fear. The memories and the fear.

"Hm, hm, hm," Germy repeated back to Brandon. "Just be there for her."

Brandon took a quick but deep breath to stave off a quick sense of panic. "Yeah."

Germy brushed his hand against his faded black jeans and took a drag. "How's that job crap going?"

"It's more of the same. I went to that meeting and networked, networked, networked with all the other supposed true believers."

Germy threw his greasy hair back behind his shoulder. "Did that help?"

"I don't think so."

"You don't need—"

"Yeah, yeah." Brandon rolled his eyes. "You know, Germy, you're on my ass as much as my parents are. Just in the opposite direction."

"The difference is that I'm right."

"I'm sure they'd say the same thing. Wouldn't your parents?"

Germy laughed. "No, they'd just tell me that I'm an idiot and my new job's not going to pay enough."

"Wait—you got a job?" Brandon asked with genuine surprise.

"Some kind of graphic arts firm of some sort. I don't know. They cared more about my hobbies than my degree, of course. It's just some temp-to-hire or internship or some crap. It starts right after I graduate in December. We'll see. I don't know what's going on."

"Well, that's cool," Brandon said, his voice rising in tone.

"Yeah." Germy pulled on the side of his jeans. "Quit worrying about it."

"Worry about—"

"You won't be washing dishes forever."

"I think it's cool that you—"

"Come on; I think we're a few Barbie burnings past formalities. Don't worry and don't compare yourself to me or anyone else. You're above this."

Brandon's heart rate picked back up. "Well, after your boss screams at you for a dirty parking lot because people litter right after you finish cleaning it, you get kinda despondent." He tried to not think about his heart. "You just want to have something to look forward to. You just want love in some form or another. You just want to have a group of friends. You just want to belong. You just want to have your own Campus Progressives or Young Capitalists to call your own."

"That's a bunch of justs. I know people have an innate desire for groups, but is that really what you want? You do have love. Damn the rest. Like, what did you do about your boss yelling at you, other than smoke an extra pack and think about relationship crap?"

Brandon smirked. "After all that, I put in my earbuds and blasted Times Zero's 'Aim to Bleed' on full and finished a few racks of dishes."

"That's it," Germy said with a hand flick. "That's all you really need. You stayed true to yourself, but you went with the flow."

"Like Ms. Gray at the lake."

"Cute reference, drab phoenix." Germy ran his boney fingers through his hair and exhaled. "Everyone wants some respect. Few people really want purpose and meaning. So, they try to find their own group and acceptance, but so few try to find their individual beauty, their own acceptance. I'm not talking about that new age junk. I mean what's real. Old age. All age."

"Easier said than done." *Clubs, dancing, mud runs, and beer,* he thought. *Connection. Belonging. Acceptance. Love. Theirs, not yours. Not you. Not you.* "Humans are social."

"And humans are logical," Germy responded. "Capable of it, anyway. It's like a gym membership for their mind that most don't make use of. They'll sign up and check-in once or twice a year, if that. You do go regularly, and that's the difference. You don't need them. What are you so afraid of that you can't trust in your own acceptance? Your own love? Appreciate Janelle and stop worrying about jobs. Just keep going, because the road goes with it. And stop posting online about how people don't care. The only ones who reply are those to whom it doesn't apply. Logically."

"I guess," Brandon responded. The sky was hazy and overcast. He thought about the intro to the Tracy Chapman song "Change." That acoustic riff. And then those lyrics.

September

"IS HE ASLEEP?"

Marianne sighed as she shut the sliding door behind her. She adjusted the phone to her ear as she pulled out the pack of cigarettes that she had been anticipating for so long. "Yeah, I think so. At least he's not in the NICU anymore." Fumbling with her lighter, she sighed again. She had been awake for two days straight. "I'll be happy if I just get a few hours."

"Welcome to the next eighteen years, sweetie."

"Gee, thanks, Mom. I heard it gets better after a few months."

"It's a long haul. Wait— did I just hear a lighter?"

"Yeah." She lifted an unplucked eyebrow. "Huh. I guess I'm not trying to hide it this time around."

"At least you waited. I still think you should breastfeed. Make sure he gets the bottle."

"Yeah." She tossed her hair over her shoulder and slumped into the white plastic patio chair. The view off the back porch featured two long, three-story apartment buildings facing each other, running up to an unkempt forest. Bugs buzzed around the fluorescent street lights. A fountain bubbled over a small, artificial pond surrounded by artificial turf. Three orange fish swam in it. Little else could be seen or heard as mother and daughter sat silently on the phone, the potent tension rising. "Mom, you know, I—"

"Yes, sweetie?"

"I know exactly what you're thinking, and you're right. I don't know what I'm going to do. I don't know what the fuck I'm going to do. I . . ." She exhaled smoke hard. "I don't know what I'm going to do, Mom."

Her mother waited for a second then said, "You're going to enjoy your job's generous maternity policy, feed that kid, and go back in a few months."

"What about school?"

"Well, sweetie, you can take a class or two each semester at community college. That will be fine. You're a decent student. But you should definitely leave time to go out."

Marianne rolled her eyes. "Seriously, Mom?"

"Not all men are like him. And who knows, there's that whole MILF thing. Maybe if you found a young entrepreneur or geeky engineer with a fetish, you could—"

"That sounds great."

"I wouldn't be a good Jewish mother if I didn't—"

"No," Marianne interrupted as she exhaled. "You'd be a great Jewish mother if you didn't. I'm having a mild heart attack over here about what the hell to do, and the last thing I want to hear from you is dating tips. I need to figure out my schedule and the next steps. It would be great if you'd be willing to watch him some when I go back to work, or at least empathize a little more."

"I'm sure your smoking is great for that heart attack."

"Oh, please." She took another quick drag. "This isn't going to kill me. You're going to kill me. Or the asshole will. But anyway."

Her mother laughed. "I know your emotions are all over the place right now. Don't worry; I'll help you. Your friends will help you. It's going to be okay. It's going to work out. Just think about those next steps."

"Yeah." Marianne flipped the long, plastic lighter between her fingers, sinking deeper into the plastic patio chair.

A car passed by the front of the complex, and a television flickered in an adjacent window. The battery icon on her phone lost a bar.

A generation sat. It looked at its predecessor and successor but could never figure out the pretext or context. It just watched its reflection on screens and on shop windows, vacillating between complacency and urgency. Perhaps the blame was with the previous generations, but there seemed to be little reason in assigning blame. It was irrelevant. So little could be done. Brandon knew the econometrics but most knew the reality behind them. Wants were getting cheaper. Needs were getting pricier. Classical economics were a whipping boy for these Neo-Keynesian outcomes. So a generation sat. Perhaps something or someone would emerge, but the doubt always voided out the hope.

Marianne quit thinking about hope years ago.

"What happened to that one guy from high school? He came for dinner that one time. Kinda quiet guy. Oh, what's his name? The one who lived in Meadowbrook—"

"Brandon?"

"Yeah, Brandon. You still keep up with him?"

"A little." Her next sigh was not of annoyance but of mourning a time lost and gone.

"I'm sure he'd like to visit the beach. Maybe he'd like to stay. Don't you think?"

"I've thought about that," Marianne responded, reaching for another cigarette then deciding against it. She just held the long, clear plastic lighter, turning it over in thought. Then she sat back and watched the light-polluted sky. "I don't know. Not really a beach guy."

"Okay, okay. He was a weird kid, anyway. Didn't really do much. Ate slow. One day, you'll find someone with spunk.

There's plenty of them. Find one of those. You have to be spunky in this world. Nice guys really do finish last."

"That's not it."

"What?"

"I mean, sure, nice only goes so far." She flipped her lighter between her fingers then stopped. "He had insight. He saw things I didn't see; seemed to really like me for me. He believed in me." Her unplucked eyebrows rose again as she lost her gaze in the air. "And I didn't believe in him." She smiled and almost laughed. "Pretty awkward and weird, I guess."

"Weird or on drugs, dear. Those will make you see things! Insight doesn't change diapers or buy formula." Marianne's mother coughed. "Don't worry; you'll find the one."

"Yeah." Marianne rolled the phone into her shoulder. After a moment, she heard crying. "He's up again. I gotta go."

***

CLOSING THE TAB OF TAGGED pictures, Janelle sat back from her computer. The temperature outside was almost cool enough to open the windows and let clean air into her small home. Her homework and books were ready for the coming week. There wasn't much else to do on a Sunday afternoon. The television, her only family in the house, rambled from the other room.

The thought of her would-be boyfriend across the country wouldn't go away. The whole notion was just another burned possibility, a beautiful thing drenched in flames. She didn't want to talk to him indefinitely, but she knew she would. It hurt to stay in touch, but compassion kept breaking through. He still mattered to her, even if he came with the requisite tinge of betrayal, rejection, and self-loathing that the rest of them did.

The thinking just wouldn't stop. She thought of kind words from Chris, but they faded away. A brother was expected to care.

Looks. Not good. Not good enough. Face. A reflection in the mirror unaccepted here or there or anywhere. The flashbulbs and pixels revealed it all. It revealed the pseudo-truth that only true superficiality could enflame beyond all reason. She couldn't stop thinking that hers was a face and a body made for repulsion, and all her failures in love and life came from this pseudo-truth.

Looks. Not good. Of course.

In her momentary plummet of self-assessment, the emanating noise of the television caught her ear.

"*Hydracutt* will shed the pounds off you in less than half the time of the competition!"

Janelle sat in her computer chair and listened to the noise. She listened like she knew she shouldn't.

"*Look* at the results! *Hear* the stories! *Know* the difference! *Be* the thin you were meant to be! *Hydracutt* can get you there with just four capsules a day. *Call* now and receive a second bottle *absolutely free!*"

She listened and didn't think. And that was the point. It ran roughshod over her cares. She just sat and listened like she knew she shouldn't. Her other four senses melded in tow, driven by the aural fixation on the noise and its promises. It drove and drove in fifteen- and thirty- second increments, first a minute, and then another. She was transfixed.

Six and a half minutes of self-destruction had passed when her cell phone rang. Her mind passed through excitement, curiosity, and then concern. It was an unknown caller. She answered on the second ring.

"Yes, this is her."

She tried to listen, but after the caller introduced himself, there was a hard shift and crash in her heart, pulling completely and horrifyingly away from her comforting self-consciousness. Something happened. Something bad.

"Captain? You said . . ."

And then she could barely listen at all anymore.

"Oh no, is . . .? No, is he . . .? You said he . . ."

Janelle fell into the large frayed blanket on her old couch as the captain spoke with measured care and stock sympathy. Silent tears rolled off of her free hand and fell on the red and purple design. Her heart broke for her brother.

Because his hands, the same hands that threw her atop his shoulders and carried her across the mountainous desert northeast of Mesa, were no more. The remaining pulp belonged to the rocket-propelled grenade, the partial wreckage of the Humvee, Staff Sergeant Jacob Carrington (KIA), and the mountainous desert northeast of Kandahar District. Post-traumatic stress disorder was a certainty. Her big brother was now a wounded mess, inside and out.

The good news was that he was alive and stable.

"Okay." She began to sniff.

The captain continued, dignified and professional, with just a little warmth.

She sniffed again and nodded. "Yeah, I'll take care of that." It was becoming more difficult for her to remain quiet and compose herself. "I'll see Chris then?" She rubbed her running nose with her free hand. "Okay, okay."

That last inflection struck the captain. His prepared response stopped for a moment, and then he added warmth and grace. He prayed and vowed to expedite the process.

When she finally hung up the phone, Janelle fell back into the blanket and let her cries flow without restraint. It kept coming.

She knew her own self-destructive thoughts would soon be back even more monstrous than before. She also knew that she would have to overcome them enough to be a loving sibling. And she knew her mind well enough to know that this was the price of love.

What she didn't know was the subconscious impression that her courage and love had left on the captain. She had been the paragon of strength and understanding, one voice of many distilled the inherent meaning of the war causalities and all who loved them straight to his inner being. It was a light that wouldn't fade. It was a light he carried to other injured soldiers and their families, taking an extra moment to lend his ear and resources however they could be lent. A light that broke through and went on and on and on.

***

GERMY WOKE UP SCREAMING AND remembered why.

Although he wouldn't share the reason with Liz.

He sat up in bed, naked, sweating, and panting, but it died down as quickly as it usually did. The sheets were in a pile between them, almost as rumpled as her dyed blue hair. She put a hand on his shoulder and tried to be comforting, but no comfort could be felt. They sat up in silence, trying to convey something that didn't exist.

He tossed his hair out of his face and considered getting a clove cigarette, but he couldn't remember where he left his lighter. As his breaths died down, he sat staring with as little thought as possible.

Liz put her hand over his chest and tried to hold him. Her breasts pressed against him through the threadbare Nine Inch Nails T-shirt that she had borrowed from him. It was a size too big on her.

He almost smiled. The feeling was one of gratitude. Still, no comfort could be felt. And he wouldn't share the reason with her. Careful repression pushed the memories slowly and firmly into the austerity of his mind.

The small hand on the clock was just past three a.m., and

the college town was as quiet as it was dark.

Liz turned back over and thought about going to sleep, no longer interested in solving emotional enigmas this late in the night. Germy knew she liked his *War Cry Universe* character hacks, so he had left his laptop running for her if she couldn't fall back asleep.

The fan blew quietly in the dark room full of school, work, and pop culture clutter. Paper plates with scraps of Chinese takeout sat in the middle of the computer desk, and the chipped, white plastic "Server JEREMY KUHN" nametag sat on the corner.

"Germ," Liz said, breaking the silence. "Let me sleep in, okay? I have to call my asshole stepfather tomorrow. I don't want to sound like I'm on drugs or something."

"Okay." Germy's jaw sat open as he tried to find something else to say. "Do you need a ride or anything tomorrow night?"

"No." She turned over and pulled her side of the covers up. "I'll walk. I mean, didn't you need to give your friend a ride anyway?"

"Yeah."

"I'll walk it." Liz closed her eyes but didn't want to go back to sleep. The concern faded, and she softly smiled. She reached back around his lean body, not sure if it was her heart or her loins keeping her awake. The two seemed to be uncommonly connected for their mutual hookup. "Germ?"

"Hmm?" He remained sitting up and staring, giving as little credence to his memories as possible. "What's up?"

"Go back to sleep or get a condom, okay?"

"Okay." He dropped back into the bed and pulled his side of the covers up, adjusting his position as he pulled. He closed his eyes and cleared his throat.

"I've got some of those pink ones," Liz said.

"I don't need pills."

She yawned. "You did last night."

He sat still for a moment. "I didn't need them then, either."

"Sure."

One of his memories opened back up. It was of his father taking him to the art museum downtown to see landscapes from Caspar David Friedrich. It was his father explaining what was meant by expressionism. It was his father laughing at his joke about Jackson Pollock. It was his father letting him pull back the string and let a light cascade of washable red paint splatter onto the oversized canvas in the children's exhibit. It was his father handing him a brush so he could carefully paint "Jeremy" onto a tile on the adjacent wall with five blue stars. It was his father holding his hand as they crossed the street.

It was before his father's holding hand became a fist. It was before the family completed the conversion from the curiosity of overexposed film to the certainty of proper palettes to be used in the foyer. It was before fake smiles were the only smiles. It was before he was beaten bloody for failing to make the baseball team, for which his twin brother pitched. It was before his parents' chosen solution to the ailments they caused, physical and mental, was medication. It was before personal connection was always less important than professional connection. It was before there was nothing left worth remembering. It was before and never would be again.

Liz shifted in bed. The purposeful apathy washed back over Germy as she pulled closer to feel his heartbeat. She didn't feel very much. He didn't feel very much. But it was enough.

"Can we go see something tomorrow?" she asked softly.

"We don't need movies."

"Just a matinee."

"We don't need matinees."

Liz pulled her arm back in mock disapproval. "Cheap ass."

"Indubitably."

October

SITTING BEFORE THE BLUE-WHITE glow of his monitor, Brandon sighed and hit "Refresh." His parents' neighborhood was dark and quiet. Now that he had exhausted his initial contacts, as well as first and second rounds of follow-ups to all his networking chances with the Young Capitalists, all he could think to do was to keep refreshing the webpages for all his online job boards.

Foundation Leadership of the Carolinas and Feeding the Triad were both updated on a daily basis, and he knew the competition was high for their positions. Nonetheless, he hit "Refresh." Each position had several hundred applicants, many of whom had more extracurricular experience than he did, even if social services wasn't their first career choice. Nonetheless, he hit "Refresh."

He kept hearing that the salaries were low for his data analysis skillset and socially-approved good feelings associated with the work only extended to volunteer activities and fundraising events. Nonetheless, he hit "Refresh." Lofty dreams aside, Randall had said it right: Brandon needed a job.

But, at this point in his dishwashing career, as in his love life, Brandon's personal expectations continually dropped. The call and email response ratios hovered around twelve-to-one. He actually felt grateful when someone took the time to tell him no.

Tonight, his only hope was that there would be one more job post to send another one of his ill-fated tailored cover letter and résumé pairings so that he would have something to tell his mother when her inevitable call to check on his progress came the following morning.

Watching the cursor glow, Brandon thought of another website to check. He typed "High Country Pantry" into his browser. After his slow internet caught the signal, he found himself on a simple, frames-based website with little coherence or color scheme. A picture of the old, blue-paneled building sat prominently in the middle of the page. He thought about how Germy's knack for graphic design might help them.

Looking to the upper right corner, Brandon saw the "Contact Us" link. He clicked on it, only to see a familiar gruff face looking back at him.

It was Conrad. Brandon smiled, happy to see him again all these months later. Then his sense of self-preservation returned, and he started scrolling down the page. There didn't appear to be any open positions, other than volunteer ones. He thought about emailing Conrad, but he twitched and told himself that he couldn't think of the right words. Instead, he clicked back on the browser and found himself staring past the webpage, lost in his mind once again.

Numbness had begun to set in until the "Programs" tab caught his eye. He clicked on it and thoughtlessly scrolled past statistics that the evaluative part of his mind would want to analyze, stopping instead on a candid picture. It struck him, and it struck him hard.

It was a boy and his mother walking out of the building's front door, taken from behind so that their faces weren't showing. The child was maybe nine years old, with a tuft of uncombed brown hair pushed up by the breeze. His mother was holding his hand with hers while using the other to hold a brown grocery bag. Peeking out of the top of the bag was a box of Penguin Puffs Organic Cereal. It was a light beige box with a blue and white cartoon penguin next to the title. Just a box of cereal, something someone thought might be good to give to someone else, peeking just over the top of the brown paper bag, just big enough to be seen in this one snapshot of what the High Country Pantry did for just two of its clients on some day or another. And a child. A child who might not be as hungry because of it.

Brandon felt his eyes slowly well up then close. He dabbed the side of one eye with the sleeve of his shirt.

Closing the browser, he thought about turning on some music or going for a walk, something to make the warmth in his chest settle back into the slog of emotional equilibrium. He understood the message that experience, common sense, and the latest takotsubo cardiomyopathy research ran contrary to the mass culture sloganeering. Because enough *real* compassion can kill you.

A sudden Castlevania-themed ringtone went off, alerting him to Germy's call.

"Hey, you," Brandon answered. "What are you up to?"

"Chilling," Germy said with his mock swagger. "You know."

"To what do I owe the pleasure at this dubious hour?"

"Come on; it's barely midnight," he protested. "I'm just getting started."

"I'm sure you are. So, really, what's up?"

Germy cleared his throat and absent-mindedly tapped his coat pocket in search of a lighter. "I've been thinking a bit today about you and all that craziness in your brain. It reoccurred to me that there is a bit of disconnect between your stated or intended objectives and your concrete actions toward these objectives. At least, as I see them."

Brandon rolled his eyes. "I hope this isn't another one of those flatulent semantic games that philosophy majors are always wanking over. We can't even talk about music anymore. Last time, we covered the apocryphal constructs of semiotic sycophants in the record industry or something."

"That's a cute try, but you left out the part about your blind deontological devotion to the principle of—"

"Germy!"

"All right, all right. It's just that you've been toiling so long, trying to score one of these entry-level positions for do-gooder stuff, and I really don't think that's what you need to be focusing on."

Brandon scoffed. "Well, uh . . . I guess not all of us can get jobs lined up quite as easily as others."

"Come on, now. That's not the point. As I've said—"

"Then be a little less obtuse, William Wordsworth."

"Fine," Germy said, reaching for the lighter in his pocket then remembering that he lost it. "To hell with all those fancy organizations and big foundations. You can't play that crap. Start with a small, local charity. Volunteer and work it."

"Yeah, yeah." Brandon shook his head. "You've said this stuff before. It's not enough that I graduated at the top of the class, and you might barely make it, but now you're going to get the career while I go passing around free labor for some *maybe, possibly* future position? Please."

"Please, indeed," Germy responded with a professorial tone. "These aren't things to expect. It's always a crapshoot for scavengers, right? So, we stick to the basics and see where it goes."

"I mean, sure, volunteering is great. But Germy, we've been over this. What difference does the low-level stuff make? And how am I going to pay for—"

"You have to do the best you know how to do. That's all you ever have to do." Germy paused. "You know, for someone who believes in faith, you don't seem to have much of it."

Brandon rubbed his temple with his free hand. "Well, for someone who believes in logic, you don't seem . . ." His voice drifted as his brain tried to recalibrate. "You're not . . . That's not logical."

Germy's strict tone changed to concern. "Is your tinnitus doing its thing again?"

Brandon almost smiled. "Yeah."

"Damn. I thought it was better since you met your friend from out west, Ja . . . Janelle?"

"Yeah, Janelle. It has been better, but I haven't heard from her in a while, so Sarah and I caught up. We actually had a really good talk. She knows her stuff, you know? She's really into social programs and helping folks. Janelle doesn't do much, you know? Sarah had this point about it being callous to not support farm subsidies, that compassion . . . compassion is, you kno—"

"Janelle's far better than that Sarah girl," Germy snapped. "That much is already clear."

"Hey, Sarah . . . actually makes a difference. We have different political angles, but she really, you know, wants to help the public sector . . . help the underserved with her career. Janelle doesn't say anything about, you know, compassion or understanding. Sarah actually wants to do good."

"So you say." There was another pause as Germy tried to bring perspective into their incompatible perspectives. He glanced around his cluttered desk for his lighter. "Mind if I ask you a personal question?"

"O . . . kay?"

"Why do you have this thing about wanting to *do good* exactly? Plenty of people out there revel in the pretension of making the world a better place, but for you, it's a personal thing."

Brandon blinked and sat back down in his computer chair, the screen's blue glow filling his face. "Hell if I know. You got me."

"I'm not trying to get you. I'm trying to actually get you."

"Yeah." Brandon glanced around his cluttered room and adjusted his grip on the phone. "I'm really not noble or anything."

"What do you mean by that?"

"I'm no more of a do-gooder than anyone. Ultimately, I'm trying to . . . get home. I mean, I always feel like I'm running in life. You know? I just hope I'm running there."

"Oh." Germy felt sudden elusive contentment. "Like baseball, huh? Ha. Perhaps. But there's more to it than that."

"Well, yes," Brandon said, letting himself open up further than before. "It's about logic, Mr. Logic. Deductive reasoning, to be exact. I don't know what else to do with my life. For professional stuff . . . I can't do it. I can crunch numbers, but I'm no hands-on techie engineer like my sister, and I'm no salesman like my dad. I couldn't build an amp, and I couldn't even sell one to a gear head at below discount price." He sighed. "For personal stuff, it's . . . I'm not sure I can be a lover. I'm not impressive. In jobs and dates, people just think I'm boring, lackluster, or some kind of fraud. I'm still trying to find home. Either way."

He nodded. "But I, you know . . . I have a little insight sometimes. Sometimes I can find what's missing or what needs to be added to make things work in ways others didn't see, like the elusive angle. But then . . ." He stopped as he realized he was starting to agree with his friend. "It's a substance problem. My style is substance, and it doesn't ever seem to be in style."

"Substance," Germy said. "So you're a substance abuser."

"Clever," Brandon replied, rolling his eyes at his friend. "But yeah . . . faith." His eyebrows lifted. "We met in Catholic school, right? There's an institution. We get through school or church, or being raised by parents, thinking on some level that we've been prepared and we're going to make it in the world, confident that our deepest beliefs will weather the world. And then our deepest beliefs become weathered from within. Faith is something to wear for most people. It's a style. It comes off when it starts to itch or goes out of style. Or, for others, it's kept on with stubborn defiance, thinking that the act of wearing it will put it back into style. As if that's the point. People everywhere act like religion is either a bad fad or a holier-than-thou badge, and they're both wrong." He looked down and felt a presence. "Faith, *real* faith . . . it's not just unfashionable. It's been covered up with institutional and personal shame."

"Indubitably," Germy responded as he pulled open a drawer to look for matches. "Shamey shame. Like how those two nudists felt before they grabbed those olive branches."

"Fittingly enough." Brandon shook his head. "I'm really just another square peg in the round hole of society. I only think I should work a nonprofit job because I can't make it in the for-profit sector. So they would say, right? And the public sector is subtly evil with its market-distorting, power-grabbing leviathan of best intentions, driving up costs, not expanding access to needs or alleviating conditions of poverty, so that's a no-go. I'd sooner quit smoking."

"So that's never going to happen."

Brandon pulled in a deep breath then let it out. "Faith, indeed. I guess I should consider your suggestion." He looked at the floor and let his sense of shame settle. Bitterness striped through it. It seemed so real to him, though it was faintly real at all. Someone was proud of him, even more than Germy was, and this negated the shame out of existence. But the shame *felt* real, as real as rocks, continuously pushing up his scarred chest and rolling back in his arrhythmic heart under his Sisyphean reality.

"You'd better."

"I will, Germ. I will. Did I answer your question?"

Germy scratched his chin then mindlessly padded his pockets

again. "It wasn't really a question. I think you have to quit running from all the definitions that fill your mind. And other people's opinions, damn. You can cherish people for who they are without taking all their fleeting judgments to heart, you know."

Brandon sighed again. "I call it social psychology."

"Meh. More structures and institutions," Germy said with an air of condescension. "But I do have a question for you."

"What's that?"

"Do you have my lighter?"

***

AFTER HE CLICKED THE "SEND" button for the last time, Brandon closed his laptop and sat back. He could faintly hear snoring from down the hall, which was all he heard from his father since moving back.

The dreary autumn evening weighed heavily, and Brandon wondered if his carefully-worded cover letters and many online application fields would ever be read. There were many distractions at his disposal: profiles, status updates, mp3s, digital movies, and applications. Apps of apps. And yet, guilt always seemed to find a way to bleed through, taunting and provoking him into action and inaction. The distractions at his disposal weren't enough to quell and deter his chaotic mind and interminable heart.

He also thought about the threshold of failure an individual could rationally endure against an inherently irrational system. The psychological need for acceptance still hungered even against something Germy had once said, referencing Krishnamurti, about being accepted into a sick society being unhealthy. He thought about the itch on his upper left arm. The ridges and hills. He thought about Sarah and hoped they had a kind of Romeo and Juliet dynamic between ideologies trying to save the world. He thought about absent Marianne. There was a comment on one of his high school classmate's Gold Pavilion page that she had been pregnant. And he thought about Janelle. Their last talk was sparse and strained, as though each of them was holding their affections guarded against each other while waiting for the world to make its move.

A feeling came over him. Pulling out his cell phone, Brandon found an unread message from Ms. Leora herself. His heart jumped then stayed still, letting care remain until he heard the word.

"Chris is coming home tomorrow. Will need to help him. Talk soon."

Brandon prayed a fleeting prayer that all was well. His chest filled up then faded again. Even if geographic and sentimental distances kept them apart, there was something there that would not fade away. Through idealized romance and the trappings of a cold world, there was goodness. *There.* He also felt conflicting notions of preconceived goodness versus being good.

"Glad to hear. All the best to him. Miss you. Always here. Goodnight and blessings."

He shut his cell phone and sat back in his chair. The Marcel household creaked as the wind picked up. An ominous sinking feeling emerged from nowhere, reminding him again of racks of dishes, student loan payments, and cover letters that would never be read, all coalescing into shame that wouldn't stop even after he scratched at his upper left arm. The tinnitus started.

Aisling.

Brandon felt a touch of hope. Even if he never received an interview or an offer, there must be something that could be done. Maybe he would consider Germy's suggestion again. *All of those with lower grades, less experience, and few innovative ideas can have their connections, their charms, and their opportunities.* Rational or not, the status quo was the status quo. One person was still one person, and the individual was where everything began. But given human nature, those thoughts carried a heavy cost. *If one truly thinks for oneself, one must be prepared to be by oneself.*

People love the idea of individuality and hate the reality. Perhaps help would come . . . but not necessarily from other people. Curses can never outnumber blessings. Something could be done. There was a touch of hope, and there was a touch of faith, and the touch of love could wait.

Aisling.

His mind and his heart rested. He sighed. The Advil room was faintly visible as his eyes drifted. Darkness was soft, soft and pleasant. Then there was a sharp but distant crack of thunder. His eyes opened again. He sat up in the computer chair and felt something dark within him. A different darkness, one of love lost many years ago.

Standing up, he ambled to the pile of sheets on his bed and climbed in quietly. He turned on his left side and imagined holding someone. It always helped him fall asleep. He thought about home. Not just a house; a *home*. A song came to mind that he had heard in a convenience store when he was still with Marianne. It was The Ronettes' "Be My Baby." He hummed the chorus softly and fell asleep.

***

"IT'S BEEN SO GOOD TO talk with you, Mr. Marcel," the human resource coordinator said with baritone depth and a hint of a Carolinian accent. "I'm impressed. Your skills, your ideas, and your passion for the Community Training Corps mission are the kinds of things we've been looking for. Just a few more questions. Sound good?"

"Yes." Brandon gulped against his rapid pulse. "Sounds great." His professional composure and cautious anticipation hadn't failed him quite yet in the past few days, but he felt that he must be ever-vigilant against his own mind's attempts to sabotage his endeavors. He angled the bottom half of the phone away from his mouth and cleared his throat.

An uncertain breeze came from overcast skies.

"Mr. Marcel, if you were to become our next program analyst, what do you think you could accomplish for the organization within your first two months?"

"Yes," he said with a quick inhale. "I would redesign and redeploy the survey assessment and third party objective metrics to reinstate internal and external reporting regimes. This means we could have midstream program adjustments to maximize impact for the clients, as well as give our supporters data to show how their dollars are making a difference. This would be especially timely given the increased giving around the holidays." He took another quick breath. "Additionally, I would take a hands-on approach to admin, um . . . administering materials in a mission-minded way, while showing appreciation for clients." He stopped but immediately picked up on the pause. "And I would assure office operating logistics are done in a timely and effective manner. I, uh . . . I can certainly make sure the room logistics are running optimally each day." He took a breath. "So . . . yes."

The coordinator continued to pause. "Mm. Hmm." He made a note. "Okay. So, Mr. Marcel, could you tell me again what it is about the CTC mission that makes you want to work here?"

Brandon took a breath and started to pace. Then he remembered the omnipresent circumstance and that there were people out there who couldn't afford basic necessities and wanted an opportunity to be self-sufficient. "Well, I . . . it's about the mission and societal change. The fact that you, um, help put people back to work, I think that's how you, you know . . . do good."

"You mean *do well?*" The interviewer paused.

Brandon blinked. "Well, do good work, to advance, you know, move society—"

"Move society forward, great. Now, Mr. . . . Brandon, all right . . . we're talking to a few people this week, and we've made some tough decisions. We had some very competitive candidates, you know." He seemed to smirk through the phone. "I'll just come right out and say they're all talking about saving the world and so on. So, Brandon, what is it that you—and I mean *you*—are really wanting out of this job?"

"Well, you know . . ." It wasn't certain whether the feeling was fear, anger, or confusion, but it was probably a mix. "I . . . you know, I like the CTC's economic model. You have these series of used media and clothing stores that have become a staple of the Triad, and that means I can get some old Hendrix records for cheap!" He licked his lip at the silence. "And of course the profits go into your job training programs, so people out there looking for jobs who are trying whatever they can to make themselves more marketable can register for one of your programs and build their skills and make themselves better candidates." He paced and padded his pocket for cigarettes. "And, with better candidates making for better employees and better business, yes, there is a real progression, and society moves forward."

"Oh." There was another pause and another note made. "Well, there's actually a client-based assessment process that you left out there, but that's fine. Yeah, uh . . ." He left his statement lingering as if to prevent a response. "Hmm."

Something like pride came and went from Brandon as he realized that his spurt of assertiveness might not have served him. He slowed his pace and held a steady hand over his pack of cigarettes, almost anticipating this conversation would soon be over, along with his only chance of a salaried job. The muscle in his chest slowed and sped back up again, and the tinnitus started. The waiting was slowly, and quite literally, killing him.

"Okay, Mr. Marcel, here's the deal." The coordinator made a last note then shut his binder loud enough for Brandon to hear it through the phone. "I've had a few conversations with the CTC team members, and I think we're at a juncture where we can talk about our decision. So . . ." In that second, there was nothing but the hum of the cell phone. "When did you say you could start again?"

Fear turned into hope. "Oh, I could uh . . . I could start immediately, actually. Yeah, definitely."

"Oh, okay. Good. Well, we'll go ahead and put together some paperwork for you. There's the standard documentation, tax stuff, benefits, and all of that. Our controller will help you out. Compensation for this position and associated skills for a nonprofit is highly competitive for the Triad area. This is going to be starting in the sixty-k range. So, I'll put together the formal offer and have it ready for you, uh . . . Can you be here first thing on Monday morning?"

"Yes, absolutely!" Brandon's body quaked with excitement and elation. "Absolutely. I'm really excited to hear that. So, I . . ." His breath pulled in and prepared to be released. "I, uh . . ."

The coordinator laughed. "Yes, you got the job. We were hesitant about this being your first full-time professional job, but your internship and trial data report were great. So good. Just know that you're gonna have to hit the ground running here. Your new supervisor, Dick, is big on putting together reports full of good news about our programs." The coordinator cleared his throat. "But don't worry; he'll build you up. So, we're looking forward to seeing you on . . . Monday at eight a.m.?"

Brandon smiled widely. "Yes, I'll be there! I'm looking forward to it. Thank you so much! And thank you to the team." He was beaming.

"We'll see you then. Take care and have a good weekend, all right?"

"You, too! The, uh . . . leaves are starting to look pretty!"

"Yeah. Sure. Bye, now."

The cell phone closed shut, and Brandon found himself standing quietly. Muscles in his core relaxed and filled with something that seemed like satisfaction, or maybe contentment. The flood of possibilities for himself and others overcame him. Paying off debts, having something impressive to tell Sarah, witnessing a meaningful change in peoples' lives, and pursuing a great mission accomplishment with a respected social service nonprofit. His financial and self-esteem worries dissipated, and the thought of *others* almost seemed to move with the inertia of new hope. It had seemed that everything was being unearthed, pulling out of the intransigent dirt of the present and toward the ecstatic air of the future.

Finally. *Finally!*

This was it. All the efforts and hopes that had remained lifeless for so long were now put in a radically different light. It was as though the first rays of dawn had finally cut through. Of all his dreams, this one dream of becoming and doing, the dream of living what he understood to be good seemed to be coming true. He had found a purpose and a job where he could make a difference, satisfying personal, professional, and even ideological goals.

Purpose. Home!

It was finally happening for him. As of Monday morning, Brandon Marcel would be the program analyst for the Community Training Corps.

The Morning Star smiled.

November

STRANGERS CHATTED, MUGS HIT THE table, and an indie rock band with a female lead singer played loudly in the coffee shop. Stark light from the clear autumn day came through the front windows as two young, well-dressed professionals sat at a table next to the window, taking their lunch breaks to catch up with each other.

They wore crisp tailored shirts. The slightly older man with the carefully spiked blond hair had a burgundy tie with an intricate designer pattern in sapphire, while the slightly younger man with light brown hair combed like Clark Kent had a blue tie with a yellow fleur-de-lis pattern.

Randall was incredulous. "Okay, you've convinced me. Go get that old Martin of yours and prop it up on Trade Street. Hell, I'll give you my Paul Reed Smith electric and combo amp. Do the club circuit thing. You, uh . . . ha. Community Training . . . what? No words, man." He tossed his hands up. "No words."

Brandon rolled his tongue in his mouth and tried to focus. "I . . . I really think this is a good start. My first week was great. Really nice folks. And my . . . I think my parents are proud." He took a sip of chai tea then sat his mug to the side. "The pay is better than most other nonprofits. I mean, I'm making over sixty, and the benefits are good. So, why do you, um . . . seem to think this is a bad position?"

Randall faked a smile and shook his head. "Do you have to ask? Sixty-k or not, you're working at a charity. Come on; a charity! Seriously? I didn't think you were some kind of libertarian-liberal hybrid." His previously welcoming eyes were becoming less so with each comment. "Hybrids, all right. I bet you want to drive one now. Are you still working with the Campus Progressives? I can't believe you took a position where you're supporting subsidizing unemployment." He slid his mug from hand to hand. "You're talkin' altruism. You gotta be kidding. I mean, it's the antithesis of rational self-interest. The virtue of self—"

"Wait," Brandon interrupted. "It's not subsidizing unemployment. Now, they do receive something like a quarter of their funding from the government, but if the liberty movement you and I support works toward ending the income tax, we can promote real economic efficiency, creating opportunities and prosperity, and for the few still needing help . . . we can cover that funding with private philanthropy." He realized he was holding up a finger as if to speak truth to an audience much larger than one. "We can steadily wean the nonprofit sector off the public funding and end the stifling regulations that cause disparate impacts and unintended consequences. But, in the meantime, we can make strides to replace government dependency with charitable opportunities; train people and help them find jobs, meet the market demand for labor, as well as service to help others with compassion. That's a demand that some free people have, Randall. Real compassion, you know, not like the fake compassion that comes through the welfare state and all the sloganeering. We can bridge the gaps and make progress—"

"Stop right there." Randall forcibly laughed and shook his head. "There's that word. Making progress for the progressives, huh?"

"No, I—"

"I understand. I get it. All that talk of compassion and bleeding heart stuff, man. I like that part about meeting market demands, though; that's rich. You really put a good spin on it."

Brandon took a quick, deep breath and ignored the careening in his chest. "I really think there's congruence here. I mean, you've got statists that insist on federal welfare and government spending to solve our problems. Then you've got your free market forces that could allow for maximum prosperity and liberty. So, why not have the public policies we both agree upon but freely choose in our personal lives to do what we think is best for each other? True private charity, you know? You know, put liberty in law, and compassion in our civic organizations."

Randall raised his eyebrows but continued to hold a firm smirk within his goatee. "Well, that sounds great, but at the end of the day, you're still a bleeding heart working at a damn charity. I think you need to pull that club T-shirt out of the closet, you know . . . one of those shirts with the Margaret Mead quote on the back. Charity? Nonprofits? Hardly congruent with a profit motive. You're still giving handouts, just not straight from the government. There's no difference."

"No, there . . ." Brandon looked out into the clear day then looked back. "I support both the principles and practical outcomes of what a liberty philosophy in a minimal government would mean. In this past decade, we saw what unintended consequences of Keynesian interventionism, along with a toxic regulatory environment and corporatist status quo, can do to the economy and to jobs." He turned away because it hurt to look at Randall. "I just think this maximum prosperity fits perfectly with a personal, free choice to help others of our own volition. Promote opportunities, not the disincentives and dependencies of handouts. I can do that by working to make sure this charity is effective in helping people find jobs as their program analyst."

"Hmm." Randall's dismissive look was turning into a scathing glaze. "Toxic environment, huh? You're starting to go into treehugger land with your metaphors there, Brandon."

"Come on; don't you think that there's room for—"

"Sounds like we're not on the same page. I think I now understand why you had trouble networking at the Nepott Club. Not feeling liberty, huh?"

Brandon rolled his eyes. "No, come on; I'm just introverted. I was thinking of—"

"Right. Introverted and sensitive. Sensitive and weak. Not an entrepreneur, are you? What you're missing here is that some people *want* to be productive. They don't need some charity to tell them how. And some people don't want to have a society of stragglers—government, nonprofit, charity, or whatever. I think that's what you're missing here."

Brandon's pulse slowed down a little. "I want to be productive. I want to provide a service. This is the private, individual, free market responding to a need. I think this service can achieve several of our objectives and transition to a society that is both free and caring, not one or the other. It's a false dilemma. I think that will make life more meaningful for everyone. I mean, don't we all want society to . . . you know, move forward?"

Now Randall's laugh wasn't forced at all. "You mean society . . . progresses? I think you just made my point." He shook his head with a taunting smile then stopped to glare at Brandon. "If you're talkin' about making life meaningful, well, there's only one thing that makes my life more meaningful— money." He stared at Brandon's face and saw only timidity and disbelief in response. The expression caused Randall to perch his mouth and grit his teeth. "That's all. Money. That's the only market we need, right there."

With shoulders slumped in the suit, Brandon strained to look up. "I understand that incentive in our public policy and macroeconomics, and money represents the exchange of value, and that this is how free markets maximize prosperity. But, in our personal lives, I . . ." Brandon's voice quivered and faded. "It's different."

"No. You don't understand capitalism. You don't support liberty. You can tell me that hippie garbage about how money can't buy happiness. Even if it didn't, I'd rather cry in my Jaguar. It can blow the doors off those pussy hybrids any day."

A quiet fell. The band had stopped playing, and the bustle of the coffee shop seemed muted and lifeless. Neither one of the well-dressed men felt comfortable anymore. One had a diminished sense of loyalty, while the other had a diminished sense of friendship.

The feeling in Brandon's chest leveled out without hitting bottom. Human nature is human nature, and he wasn't ready to cut the emotional loss of this aborted friendship yet.

"Yes, Randall, you should have that freedom. And I should have the freedom to choose to do good in my personal life as I understand it to be—bleeding heart or whatever. To do so by my own volition without any imposition. To do—"

"A bleeding heart isn't functional, Brandon." He went to take a sip out of his coffee mug and found it empty. "I guess you weren't the true believer that I thought you were. Fine. I mean, why weren't you honest about it up-front?"

Brandon shuddered as he remembered hearing this same doubt and accusation from Sarah. "I was. I thought we could have an intellect—"

"Whatever." Randall stood up and grabbed his sport jacket, still shaking his head as he tossed it over his crisp shirt. "Compassion is a cute, fluffy crap concept. You've got to grow up. Get a real job that's not trying to rip me off to help people or whatever. Good luck, I guess. You aren't what the Young Capitalists are about by sheer definition, so take that however you'd like."

Brandon remained sitting. "I really . . . Um, good luck, then." He audibly sighed as he watched his would-be friend walk away. A forced hope for connection pushed through his quivering mouth. "Hey, if this gig doesn't work out, maybe you can join me for a different kind of gig on Trade Street. You know, bring your Paul Reed Smith and we can jam."

"Ha, yeah. Don't wait up."

***

THE WEATHER IN THE VALLEY of the Sun had become seasonally pleasant. Janelle sat on her back porch recliner to enjoy the clear and almost cool air of the Thursday afternoon. Someone's dog was barking.

She checked the back wall for more cracks. The roots of her neighbor's pine were undoubtedly causing trouble from beneath.

She went to pick her upper lip. Just before she started to worry about leaving her brother alone, the melodious jazz chime of her phone went off.

"Hey . . . Janelle?"

"Hey . . . Brandon." The playfully mocking tone of her voice masked both a great anger and a great relief. "It's been a while. What kept you?"

"Jan, come on; I figured you would want more time to, you know, take care of Chris and do what you need to do." He was more nervous than he thought he would be. "And uh . . . I don't know if you've seen my profile, but I got that one job, so I'm getting adj . . . Hey, you know, it's always been a two-way street, so . . ." He paused and exhaled. "You know I'm always here when you need me."

"Oh?" Her talent at saying so much with such a small change in inflection was as evident as ever. She herself wasn't sure if she was fuming, but she hoped it sounded that way.

"Yeah, we're both busy, but I think there's more than a two-hour time difference keeping you away."

Brandon wanted to step out for a cigarette but remembered that his parents would be home soon. The Advil-colored room weighed on his head, but he reminded himself that he would go apartment searching along the bus route on Saturday.

He started to pace again. It was a wonder that the open space of the room didn't have an actual track worn into the beige carpet. He worried that his success was only ostensible. And he worried about what Janelle thought.

She sniffed. "At least you can quit posting complaints about not being able to find anything on your profile."

"Nice." He shook his head. "I'm trying to make my way the same as anyone else. I'm not trying to be anything great. I just want . . . well, you know."

"Yes, I do." She adjusted her position in the recliner. "And for what it's worth, I'm glad you finally have the stability." The tips of her fingers found themselves back at her upper lip. "But I can only give myself so much, you know? Being the perpetual shoulder through the lonely and hard times takes a toll. I've been there for you since before I heard your voice, and you know I'm not going away anytime soon. Even if, uh . . ." She tilted her head back and felt a lump in her throat. "Even if things between us aren't going anywhere."

He stopped pacing and closed his eyes. "I am, too. Always. I'm not going away. But as far as feelings, it's . . . You know how I feel about all this, and it's—"

"Yeah," she interrupted. "I know, I know. It's not from those crazy dreams you have or some other woman. I know the way you think and the way you feel. I mean, give me some credit here. Have we met?"

Brandon smiled. "Well . . . in a sense, yes. In a sense. I wanted to be clear and all."

"Yeah, yeah. Well, that's fine. I—" She had picked her lip so hard that she had cut her own words off. "I . . . know I'm holding on for something, and the hell if I know why it is, but . . . I guess no one can really help how they feel."

"To a certain extent, I think." He stood up taller and took a breath. "Reason can help us to sort this stuff out. Emotion or passion may be the flesh of life, but rationality and logic are the bones."

She laughed. "Oh, a physiological metaphor. I like it more than the sports analogies or unusual euphemisms. You really are stepping up in the world, Brandon Marcel! Good for you."

He chuckled. "Well, I wanted to make sure we're cool and all. And I have to try to be witty because my wisdom doesn't serve me."

"I see. Nice try." She made a concerted effort to take her hand away from her face, but she knew she would go right back to picking. "Yeah, that reason and rationality stuff does help sometimes, putting the emotions in a reality check." She looked out into the sunshine. "They do put things in context."

Her gaze faded, and her voice softened. "Actually, there has been a development on my end. Some news. I've been meaning to talk to you about it, but you haven't seemed available."

"Well, I . . ." Brandon had a realization and panicked. "Oh no, is Chris okay? Is he—"

"He's . . ." Janelle paused. "No, he's . . . stable, at least." She sighed. "It's going to be a haul. His . . . arms are okay and all."

"Thank God."

"As much as to be expected, at least. And everything else, well . . ." She sighed again. "It's going to be a haul. We spend time together, of course, kinda . . . we talk a lot. We watch classic movies. He likes Gregory Peck flicks, but I'm more into Jimmy Stewart." Nails tore small bits of skin away from her lips as three sharp emotions converged, revolving and piercing through her chest as she waited to tell him. "Yeah, Chris is as good as can be expected. Of course, he's never going to be the same. I'm always worried about him, especially when I can't stay with him. His eyes are just . . . Well, it's a haul. I know he'll push through, though. He's strong. But, yeah, he's as good as can be expected, yeah."

"Good, good." Brandon nodded. "Yeah, if there's anything I can do, I . . . you let me know, dear. I'm here for you."

She frowned. "No, Brandon, you're not."

"Wait—what?"

"That's the thing—you're not."

He squinted and rubbed his temples. "Okay, as you said, we've both been busy, so you know I—"

"Yeah, and that's also to my point. I know you well. I know you too well. I know that we're going to stay in this pattern of being long-distance confidants indefinitely, but that the connection isn't going to go the next step, romantically or otherwise. You think you have the noblest intentions for your nonprofit career, as well as being a great friend on the way to being a great lover, but that's not the whole story."

"No, I . . ." His posture loosened, and he started to pace again. "I know I'm not perfect and certainly not noble, but it's about connection. It's about breaking out of this callous mess of a society, about finding something substantive and meaningful in a sea of irrelevance. Culture and its media become increasingly complex, and yet the simplest messages . . . the simplest meanings are diminished. But truth—real truth—is both infinitely complex and astonishingly simple."

"See? That's good wisdom. You don't have to be witty. And I

definitely think you've got that paradox down." She feigned a throat clearing. "But see? You're doing it again."

"Doing what?"

Janelle rolled her eyes. "You're making the issue about everyone else and society at large again. You're forgetting that we're talking about me and you."

"That's the context. That's why I try . . . That's why I think what you and I have is great, even if it's not quite what either one of us originally envisioned." He put his free hand on his hip and looked downward. "So, what is it that I'm missing? How is it that I'm not there for you when I'm always a phone call away?"

"You don't trust me." She let the pause stretch. "That's the thing about you. Yeah, you care. Yeah, you're trying to do the right thing . . . Sort of. You may think you're trying to connect, but underneath that, you're afraid. You're afraid, and you don't trust. That's why you took so long to call. You needed that time to pull back." She let a second pause stretch, soaking the knowledge that she was right. "And after a few months of the best friendship either one of us has ever had, I think that means something. What it means is that you're not going to trust anybody. And that means you're not going to let me in, so you'll always keep your distance, geographically and otherwise. So, you're not there for me either way. You're not really there at all."

"No, I . . ." Brandon looked down then looked back up again. "I'm trying to . . ." he stammered as his waning sense of pride in his societal insight melted into the vexing notion that he wasn't as self-aware as he thought he was. High vexation, given the implication that this meant he had been callous toward his most benevolent friend of all. "Okay, fine. So, I guess I'm not enough of a head case after all. What am I supposed to do? Sarah says I'm too open and too intense, but you say I'm too closed off? Even if that's true, there's not much I can do about it. It's subconscious and elusive. I've had enough therapists and meds try to fix this ridiculous brain and it only gets worse."

"Not always." True to other conversations with all her friends, Janelle reached the point in the conversational cycle where she felt less challenging and more empathetic. She closed her eyes and let her gesturing hand slowly descend through the dry air. "Lightning could strike. Good can come for doing good." She almost smiled at the idea. "But you can't expect it. It's not up to you. What is up to you—I think the one thing left for you to do, the one thing left for me to do—is to free our minds; take the leap of faith. You need to finally let go and love without any kind of expectation of how it's supposed to be." She cleared her throat in earnest. "If you want to do good, then do good and let that be that. Make sure your big, new job actually helps people find jobs." She felt a twinge of doubt. "Don't . . . don't let them skate by. Make sure they use those hard numbers you talk about." It subsided. "Be more patient with your friends and family, because we're only human. You can't really do good if your intentions are being distilled in fear. Fear of misunderstanding, being judged, or things not working out how you thought they'd work out. You're worried about that crap all the time. Doesn't First John say that perfect love drives out fear? So, the more afraid you are, the less likely you are to actually be good, and so the less likely you are to actually do good."

"Okay." Brandon sighed. His instinct was to find some objection or exception, to point out how any advice of any kind of intention was limited or short-sighted, but he couldn't. "I wish my thoughts didn't come between us. Strange thoughts. I think it has something to do with fifth grade and all that. Growing up, I always felt, y'know . . . the goodness. The love broke through like sunlight. I was weird, you know? I sucked at sports. I didn't like pizza. I didn't want to wear any labels. I liked old rock music more than the popular nu-bands and hipster stuff. I taught myself guitar. I got along with adults rather than my peers. My cat was my best friend. I was just . . . weird. And I wished I wasn't. I think my mom and dad loved me, and so, whatever arbitrary demands of suburbia or human nature emerged, I could . . ." He gulped. "I could usually feel love breaking through, but on its own terms, so I waited and waited. And, at some point, I stopped believing, and I . . ."

Janelle let him drift into silence. She felt his heart from some two thousand miles away, bruised and beating before her, frantic from an overactive mind. The moment came and went. Her timeless patience and willingness to hear were matchless. The years of yearning had honed these skills to deal with the toughest and the softest. She heard them all.

"I'm sorry, Jan, I'm sorry. I've dumped years of this on you in a matter of months. The same nonstop thinking that gives me insight also drives me mad. It's my greatest strength and my greatest weakness. My guardedness is false. I'm a raw nerve. I'm trying to apply reason to these emotions and the bone's cutting the flesh, I guess. You can't toughen a raw nerve."

She laughed. "You really do know how to torture a metaphor. Quite literally, as it seems."

"Ha, yeah." He lowered his head. "But I am sorry. I do appreciate you, I do. But I can't seem to show it. I can't seem to break that guard or wall, and I just don't know. And above all, I . . ." The tension built and fell again. "I don't know why I can't be there for you, emotionally or, you know . . . romantically."

"Romantically, huh?"

"Yeah." He adjusted his grip on the phone. "Like my last

therapist said, if it's the ultimate connection I seek, to have a real home . . . there's only one kind of relationship for that—romance, marriage." He shook his head again. "And I'm afraid she's right. It's been that way all along. It's that one missing piece, you know?" His silhouette against the wall stayed stationary. "And I think you're wonderful and lovely and the best. I mean it—the best. But I . . . You know how I feel, unfortunately."

"Yeah." She sat back in her recliner and took a breath. The appointed moment for her revelation had come. "Romance. Yeah, about that. You know how I said I have some news? It's about that."

Brandon looked up as if to see her. "What's up?" His heart beat faster.

"So, yeah, guys." The torn skin of her lips came apart as she developed a kind of smoldering smile. It was a foreign feeling to her face. "A few weeks ago, I was talking with my criminal psych group after class, and this guy walks up. He had on an Iced Earth T-shirt and these . . . designer jeans? And the hair. I mean, it's like he shined."

Brandon's chest turned. "Oh, yeah? You met a guy?" He thought he would be happy at this turn of events, but there was something about her description that did not feel right.

"Yeah. He had this slicked blond hair. He's built, but not too built." A curl formed in the corner of her lip as she turned over and faced the sidewalk. "I told him I liked his shirt, and we talked about the upcoming Kamelot show. He's not into the"—she lifted her hand in aimless gesture—"Psych profile and deep stuff. Some music. He's kinda . . . laidback. He's a programmer; makes a good living. He works his own hours and dresses how he wants." She kept smiling. "So, we went out last weekend, and he took me around town. I haven't really been to many bars, so that was nice. He even kissed my hand when he dropped me off. I like his dark eyes."

No, Brandon thought. His heart slowed, and the pain in the side

207

of his head acceded for a moment. Something was not right. The idea was certainly right—he wanted her to find someone who could make her happy, as he so emphatically believed that he himself could not. He couldn't think of exactly what in her description was wrong, but the feeling was as powerful as a reason. It felt entirely wrong.

"So . . . I'm going out and meeting people. Didn't you tell me that would be good for me?"

"Yeah, yeah, I do think that's a good thing." His objection burned, but he didn't understand it, let alone know how to express it. "I do. That's cool. So . . . what's this guy's name?"

"Caleb." Her excitement blunted the uneven tone in Brandon's voice. "Caleb Sterling. Why?"

"Just . . . for reference." He decided to back away as naturally as he could try. "That's cool. So, when's the next date?"

"Actually, we've been talking and, uh . . . we're kinda together, actually." She waited.

"Oh." There was something like guilt in his concerns for her and for himself. He thought of a few different responses, but they all sounded counterproductive. The one he went with sounded sarcastic. "Congrats."

"Is . . . everything okay with you?"

"Yeah, it's cool."

"Well, you had an opportunity."

"No, I just—"

"I know we haven't felt the same, but we are . . . like long-distance best friends, right? I thought you'd be a little happier for me."

"Yeah, I . . . I'm just tired. We're good." He tried to calm himself. The sense of being torn from this bearer of hope was adding an anomaly to a growing sense of distance within him.

"We're good. Maybe we've become too, I don't know . . . emotionally close for friends? We don't quite know what this is." He couldn't distinguish the concern between his own self-preservation and care for her. But, in a quick rumination over this dichotomous dilemma, he found an apparent answer. He shuddered.

"You know, maybe . . . maybe we should chill for a little while. Just take a break, you know? Kind of go off to our corners, cut our contact, not call or email each other for a month or two, just to clear our heads, I guess. Just for clarity." He cleared his throat. "I mean, I know I've been spotty. I think head-clearing may be good for us."

"Hm." Janelle felt a haunt in the notion and consciously kept her hand away from her lips. "I don't know. Maybe. We can try it, I guess." She took a deep breath and turned back over in her chair. Her heart felt warmth. "Although . . . maybe the opposite is true. Maybe meeting each other will work out what we are."

"Meeting?"

"Yeah." She adjusted her grip on the phone. "I'm actually putting together a New Year's get-together. I found a few people up for it, you know? Probably has to be dressy. I have this nice, royal blue dress that I haven't worn since I was a little . . . younger, and . . . it would be really good to see you. I mean, you know, to add a face to the voice. Pictures aren't . . . It would be good. I can pick you up at the airport and drive us around. I know you're not super comfortable with driving. Flying's okay, right?"

"Oh. Uh . . . yeah, flying's fine. I'm making a quick trip to Florida over Thanksgiving."

"Marianne?"

"Yeah. She gave me a call, but . . ." Brandon's heart cooled. The hidden pit of apathy within his mind smothered the thought with equal parts ignorance and selfishness. "I might be going to this conference for work around the first week of the year, so . . . I don't know. I'm sure we'll meet eventually." Something kicked his heart.

209

ASHE

"Caleb's going to be there, I assume?"

"Yeah, Caleb and his friends are coming. It'll be great. I've already got party favors and some things for us planned out, I guess. Yeah."

Caleb was a neighborhood away, a country closer to her than Brandon. For her, the relationship distance had finally closed. It made her happy.

"You know, Caleb believes in the kind of things you preach about—compassion, understanding, and forgiveness. I think you'd like him. He's the real deal. He tutors people at school for free and does all sorts of volunteer stuff. He's fit, too. Kind of makes me think of all the stuff you like about Sarah." Her sardonic tone was never more purposeful. "I thought you'd like that comparison."

"Yeah." He couldn't shake the feeling that, despite both of them having long-sought opportunities, there was a strong sense of mourning. Something really didn't feel right.

"And . . . he's there. He's there for me." There was an outer limit to Janelle's emotive mind. She sensed pieces waiting for the time to fall into the design. "But fine. I guess, uh . . . take care during our little break. We'll catch up after my party, maybe? Sometime early in the year, I guess. Take care, Brandon. Do some good at your job. Don't let them skimp using your data. Facts are important in the feel-good realms, right?"

"For sure. Will do. Be careful during this break and . . . just be good." There was something illuminating in Janelle's invitation. Something ultraviolet. But his heart had cooled, and so he ignored it. He had deliberately pulled at the shroud of darkness now beginning to come over them. "But, yeah, we'll meet one of these years."

"Yeah. One of them." She shrugged the embers off her heart. "Have fun in Florida, travel well, and be careful. You can

210

start working on that head-clearing by not getting that bleeding heart of yours broken."

"Yeah." His body finally relaxed. "I will try. Take good care, Jan."

"You, too."

***

THE OFFICE WAS MONOCHROMATIC GRAY. The cubicles, the wall accents, and the carpet were all this shade or close to it, aching beneath fluorescent lights. The gray seeped into the pastels of Brandon's naivety and dress shirt. The only attempt to break it consisted of carefully framed pictures of Community Training Corps clients and volunteers hanging on each wall. A white woman laughing, black teenagers organizing shelves, a Latino man with one tooth short of a full smile. The faces illustrated diversity, but according to the demographic profile report that Brandon had pulled from the database, they were hardly representative.

With neat piles of papers growing on the work surfaces of his cube, he laid a freshly printed document next to his keyboard and leaned back. The ceiling had hundreds of tiny little dimples in each tile, like a chaotic score composed in Braille for a goaded din louder than the murmurs, *click-clacks*, and shuffles of the office.

With a carefully prepared "CTC Monthly Metrics: October" report in hand, Brandon felt a strong sense of purpose that he had never felt before. He was neatly groomed and nicely dressed, topped with a fresh mind for the professional world. As ready as he consciously felt, his mind still wondered. It wondered about timelines, expectations, and definitions of client success. It wondered most of all about meaning and purpose and home, which always led to the visage of the woman.

And it worried.

For good reason.

"You stay up late partying?"

211

Brandon turned around in his desk chair, blinked twice. "Hey, Dick. No, I don't really . . . I just, uh . . . I got the report together so it's ready for you. Yeah. So . . ."

The stocky, middle-aged operations manager wore a red and black striped Polo shirt and an aggressive stare. His dark hair was combed away from his unseasonably tanned face, and his lips maintained a constant pursing. He knew that Brandon, the most recent employee in an organization with high turnover, was intimidated. And that was the point.

A gulp started, but Brandon forced it away. "Yeah, I—"

"Gotta make sure you weren't dozing off on me." His voice had a Northeast dialect with a monotonic edge to match the office décor. "You need to get that report together and see me about it, pronto. Got it?"

"Yes, ah . . . it's ready right now."

"Really? Okay. Come over." Dick promptly turned and walked away with a subtle stomp.

A few seconds of shuffling papers later, Brandon picked up his report, an extra copy, and a pencil. He nervously stood up and walked along the outside of the cubes.

Entering Dick's corner office, Brandon pulled out a chair from the desk, nervously tugging it over catches on the carpet. He sat down and handed Dick a copy.

Dick looked at the cover page with the plain "CTC Monthly Metrics: October" title for a moment, muttered something, and then turned the page.

"So," Brandon started, "I made sure to follow the template from my predecessor but added a few more measurements that will make our numbers more scientific. That way, we can really pinpoint where we . . . have issues. There are a few issues, but I'm sure we can make the necessary program changes so we really have an impact. Take a look here . . ."

Dick looked up for a moment at Brandon then looked back down and read with perfunctory attention. He turned another page, and his gaze skipped from graph to graph, narrative to narrative. He coughed.

"So . . . for the Back to Work program, we had just enough clients in the sample to make an inference on the population, and . . . it was still a positive change, showing they apparently did learn a little about their trades. But . . . there was quite a bit of variation, as you can see there with the high standard deviations. So . . . the correlation coefficients were low and . . . as to whether or not there was improved knowledge for our clients versus the labor statistics for the region, it was positive . . . but still not quite, uh . . . it was still not . . . statistically significant. At any alpha, actually. I'm afraid it's the same on job placement figures, as well."

Dick paused halfway through a page turn and looked up. "And . . . what does all that mean? I need a story, Brandon. We need metrics that tell a good story."

"Well . . ." Brandon sat up and gesticulated with caution. "It means there was an improvement, but not . . . not enough that we can't attribute it to chance." He looked up and blinked, but his boss did not. "If we look at the individual modules, I think the problem is—"

"Come on; this is a simple question." Dick jabbed his index finger onto a figure in the middle of the page. "This score looks good to me. So gimme the good story."

"Actually . . . there may be multicollinearity in that data. The sample was small."

"Multi-what?" Dick rolled his eyes. "Throwin' around big words, huh? I don't buy that crap. Come on; the client scores improved. Answer a simple question: what's the story?"

"No, that's the thing." Brandon lifted his hand to comfort the racing in his chest but realized what he was doing and put it back down. "Failing significance testing indicates that we can't rule out chance, so the improvement in client scores is not statistically . . . It means that for these variables, there was a modicum of—"

"You gotta be kidding me." Dick shook his head and pointed at another figure. "I mean . . . you're sayin' that 115 over 40 is 2.9? It's 1.9! Come on; that's basic math! If you wanna go to that national conference in New Mexico, you gotta do better than this."

"I . . ." Brandon's tinnitus started, and he tried to explain once again. "I don't think that's right, so let's . . . Okay, I'm sure you had this when you got your MBA. Statistical signfi—"

"Oh, you're gonna to try to put this on me?" Dick scoffed. "I know data analysis, okay? It means basic math and good conclusions. If ya wanna get technical, we need analysis of, uh . . ." Dick looked up as he recalled his stock business-speak. "We need data systems using key organizational, operational processes and, uh . . . positive quantitative reporting for management to make key decisions on, uh . . . how we're going to expand our organization statewide with our best administrative practices and . . . and our operational processes and practices. See? It's simple." He leaned forward with a gaze of hostility. "So, you can talk all of this multi-significant-whatever, but you haven't even developed any stories or conclusions. You haven't done anything except copy some formulas you had in school, and then sit there and shake. You got no confidence. And that's because you barely meet the job qualifications." He scoffed again. "You can't even do basic math. You embarrass me."

"I . . ." Brandon's full-bodied panic subsided as reason began to take control. "The conclusion is that most of our programs haven't made a significant difference, and so they must be changed. In this report, I pinpoint exactly which materials in which modules went wrong so we can make midstream corrections. Some of the material doesn't align with our course objectives at all. For example, if we're counting the number of new applicants as an organization-wide metric, but a third of our clients report that they are looking for advancement rather than a new job, we shouldn't—"

"Oh, really? It's our fault? You gotta be kidding me. Quit trying to excuse your failure."

Brandon took a quick breath. "I have not failed. I've met my job description's goals by using research-backed data analytics methodology with data quality control tailored to your reporting regime, and now I'm making my recommendations to you based on those measurements for each individual class and program. Those are conclusions."

Dick scoffed. "Sure, keep tellin' yourself that. Not giving us anything useful."

"More to the point, the programs aren't following the evidence-based practices from the literature, so these results can't be surprising. The surveys this organization uses aren't capturing client feedback because we have double-barreled and many repetitive questions that lead to survey fatigue, not to mention the esoteric jargon that most people don't understand. I use statistics terms with you because . . . I thought you've had that coursework. But the surveys need to be updated. If you allow me to edit and deploy new surveys with industry-standard methodology and widely-used language, we can truly capture our client feedback and—"

"Oh, no, no," Dick interrupted as he pointed his finger. "So you wanna change our surveys, huh? The surveys aren't the problem. You are. Don't give me your smartass talk. We have standards around here, including basic math and not using made-up crap. Get with the program and be a team player. You're not making a good first impression around here, okay? You're always sitting around, all quiet and hunched over some spreadsheet. That's not good, okay? Your report doesn't tell me nothin'. Wanna try again?"

"This . . ." Brandon spoke up even as he shook. "P-value measuring for statistical significance is a tool to scientifically measure if there's a signal in the noise of data. And regression . . . for instance, in the Trade Guides program, I used the regression correlation coefficient to show that Phase III attendance actually is correlated with increased scores, albeit with a low R-square. That's good news. The story is that our Phase III program significantly increases job readiness. We can build on that and actually make the program effective if we do a client needs analysis to—"

"Needs what?" Dick forced a laugh. "You need to do what you're told. You wanna ruin our Charity Star rating, huh? Whatever you call work, it's not helping us grow the organization."

"Mission expansion does not necessarily mean mission achievement." Brandon closed his eyes for a moment. "In the long-term, what I propose will improve our rating." He opened his eyes again and looked directly at Dick. "More importantly, it will help people find jobs. That's the mission of this organization, so let's focus on that. And your . . ." He hesitated. "Your tone is not helpful for anyone."

"Oh, here we go. Great. Now you can't take being criticized? Your generation and your fragile egos. You can't take the heat. Well, that's the way things really are. I'm not going to sugarcoat things for you, okay? I'm direct," Dick said with a near spit. "I tell it like it is."

"I understand scrutiny better than y . . . you might think. I scrutinize myself . . . more than you do. The bashing doesn't help anyone. I think this . . . management style lets personalities get in the way of the work."

"Ha! Then we both need to be harder on you. You're naïve." Dick scoffed. "Think for once. We have a good thing going here. Our funders love us. We're finally ready to expand statewide, but we need to make our name at the national conference to get the funding." Red was taking over his tanned face. "And then YOU come along and charm the HR coordinator and want to mess up our survey and then sit there and shake when I call you on it." His volume increased into yelling. "You know what? I'm not gonna share these so-called statistics. I'm tossing this piece of crap. I want a new report tomorrow. One using our tried-and-true template. You better learn real math real quick."

"Wha . . .? But . . . I . . . I'm using standard program evaluation methods; why . . .?" Brandon looked down and took a deep breath. "Look at the nonprofit management literature for yourself. The current program model isn't making a difference and isn't even stable for the long-term from a funding perspective. Most large funders want viable data analysis. Their program officers are trained to look for it. So if we analyze—"

"No." Dick picked up the report and threw it in his trashcan. "You're no analyst. I know analysts from over twenty years of successful corporate finance, and you're no analyst. You like this job? They call it a probationary period for a reason. It's make or break. So do it again, use our regular reporting, and find the story. Good conclusions. This is simple."

Brandon looked at his supervisor in the eye. "Could you define my shortcomings?"

"I . . . What?" Dick leaned forward with his gut against the desk and pointed at Brandon. "You listen good. I already told you. You do what I say, got it? Don't make me get disciplinary on you for insubordination."

"True discipline comes from within," Brandon mumbled.

"What?"

"True . . ." Brandon took another deep breath. "Never mind."

"That's what I thought." Dick turned toward his computer. "We're done."

Brandon picked up his copy of the report and got up. He clumsily stepped around the office door and walked back to his cube. He sat down and looked at his shaking hands. The nerves continued to jolt through his chest as he shook his mouse and typed his password. He turned his head toward the gray fabric of the side of his cube. There was no focus. He simply waited as his mind and body eased back from the edge.

"Quitting time in a few minutes," a coworker in her thirties said as she passed by Brandon's cube. "Do you need another ride home?"

Brandon blinked. "That would be great. Thank you. The bus, uh . . . The bus hasn't been . . . consistent." He was having trouble calming down, and it was obvious.

"No problem. Your neighborhood is on the way for me." The coworker looked out of the adjacent windows. "Whoa! It got dark fast. Daylight savings always does that to me."

"Same here."

He stood up and shared her view of the Piedmont from the fifth floor of their hilltop office building. There was a sight of small structures on barren hills under a twilight sky. It reminded him of a pre-Renaissance fresco of Bethlehem that he had once seen on a school field trip. The town teemed with headlights and foot traffic, little lights in the dark looking for shelter.

Brandon's mental radio began to play the ambient sounds of guitarist Joe Satriani's "Midnight." Darkness was never quite

218

upon him the way it was in this florescent cage, especially after an interaction like he had just had. It made no sense.

And that was the point. Meaning faded away. Trying to hold onto it was like grabbing at the surface of a large, flat, smooth, wet rock. Compassion was irrelevant and hope was a four-letter word. Home was farther away despite every message in society indicating the opposite would occur from all the choices he had made. He could feel his landscape of scars beckoning for him to come closer, to come all the way. Darkness was becoming inevitable. He knew he needed a light, a speck of light, from somewhere. From someone.

"Doing anything for Thanksgiving, Marcel?" the coworker asked.

"I'm . . . Oh, yeah. I'm visiting an old friend in Florida. Sorry. Brain fart. And you?"

"Staying home with the family."

"That's good."

***

"MY MOM STILL LIKES YOU."

Brandon laughed as he closed the door behind them. "I don't know about that. She still scares the hell out of me. Maybe that's my inner teenager."

"She likes you enough to take Brant for the night," Marianne said as she tossed her keys on the coffee table and dropped her purse next to the couch. "She might be scary, but she's not stupid."

"Fair enough. And she does make a good sweet potato casserole!" He nervously shifted his weight and tried to not stare at his radiantly beautiful ex-girlfriend. "I've been meaning to ask you something. How has it been, you know, being a mom and all? I know you . . . weren't wanting kids back in the day. Like you said after our, y'know . . . scare."

"That's another kind of scary." She stepped into her kitchenette, opened the refrigerator, and pulled out two bottles of

219

beer. "You know how it goes. I'm not going to stay the same person forever. And nothing changes you like having a child. Puts things into perspective, you know?"

"Yeah." He smiled as he slowly sat at one end of the big brown couch, feeling the soft plush as he eased down. "I would think so."

She came around the corner and started to hand him a bottle. "Wait—you don't like beer. Oops. Hey, more for me." She set them down on the coffee table, pushing aside her Dalí hardcover book. "I have some really great water! It's filtered and everything."

"Perfect." The fact that she remembered his preferences was endearing. She always seemed to remember. "Brant is a sweet little baby. I figured you'd be a great mom."

"We'll see about that. Still getting used to it." Marianne filled up a glass then brought it back to him. "Oh, I wanted you to hear my speakers." She went to the laptop on her messy desk in the corner of the room, shook the mouse, and then clicked on an audio interface. Pink Floyd's *A Momentary Lapse of Reason* album started playing. "I know you defend later Floyd. But, yeah, being a mom, it's something else," Marianne said as she popped open a bottle and sat down on the other end of the couch. "Tough. I don't sleep much. Not that I ever really did." She reclined and tossed her long hair with her free hand. Her loose, unbuttoned black sweater fell on either side of her heather gray T-shirt. Those deep brown eyes that Brandon remembered now stared back at him. "It's good. Cute kid. You . . . never quite see yourself in this situation until it happens." She took a swift drink then sat up to put the bottle on the coffee table. "I did all the right things. Well, almost all. I went from straight-A's and job offers to being a single mom and unemployed after a few wild nights. Wonderful."

"Some people do all the right things but are dead inside." Brandon took a sip of water and held his glass. He listened for David Gilmour's signature guitar tone playing blues rock over synthesizer atmospheres. Music often reminded him of past relationships, but by being with Marianne, the past was present. "Even if someone pulls off a picture-perfect transition to adulthood, many of those types are more uptight than me, with fundamentalism or materialism or some other twisted mentality at work."

"I guess." She sat for a second then laughed. "You always were uptight. Did you know we used to call you Dog Whistle when you weren't around?"

"Yeah, Germy told me." He chuckled then spoke with sardonic inflections. "Apparently, my ass was so tight that if I were to fart, only a dog would hear it."

Marianne laughed again. "Oh, come on. You know that's funny!"

"It is." He smiled, took another sip, and then set the glass on the table. Late November wind blew across the fountain's waters outside. "But you're whip-smart and always worked hard. You make things work. And you will with this." He sat back farther. "I was uptight and I did all the right things. But all I have to show for myself is a supposedly fancy job, working for a screaming profit-driven manager of a nonprofit organization who must have majored in sycophantic jackassery while rushing Tappa Kegga. They're more interested in the status quo and securing their bonuses than using data or mission achievement. He says I'm just naïve."

"You're only a little naïve. Definitely idealistic under your angst, though. Just like you were in Scouts. You were mad that they kept voting you down for Order of the Arrow and wouldn't help you with your projects after you helped them. Now . . . at least you're making decent money, right?"

"Yeah, but it's . . . I'm kind of surprised that they even have tax-exempt status from the way they run things. I'm not sure it can even qualify as a charity from the bare-minimal program delivery. The effectiveness figures are sad. If we had to rely on private fundraising or foundations instead of federal grants, comparable charities elsewhere would snatch the big prospects up by showing themselves as more effective. Most program officers would look closely into our management-designated effectiveness reports and see that they're simply not making much of a difference. Reporting for our grants is a mile wide and an inch deep."

"Doesn't sound like a good nonprofit to me." She quickly finished off her beer, tossed it on the table, and then turned back to him. "Babe, if you keep searching, maybe you could find a nonprofit that actually wants to be effective."

"Eventually. It already took so much time and effort to get here." Brandon closed his eyes, feeling the presence of Aisling, and rubbed his face. "I've been trying to connect in other ways. I've been into politics in the last year, y'know . . . asking how to make the world a better place. I went from that white suburban progressivism to a more liberty-focused, voluntarism thing, but I can't find meaning there, either. They all have big ideas without application. The devil's in the details. And big egos, too. Self-congratulation permeates all political ideologies." He sighed.

"Thankfully, there's more to life than work or politics. What about personal stuff?"

"Well, I'm also trying to figure out what the deal is with my family. It seems like most families value conformity, as if caring for each other necessitates blind devotion to traditions and trends. So, I try to get a sense of connection with friends, right? Germy's pattern is to give me a piercing truth of some sort and then blow me off. You know him; he's always been half-in, half-out. He'd save us all if he didn't have to run off and get laid." He shook his head. "And then there's my new friend, Janelle, who's . . . good, I guess. But she lives on the other side of the country, and I . . . I don't know about her." He sighed again. "Of course, there's always romance. You really know me there, huh? This girl I've known for a while, she—"

"That Sarah girl?"

"Yeah. She's . . . well, pretty much everything I've ever looked for in a partner—smart, gorgeous, good taste in music, reads Tolkien, really involved in clubs and volunteering. We don't agree on politics, but I think that's a beautiful thing, you know? She, you know . . . she believes in helping people and is looking for a career in social services, like me. We make less money but serve the underserved." He shook his head. "She's standoffish, but I really think that's the kind of girl who could . . . you know, be the right one."

"You *think*? Brandon, have you tried feeling? Both are important."

"Feeling, yeah. That gets me in trouble more often than not, you know. But I get your point." Brandon smirked. "Because, here I am, a pile of emotions bitching up a storm to someone who has overcome all sorts of situations, someone who always makes things work." He scratched his side through the tattered blue fabric of his summer camp T-shirt. "And who makes me feel like I can make things work."

"I like that." Marianne curled into the couch, looking intently into his eyes. "I always liked your tight-ass hyper-analysis, by the way. You're not always right, but at least you think things through. People can have all the egotistical pretentions they want. That doesn't mean they give a shit." She played with her small earrings. "Whereas you give too much of a shit. You'd be fine if you remembered to chill out. It works for me. Too much, I guess."

"I try sometimes." He scratched his chest and turned to look at her. "And I'm thankful. I think I've been right about a girl at some point in the past." He paused. "Maybe once."

Marianne looked at him and smiled. "Yeah, maybe." She continued to play with her earrings and looked away, her face fading. "I don't always call them right myself. I mean, obviously." She looked down.

"Dear . . ." He wanted to slide closer to her. Self-consciousness prevented him. "You can't blame—"

"I got too wrapped up in the moment. You need more moments like that. I guess I need less. He was a pretty slick guy, you know? Cool guy, life of the party, not even a pinch of self-doubt. He had this shine to him. Aloof, just like I like 'em. Real cool guy."

"Yeah." Something in Brandon's subconscious mind went off, but he couldn't focus on it with his self-consciousness in full force. "They say confidence is everything. Even good girls and guys can't resist it."

"We can't help who we like." She sat up and opened the second bottle. "I swear there's a factory somewhere that spits out guys like him." She took a fast swig and nearly slammed the bottle back down. "Confidence, as you said, is everything in the attraction game. As if confidence is better than being a decent human being. So fucking special. So fucking typical."

"Yeah."

"Not like you."

Brandon's heart beat faster, and suddenly the world was more chaotic yet made more sense. The one coherent thought he had was Germy telling him about Søren Kierkegaard's concept of the teleological suspension of the ethical. He wasn't sure what it meant but knew it had something to do with the nostalgic beauty before him that was so wrong and so right.

"I love you." Her eyes met his and wouldn't let go. "I've always loved you." She closed her eyes and grabbed her beer, finishing it with her infamous speed before setting it back down to finish her thought. "I know we can't be together. I can make things work during the day, but by night, I want to be so wasted that I can't remember it. You've never been able to handle me, so I know we can't be together. I still admire your mind almost as much as I admire your heart. But you always need some kind of emotional support, and now mine's reserved for myself and my son. I know this sucks given what I put you through in high school, but I had to say it."

"It's cool, it's cool. It's good to finally see you again. I love you, too. I—"

"You." Marianne threw her legs around Brandon, straddled his body and covered his lips with kisses.

His heart beat harder through his chest and into hers. For once, the panic was worth it.

He felt her arms around him, pulling him closer and enveloping him completely. Her tongue was as tenderly penetrating and energetically lustful as he remembered. The taste was of cheap beer, cherries, and sheer delight. The line between the physical and the emotional blurred and then dissipated in a way he hadn't remembered was real.

He slipped his hands around her back and pulled her closer. He felt her breasts push firmly against his chest. They kissed, and they kissed. Wet kisses welling up the warmth within his heart. It was wet, and it was mad. It was something that neither one realized how much they needed it until they had it.

And it felt so damn good.

As the trance of lips escalated, she pushed her hips harder against him. They each remembered where such moments would lead.

She broke their kiss and held the side of her face against his,

225

whispering into his ear, "Come on."

Brandon's blinding elation subsided enough to elicit her meaning. "I . . . love . . ."

"I love you, too. Always have." She pulled back and started to get up before abruptly stopping. "Let's get a—"

"I . . ." Through all of this moment and everything within it, there was something right and something wrong. He didn't know if it was wrong for her or him, for both or neither, but there was something that couldn't be right with what would follow. "I've thought about this and what it could mean. I would love . . . It would be wonderful. There's no one else I could be with but you." He looked away. "I don't think . . ."

She remained still and looked at him as though he was a new canvas; not to be worked upon, but interpreted. "We can't do this, can we?"

His head started to hang. "I don't think we . . . should."

"*Should?*"

"I guess."

Marianne slumped down next to him on the couch, closing her eyes in an unnamed expression. "I wasn't sure. Felt good."

Brandon leaned into her, leaving his hand on her thigh for affection.

She brought her hands to her face then dropped them down again. "It's not a good idea."

"Right now, I see the girl I met in those young years. I can't describe how happy I am to be with you." He lightly shook his head. "I don't want us to tease or delude ourselves. It's what so many do at our age. Holding on to a temporary emotion or sexual interest to tide them over the years of loneliness and lack of something real. Thus the divorce rates in recent years." A gaze formed between their eyes. "Moments like these are as much as we can hope for. We learned years ago that sex is . . . worth it if it's . . . meant to last."

She lost her gaze as she rolled her eyes. "Maybe. But I think you're still waiting for Sarah."

"Well, I . . . I mean, you still mean so much—"

"It's okay." She sighed and sat still for a moment. Then she shook her head and leaned into him, cuddling close on the couch. "You have your reasons. I have mine."

He took her hand and held it to his face, feeling the light calluses of her fingers. She gave him one soft kiss, and then they held each other. The thoughts and feelings were shared and known. There was uncommon contentment. The years were theirs, and their love was real, but the romance was made of impermanence. They were not meant to be together. They were once and once again. This time together was meant to be limited.

"Come on," Marianne said. "It's getting kinda late. We should get some rest."

***

WAKING UP TO THE SOUND of an electric violin and a harpsichord, Brandon found his arms around his girlfriend from years past. He felt something just short of complete. She was still asleep as Emilie Autumn's "A Cure?" played softly on the laptop speakers.

Taking a small breath, he held Marianne's scent like a talisman before a journey. A moment later, she awoke and turned around to find his lips. They kissed. And kissed. It was thrilling yet peaceful. Their hearts beat together in such temporary tranquility.

And then they spent a perfect day together. They went to the Dalí museum, had lunch out on the pier, fed the birds, went to her mother's house and spent time with baby Brant, made Cuban sandwiches for dinner, played pool in a dingy bar, and ended with a long talk about old times, conversing and smoking into the night.

They fell asleep on the couch, holding each other and dreaming of a life that would never be.

The invigoration was palpable for each of them. It was as if they had broken free of their own circumstances, all social and emotional pretenses, and were able to just be with another human being. To be special to someone else who understood.

The visit was short by design. They didn't want it to end, even though they knew it must, for internal and external reasons alike.

When she dropped him off at the airport the following morning, Marianne didn't have much to say to Brandon. He didn't have much to say to her. They thought of it as a piece of time that needed to be. They knew this kiss would be their last.

"Thank you."

"I love you."

"I love you, too. Always will."

"Always."

"Take care."

They would need it far more than they realized.

December

"IS IT GOOD?"

Brandon took another small bite of filet mignon cooked to medium-rare perfection. He found the glass of petite syrah to be a fantastic pairing. The virtuoso violinist, perched by the restaurant's outcrop overlooking the nighttime city, was playing one of Brandon's favorite caprices. All the patrons were well-dressed, and some looked vaguely familiar.

As Brandon went for another sip, he looked to the figure across the table. Comfort interlaced with terror. It had a face much like his own, only without eyes. It was a face beyond death.

"Is it good?" The question reverberated with a menacingly even tone.

Brandon put his glass down. "It tastes good."

"Then it is good."

The violinist struck a high, piercing note and shuffled his fingers rapidly down several sequential scales. He finished the caprice to light applause.

After a quick bow, a group of supporting string musicians appeared around him on the stage. The pianist sat behind him and prepared his hands. They began a performance of "Danse Macabre" by Camille Saint-Saëns.

"Oh," Brandon said in a lucid daze. He turned to face the performance. "This was on that classical music CD I would listen to when I studied math. Then . . . I ran away from home that one weekend after . . ." He took another sip of wine. "I ran all the way to the river that day, trying not to think, and this was stuck in my head. I watched the river flow while hearing this in my head. Upon the hillside . . . I saw gravestones. Whitewashed gravestones." Looking back down at his plate, he went to cut another bite. "And then I went back home."

"Authority." The figure grinned and folded his hands on the table. "One might say about that. What else is on your mind?"

"Well . . ." Brandon took another bite and looked up toward the ceiling, seeing soft lights hung at various lengths around the club. Even though he could see quite well, these lights struck him as especially artificial. "Friends. I remember friends growing up." He chewed through his reminiscence. "They'd call and say they were coming over, so I would wait for them and wait for them, watching the clock in the living room. I'd just pace around, waiting." A second passed as he stared. "And if we were going to meet at their house, I'd ring the doorbell right on time, but they would either take like ten minutes to get to the door, or they weren't home. I always wanted to see them more than they wanted to see me." He scratched his upper left arm. "They were certainly never around when the bullies were."

"There's a friend for you." The figure reached for his wine glass and let the boney tips of his fingers rest on it. "You always tried so hard. Just find other friends." He picked up the glass with a slight tilt. It was as if he wanted the deep red drink to be something else. "You believe too much."

Brandon continued to stare into the ether. "I've always wondered about that." He looked down and shrugged. "I've always had a real friend when I'm in real need, like my cat and Germy. And even when they weren't around, in the darkest nights, it was like . . . there was this . . . dream of a woman who was always there. And when I really listened, I heard her. I knew it was okay, or it would be okay. Then I remembered what's important."

The man seemed to lift his eyebrows then ease into a soft smirk. "So, what is important, then? I know you've been thinking about that. Your thoughts console you amid the disappointments of your beliefs. Good. But have you figured out what you're going to do?"

Brandon sat back and put his fork down. "I couldn't go for the meds. I'm not sure what to do with my career. And I've been waiting for a relationship, but . . . I don't know. You know, I have this really good friend now. We're still figuring things out, but there's so much good there, so many ways we can help each—"

"Oh, her." The man sighed then chuckled. "That girl way out there. She might as well be beyond the light, you know, given all that distance. I can tell you that she's as unstable as they come. Just watch, she's going to pull away from you. She's going to fall harder for the new guy and turn away from you. Why not make both of you happy and let her go? Sarah actually goes out and does things. The reason she doesn't like your openness is because she's interested and knows that only makes things uncomfortable and awkward, so go with her flow. She shares your beliefs, and she cares. I'm sure I don't have to tell you that her looks don't hurt, either." He laughed. "That's all I'm saying. Just watch, that other girl way out there, the one you haven't even met, is unstable and doesn't actually care about you."

Brandon took another bite and talked with his mouth full. "I don't know. We'll see."

"So, what about the job?"

"The job? My boss is a prick, and the organization is hardly doing any good. I don't know why I'm there."

"Brandon, this is an easy one. We know that no one is perfect. No organization is perfect, either. You'll definitely find a good one later on, okay? Right now, learn to overcome your boss by beating him at his own game. Quit being the bearer of bad news; no one likes that. Warm up to the executive director by telling him what he wants to hear. He'll recognize your talent and invite you to conferences. You could even get promoted! Take the prick's job." The man gave an assuring nod. "You're making real money when your mother said you couldn't! And you could make more. You can always use that to donate to better causes, right? Focus on getting ahead. It's still a good path. A more refined good. That's what it's about." He took a sip of wine.

"Well, I . . ." Brandon sat and began to stare at the table, his brain suspended within him. "I want to do good, but it . . ." He hesitated, feeling a jarring within him. "It seems to . . ." The words bent and buckled like a bridge collapsing. He identified a small thought that resembled a cornerstone. "Well, it doesn't sit with the whole con . . . science . . . faith."

"Right." The man grinned. "I keep forgetting about the prevalence of superstition even in the postmodern world. Brandon, you use scientific principles when analyzing statistics in your academic and professional life. You even think analytically about everything in your personal life. So, why don't you rely on science, evidence, logic, and reason for the universal questions?" He laughed. "But no, no, it is good to have groups like Sarah's groups, church groups, and so on. It's all about camaraderie. Focus on being happy with people and not on rituals; they're outdated customs. Faith is about people and being happy. There's nothing greater. Don't let 'believer' become a synonym for 'sucker' because you don't know how to enjoy yourself. Good people and good organizations will come around in time. That's how you make a real difference. They're all a means to an end."

Brandon's eyebrows rose. "I . . . I haven't quite thought of it that way."

And just then, the performance changed in tone. Somber, minor notes faded away and a new beat began. It was a capricious and almost fun piece, full of grand and quirky notes. The string section sounded almost delightful. And then the night didn't seem quite so dark. His heart lifted.

"You know . . . yeah. Happiness is a choice. So . . . what's next?"

"Say yes! You'll soon have the opportunity to finally get ahead and show everyone what you're capable of doing. Job, dating, everything. Just be open to doing what you have to do to take it to the next level. It's a means, right? Don't get caught up on your preconceived principles. You know that . . . eventual outcomes are what matter. Intentions and enjoyment will eventually lead to a greater good. You'll soon get a chance at your job and, well, maybe with the girl. You know, the one, the real deal. How about that? It can happen if you keep your eye on the prize. But you'll have to be confident. Confident and happy. That's a win-win, Brandon. Say yes to the opportunities. Next thing you know, you'll be settled. You'll finally be settled."

"Settled?"

"Home." He took a sip and watched Brandon's reaction.

Brandon sat back in his chair and listened to the major scales gradually ascend. He turned over the man's last word in his mind like a coin in a gambler's hand. The greatest prize was being offered. The odds were unmatched. It was better than likely. It was nearly certain. It might as well be certain. It was certain.

Hope swelled within his chest, displacing the doubt with a synthetic serenity. The feeling was better than the food or drink, better than the lavish surrounds and sounds, better than his lucid clout endowing him with the knowledge that this was all within his control. He had previously come to complacently accept that the entire world was built to control him; to first build up his dreams and then assure their impossibility, to accept that one was powerless beneath the many powerful. Choice seemed irrelevant . . . until now. Free will was most especially irrelevant . . . until now. Now he knew the choice was his.

With the divine roulette of great chance and greater promise in his hands, all that remained was a burning question.

"And if I don't?"

The man put his hands on the edge of the table and stood up. "You know. Remember that time back then? Yes? No? A little? A little. Well, imagine that morsel of awful horror in exponents." He looked into Brandon's eyes with his own vision of corporeal nothingness. "After that, your choices will run out. Either way, it will be over soon. Very soon." He laughed. "And that's good."

***

THE ROOM SWIRLED IN BRANDON'S delirium as he threw off sheets and stumbled out of bed. He felt like he had a hangover but didn't remember having a drink. The impulse to check his Gold Pavilion account was especially strong. He rubbed his eyes as his computer booted.

At the top of the feed, there it was: an entire thread in the Young Capitalist group about him, apparently left public so that he could see it even though he had been removed from the group. Palpitations erupted, especially after seeing that the original poster was Randall himself.

"*Watch out for snakes in the grass, y'all*," the post started. "*I thought Brandon would be our next true believer to argue statists on economics. I was even hoping to jam guitars with him. Turns out he's a bullshitter. Just another bleeding heart who talks a big game, but it's just talk. Dude works at charities. I don't need a handout. Do you? Keep away from statist shitbags.*"

The first comment concurred hard, but on other grounds. "*Surprised but not really. He's one of those betacuck snowflake types. You can tell he doesn't work out. When I shook his hand, I thought I'd crush it. Weak will and weak body. Maybe screen recruits harder?"*

And another. *"Sorry, Randall, this is on you. Just cuz someone plays guitar doesn't mean you should be their friend. Probably can't play for shit anyway. Nothing of value was lost."*

And another still. *"Haaaa haha you got punked by a progressive. What did he want, anyway? Talk us into donations? Hippity, hoppity, get off my property, you damn leach. Next!"*

And so on. And so forth.

Through the chaos of heart and mind, Brandon had to tear his hands away from the keyboard. He started and deleted three comments before standing up from the desk. All he could do was stumble around the room. The aching anger, self-hated, and cacophony of palpitations formed a pit in his chest. He shook in his pain. He knew this reaction would be exactly what they wanted. It didn't matter, though. He screamed and pounded his fist against the desk, the feelings of brokenness and worthlessness raging.

After minutes of fury and panic, he felt two paths out of the emotional chaos. One revolved around his job. The other around Janelle. He felt entirely divided, so he decided to sit down, figuratively and literally. He simply sat on the floor like a child. Nothing to say. Nothing to do.

For now.

The Morning Star watched.

***

FLICKING THE ASHES OF HIS black clove cigarette out of the driver's window, Germy sat quietly at the red stoplight as Brandon ranted first about the Young Capitalist group thread and then about his boss.

Germy wasn't used to not feeling the wind in his hair. It had been cut short and plain at his parents' firm demand.

The thought of one of his girls came and went as he drummed

his thumb on the steering wheel to "South of Heaven" by Slayer. Gray clouds of the early morning held above them and the bare trees as harbingers of the coming winter.

"I mean, I don't understand how someone can make six figures and not understand pie charts," Brandon said as he tapped his own ashes out of the passenger window. The embroidered Polo shirt under his black peacoat felt rough on his skin. "I don't understand it. But we're supposedly the generation whose expensive education isn't worth a damn, and we're too entitled, and so on. We're entitled to participation trophies, but they're entitled to cushy pensions. I'd gladly trade. Not to mention this tenuous, would-be recovery. Thanks for the plastic."

"Boomers." The stoplight turned green, and Germy hit the gas and turned up the bass mix. "You know how much I look up to my folks, of course. Then again, I don't think the kids these days have seen a vacant stare they couldn't share. Or a new indie band they didn't think was better than everything since the Beatles. There's like an ever-shortening duration of acceptability for actually liking something. It's going to get to the point that it's only cool to like bands that don't even exist. Bands that take their names from random words and numbers, like in the late 90's, but worse."

"What's your point?"

"All I'm saying is that they can all stick it in the poop chute—boomers, zoomers, doomers—for their own reasons."

"Uh, I suppose." Brandon took a quick drag and looked over the rows of strip malls. He wondered if Sarah would respond to his latest text. It was his most sincere attempt yet at sounding casual while not being casual. "One generation's crap to the next. And I'm about to get another serving."

"I'm telling you, if your boss is going to be immature, you

should be immature right back." Germy took a quick drag and exhaled hard. "Go in there and take a dump right on his desk. That'll learn him. Poop chute riot. That's my kind of swing."

Brandon laughed. "That'll go over real well. Like a . . . fart in church, but . . . yeah. Talk about late 90's, Germ." Wisps of smoke flowed out of the corner of his lowered car window. "How did graduation go?"

"Yeah. I didn't go."

"Really? I know how you feel about traditions, but how did your terminally status-conscious parents take it?"

"They took it in the poop chute."

"Well, you're a barrel of scatological humor this fine morning."

"I figure our old friend Dante would appreciate my verses. I read his comedy, but it wasn't that funny. Certainly not divine. You know, I tasted God's shit one time."

"Germy, for fu—"

"It tasted better than mine."

"Seriously!"

"Now, that was divine. I call 'em like I see 'em. I can't help it if my parents, indie bands, and your boss are downtown with the brown sound. They're all pricky-dick bumscuzzle."

"Seriously." Brandon shook his head with a smile and tapped the last few ashes of his cigarette out the window. The haunt of arriving at the office was coming over him stronger than before. He found the razorblade distortions of the Marilyn Manson song starting and the holiday scent of Germy's clove smoke comforting against the thought of the office building on the horizon. The palpitations started. He tried to ignore them. The woman's face wouldn't appear in his mind's eye. "Damn."

"Stop worrying."

"You do know me well."

"Indubitably."

237

"What the hell do I replace it with? You and Janelle still don't have an answer. But Sarah would say—"

"Ho, no, no, merry Christmas for you. Sarah's a lump of crap."

"You mean coal?"

"Same difference."

"That's quite a bit of certainty coming from Mr. Abstract over here. She's still more involved."

"There's not much to abstract with her. Involvement doesn't mean anything by itself." Germy shook his head. "You don't have to replace the worrying with anything, let alone whatever we say. Including this." He chuckled. "There's my magic koan for the day." He took a quick drag before he took a sharp turn into the parking lot. "Although, you are going to have to face this by yourself."

"What do you mean? I'm almost always alone while you're out there drinking and screwing like there's no tomorrow."

"Well, there may not be one, and I don't mean alone but still checking your Gold Pavilion and phone constantly. I mean *alone*." He sniffed as he pulled up to the curb. "I'm going to be training for my new job next week, and I've got my own crap, so I won't be around much. I won't be around to give you a ride or anything, so . . ."

Brandon heard the shadows in his friend's voice. "So, what?"

"Just, uh . . . just be cool in the days ahead. Quit obsessing and be good. You gotta, you know . . . do what you should."

Brandon stuck his cigarette butt in the ashtray, grabbed his leather folder, and then opened the door. "Thanks for the ride. I'll catch you on the dark side. And I'll drop a stinky one for you."

"That's right." He cleared his throat and looked down as

Brandon shut the door. "Be good, brother."

***

THE CORRELATION COEFFICIENT WASN'T HIGH enough. Brandon ran all the numbers on the spreadsheet again, but the standard deviation was too high and the final scores were too low. He checked each figure three times. He clicked through the formulas—always the same results. The lump in his throat grew harder when he remembered Dick saying that these figures would be shared at the conference. With a correlation coefficient directly beneath the acceptable range, there was no way to say with confidence that there was a statistical relationship between participation in the Community Training Corps program and employment offers.

Tapping the space bar, he rearranged the placement of cells in a ruminating gesture and raised the significance level all the way to 0.1. But the very last cell in the very last corner remained red. He wondered what to do.

"Watcha working on, my man Marcel?"

"Oh, Rob," Brandon said, startled by the tall and impeccably dressed executive director suddenly appearing behind him in his cube. Rob's always casual verbal expressions contrasted hard with his always formal appearance. "Yeah, I . . . I was finishing up the most recent job placement data that Dick and I were working on." He wondered if ending a sentence in a preposition would be noted. Dick had subconsciously trained him to know that management's big mistakes were more acceptable than his little ones. "I'm getting them prepared for the upcoming report."

"Yeah," Rob said as he leaned over to read the figures on the monitor, resting his hand on the work surface. "He was telling me about that. I know he's trying to build you up and make you into a real fit here, so I'm hoping to see some good stuff."

He leaned closer with his eyes holding a slight squint. "Hmm,

239

yeah." He tapped his finger twice. "I know how these stats work. I've seen what good numbers can mean at a Fortune 500." Rob's tone made a sudden shift upward, belying the meaning underneath it. "I, you know . . . Brandon, I was really hoping to see something a little more . . . helpful than this. A better story."

Through the wreck of his ears and his chest, a thought occurred to Brandon. It came suddenly and gave him a burst of forward momentum. His heart calmed. Then there was a thought of the woman's face. He dismissed it as a self-imposed distraction and opted for newfound confidence.

Confidence and happiness.

"Actually, Rob, I just thought of something," Brandon said with an almost loud projection. "We could, uh . . . instead of using their first session scores, we could . . . assume that their baseline scores . . . are zero. Because, you know . . . the program is a new start for everyone, so the scores aren't accurate anyway. That should bump up the correlation coefficient."

"Well . . ." Rob thought for a moment and smiled. "I think you have a point. I was going to say . . ." His voice trailed away for a moment. "Nah, I think . . . you're right. We don't need those numbers in there. Right, my man? Doesn't help anybody. And we want to help!"

"Yeah, Rob, that's what I was thinking." Brandon used his cursor to carefully highlight a series of columns on the left side of the spreadsheet. He reached across the keyboard to the "delete" key, which seemed farther away than ever before. This action wasn't second-nature; it was very deliberate. His ring finger came down almost slowly. And with a light tap, all the participant responses for the first session were gone. Instantly, all the figures increased, the standard deviation went down, and the correlation coefficient jumped up enough to fall into the threshold of statistical significance at 0.1. The very last cell in the very last corner turned green.

"Yeah, look! They weighed down the results anyway," the Executive Director said as if he didn't know what was going to happen. "We want to tell the story of people building better professional skills and learning how to find a job, so we just include the, uh . . . relevant scores. Everyone starts at zero, right? Yeah."

Rob leaned closely to whisper. "Keep this up and Dick will have good reason to be jealous. I know your math is tighter. You'll make six figures." He stood up straight annunciated proudly. "Excellent analysis, Brandon. Our trainers will be proud of these numbers and happy to know their work really is making a difference." Stepping back from the cube, Rob stretched. "Just doing some good, you know?"

"Yeah," Brandon responded. The weight in his chest lifted. Something in his mind faded away. He felt levity and an alien comfort. And he felt excitement not only at the subtle prospect of advancement and vengeance being offered, but more than anything, the approval from authority. "Yeah, definitely!"

"Good work, my man, good work. Just, uh . . . report the improved scores."

"Got it, Rob!" Brandon scratched under his collar. For some reason, the fading image in his mind's eye was replaced by the thought of Sarah and wanting to kiss her under a cascading shower. He blinked and refocused on the spreadsheet. "So, yeah, I'll get a report together and give it to Dick so he can share it at the conference."

Rob laughed. "Oh, I didn't tell you about that?" He turned and leaned against the edge of the cube. "I talked with Dick, and . . . I think you're ready for the conference. If you're free for the first week in January, of course."

Brandon's face lit up as his confidence multiplied. "Oh,

absolutely!"

"Very good. We're going to be flying down early on New Year's Eve, get there in the afternoon, have some fun downtown for a few days, and then hit up the conference before flying back on the sixth. You'll learn about a bunch of other nonprofits and funding opportunities in time to apply for the coming fiscal year. And you'll get to share this great news to foundations and philanthropists from all over the country!" Rob nodded a proud smile. "They can hear it from you firsthand. That's great. Yes, this is exactly what we need to get real exposure. People will be talking about CTC. With another big grant, we'll be able to expand statewide!"

"Awesome!" Brandon caught himself in a rare moment of zeal. It felt unfamiliar to the point that he felt like someone else.

The gray around the cube seemed to move.

He blinked and looked back up at Rob. "I'm excited about it. I'll work out the details with Dick."

"Great work, my man. I knew you would turn out to be a good hire." Rob started to walk back to his office. "Keep it up!"

"Thanks, Rob!"

The Morning Star smiled brightly.

***

PULLING BILLS OUT OF HIS wallet, Brandon looked up and saw a pretty face. He dropped a five-dollar bill and a one-dollar tip on the deli counter next to the miniature Christmas tree with small glowing lights. There was unusual confidence under his poise.

"Sarah," he said with a steady grin and opened arms. "It's been a while. I figured you were tired of my messages."

"Oh, you," she said with a laugh as she fell into his hug. A red scarf with brilliant gold accents sat easily on her impeccable charcoal business suit. Her modest use of makeup left the mole in front of her right ear untouched. The strawberry blonde hair was now cut shoulder-length. "You know I'm bad about responding to everyone." She grabbed her food tray order from the counter and waited with him. "Well, look at you in your wool coat, nice white shirt, and tie. Aren't you all grown up now?"

"Yes, indeed," Brandon said playfully as he leaned against the corner. He noticed the mole and let himself be allured by it. And by her. "I thought I'd try my hand at a grown-up job, so I ditched the T-shirts and hoodies for something more professional."

"That's good. We've all got to do it eventually. Did you finally get a car?"

"Not yet. I'm saving money by taking public transportation. That also helps the environment, right?"

"I guess," Sarah said while shaking her head. "I think it's because you don't like driving."

"That, too."

"I knew it! Not always so virtuous, huh? Wait, where are you working again?"

"I'm down the street at the Community Training Corps, a few floors up at the business park there. I'm their program analyst. I started a little over a month ago."

"Oh, yeah. Good organization. I drive by that park on the way to my office up on Stratford."

"That's cool! We're not far apart. I'm glad you landed in the Triad." He looked away and back again. "But yeah, I'm happy to be working for a great mission that helps people find opportunities, you know? Putting compassion and understanding to work, right?"

"Sure."

"So . . ." he started but compulsively turned to see if his order was ready. "So, the last I heard, you were also looking to do that kind of work at a regional nonprofit. So, did you . . .? Is your job up there on Stratford one of those nonprofits, or a public sector gig, or . . .?"

"Yeah," she responded, her face having little expression. "I'm actually working for-profit. I'm a financial consultant for Vazio & Leer's new office. They liked my math skills and all my club leadership stuff, so I started there. It's been really good so far."

"Oh, I see," Brandon responded with surprise. He felt jarring cognitive dissonance between thoughts of her speeches and her career decision, but he dismissed the feeling as naivety and ignored it. "That's cool. My sister's an engineer on their R&D side, and she seems to like it. They have good insurance and retirement plans, and of course, the pay is good. Or so I've heard."

"It is good," Sarah said as she looked away. "I'm one promotion away from six figures. Not bad for my first full-time job, huh? Thank goodness for the federal bailouts, though, or the whole company might have gone under."

Brandon winced. A second later, he noticed his lunch order on the counter. He thanked the clerk, took the tray, and then walked with Sarah to the booth in the window nook.

Most of the sky remained gray, but there were a few spots of blue out on the horizon. Cars maneuvered around busy shoppers and workers on lunch break. A driver honked.

Brandon and Sarah took off their coats, sat down, and settled into their impromptu date. A barely audible holiday song played in the ceiling speakers.

As they talked and ate, there was a moment when Brandon looked at Sarah and caught her in a glance. They shared a flicker of thought. Then she leaned into the table, and he realized that this was the first time she had come to him and wanted to spend time with him. Something was there. Something was waiting. In her gaze and gestures, there was a magnetism that wasn't there before.

It was there now, and it was finally mutual.

"I've got to give it to you, Brandon. That sounds like a social justice-friendly position you scored."

"I guess you could say that."

"That's good. I'm still active at a few different organizations. I'll have to see what's going on at CTC. The youth group at church is throwing a party, if you're interested."

"Oh, yeah?" Brandon took a bite then covered his mouth with his free hand.

"Yeah. Still meeting on Saturdays, coming up with projects. Actually, we had this one spaghetti dinner a few months ago that turned into a big food fight. It was so much fun!"

"Aw. That does sound like fun. You can't take yourselves too seriously, right?"

"Exactly! Life's about being happy and having fun." She took a sip of sweet tea and looked outside. "It helps to have a positive attitude. I can't stand people who are all down and depressed, you know?" Sarah licked her lip. "I like to spread good vibes. We don't want people to feel too sorry for themselves. No one wants that. Even if someone's going through a rough patch, being happy and grateful can only be a good thing."

"Uh . . . yeah, yeah." Something in her comment stoked cognitive dissonance again. He continued to ignore it. "Right on. We've got to be a good influence. Social service can have all the program people, fundraisers, analysts like me, and volunteers, but it's like . . . all that's just work unless you do it with a smile, right?"

"Exactly." Sarah took a bite and held a steady grin.

They felt the cheer from people's red and green garb to the paper snowflakes hanging all around the deli. The tune over the speakers became clearer, emerging as a jazzy version of "Greensleeves" from John Coltrane. It reminded Brandon of enjoying Coltrane's "A Love Supreme," while it reminded Sarah of mood music for intimacy. She thought of past lovers. Brandon's new demeanor gave her new ambitions.

She looked at his slight stubble under his now smooth smile. The only thing left in her way was a modicum of deference to the intellectual comforts of her ideology.

"So . . . Brandon . . ." she said as she finished picking through her teeth with her tongue, "I'm liking the new social justice job, and you really should come down to the church group, but I was curious if you . . . still felt the same way you did before. I saw a post about the Young Capitalists on your Gold Pavilion and some conservative article about the debt ceiling. And, well . . . I guess I was hoping you'd reconsider what they stand for versus what we stand for."

"They? Oh, yeah . . . about that." Brandon held a finger up as he took a quick gulp of water. Before he was ready to speak again, it occurred to him that this was something of a test and that his rejection from Randall could endear him to Sarah. It also occurred to him that intellectual honesty required honesty about intellect. "Yeah, the Young Capitalists. I did try to get involved there, and uh . . . yeah, it didn't work out for me. Not much compassion and understanding."

Sarah chuckled. "Duh! We're talking about people who want to balance the budget on the backs of the poor. What did you expect?"

"That's a good question." He nodded and looked out the window. "Yeah, there wasn't too much . . . acceptance." There was a faint and uncomfortable thought encouraging him to loosen his lips. And yet, the longer he sat there, the closer it came, casting light on his increasingly hardened heart. He didn't want that. He wanted her. And now was the chance. *NOW*. "It, uh . . . yeah, I'm not quite sure how I feel about the capitalist approach to social justice."

"They want to get rid of government programs across the board, slashing critical government assistance programs. No capitalist cares about anybody but themselves."

"Yeah." He didn't want to disagree with her. He didn't want to counter an effortlessly graceful and intelligent woman in favor of the arguments from a group that had rejected him, but his thoughts betrayed him.

You can't equate personal morality to categorical policies. There can and should be a discourse on the effectiveness of public and private programs. And the strings attached, red tape, and litigation risks diminish efficiency. Public sector service outsourcing creates dependencies among private charities and their clients, including . . . my new job. Dammit.

But if the foreign military empire was cut to constitutional constraints, more federal debt could be paid, and the tax burden could be lowered. And lives saved! A more prosperous society would naturally allow more private philanthropists and foundations, some of which would fund private charities that were more nimble and more effective than government assistance or . . . my new job. Dammit.

His own organization was rife with inefficiencies, and the "Impact" webpages and annual reports of other organizations were much more substantive, but he didn't want to think about that right now. Sarah Shea-Trivette herself was looking at him straight in the eye and waiting for him to say something. He wanted to think about witty retorts that would endear her to him, not the opposite.

"I . . . yeah."

"Hmm?"

Brandon used a nervous bite of his sandwich to think of a few things to say to abort the unwanted thoughts that threatened his chances with her. He thought about stressing mission importance. *"When the sectors work together toward the same mission, we can meet the needs of all"* would be an agreeable thing to say. *"Make a difference, help people, be the change you want to see in the world,"* ad infinitum. Platitudes. *Mix a little smart talk with a politician's penchant for the dramatic, and her heart and/or loins will invite you.* It didn't matter if the words meant anything at all, let alone if they led to effective action in terms of advancing opportunities and expanding access without detrimental opportunity costs.

Platitudes are only a problem if people don't believe them. So, say it and say it well. You're getting better at it. He wanted to follow this thinking. If it weren't for *that face* and his damn internal dissension, he would tell Sarah some damn good platitudes. He would be in the *now*. He would be in the moment for himself and for her smoldering smile and her mole. It was the thoughts. It was the thoughts and the feelings and *that damn face.*

"What is it, Brandon?"

"Nah, I just . . . Sorry, had to finish that bite." He scratched his chest and tried to focus on Sarah's face instead of *that face.* There was a truth burning within him, but he didn't want the truth. He wanted Sarah. "Nah, I just . . . There are some cuts that are too drastic, and we . . . we can fight for social justice and make a difference if we . . ."

AISLING!

"What?"

"I . . ." Brandon's gaze gave way, and he caught himself staring into his own thoughts. He couldn't turn away. He would have to make a choice: say something pleasing or say something true. Take a chance for "love" or love. Or lust. It was a blur of evolutionary psychology, cultural conditioning, economic theory, sociopolitical ideology, moral perceptions, and a rusted pile of personal reasons. It was between "good" and good under mass uncertainty, and he would have to make that individual choice *now*. "I think there's . . . room for . . . different . . . views."

Sarah's smile slipped a little. "What do you mean?"

"It's just that, well . . . the question is not of *what* or *why* but *how*. There are different methods between government and civil society, and you and I agree on what to do and why to do it. Improve access and conditions, right? We both want to expand career opportunities, provide basic needs for families, improve childcare quality and education, assist the homeless, feed the hungry, clothe the naked, visit the imprisoned, and so on. What if charities are being stifled by govern—"

"No, hold on." Her grin became sarcastic as she finished chewing. "I've heard this before. This whole thing about just letting the private sector take care of people, as if that worked." She dropped her sandwich on the paper wrap, rubbed her fingers on a napkin, sat back, and folded her arms. "I was hoping it was a phase you were growing out of. I guess I was wrong. Newsflash: people don't care. People are selfish and corrupt and are capable of terrible things. You can't fight greed in-person. You can only do it by policy. That's why we need a strong public sector."

His heart sank with his shoulders, but his mind was resolute. "Policy to address character flaws. So . . . people can do terrible things, so let's concentrate their power in a central government?"

"Uh, yeah?" She rolled her eyes. "A government is accountable to people, unlike some little charity."

"So . . . people can do terrible things, so they need to be held accountable by people?"

"Oh, how cute," Sarah scoffed and threw her hands up. "Did working at your fancy, new job convince you of this? Do you really do that much good?"

"No," he responded. "We don't do nearly enough. Incidentally, our private charity program success metrics are bound by public funding we receive, which effectively renders us a subsidiary of the government. And the government's program success measurement for this program is any improvement. In my professional opinion, I don't think that improvement means anything if it's not statistically significant with a good p-value, for starters."

"Oh, so p-hacking? Real smart. Whatever." Sarah abruptly balled up her half-eaten sandwich in the paper wrap. Then she folded her arms and turned her now frowning face into a weapon against him. "I can't believe I thought you . . . Whatever." She paused and stared at him. "You know what your problem is?"

Brandon folded his hands on the table and looked down. "By all means."

"You're full of it. You're a fake. You have this whole thing about 'do good,' but it's all a front for your insecurity. You're so insecure you can't even talk to a girl without getting nervous, so you prattle on with all your little ideas. You can't have a normal conversation without interjecting them. I know why you do it. It's because you're needy. You're emotionally needy. It has nothing to do with acceptance or beauty as you'd like to believe. I know you don't want to hear that, but it's the harsh truth that you have to accept. The first few dozen unanswered text messages and emails should have tipped you off. And I think you're a-okay with being a weird, sensitive introvert, because you think it's virtuous or something. Brandon, sensitivity is weakness. Do you want to be weak?"

"Well . . . the Young Capitalists said the same—"

"You're weak, and so that makes you afraid, and that causes you to be needy and clingy. And you put everything out there. That's how I knew I couldn't trust you. Openness isn't honesty, Brandon. And I can't trust someone so desperate that they would create this front of trying to 'do good' to impress potential friends and girlfriends. Oh, such a good guy. Such a nice guy. I saw it last winter and thought you'd mature with graduation and a job but you're still doing it. Why are you so desperate to make friends, anyway? Is it because you're—"

"It's because I want to settle down and come ho—"

"No, no, don't even start. You're not after some normal life. If you were, you could hold a normal conversation and not have to talk about all your feelings and ideas and all your problems. I bet you think you're this perfectly nice guy. You don't actually care about compassion or understanding. Don't look at me like that. You know it's the truth. You don't care about helping anyone but yourself, because you're trying to get over your own insecurities. Hearing your latest little ideas today proved it. It manifests in all your supposedly complex and deep ideas."

"Sarah, doesn't understanding require—"

"Can I finish? See? You can't even hold a normal conversation. I mean, look at you sitting there. You're nervous. You're nervous, and you're so awkward. You're so insecure that you cling to people because you think, if they express themselves the way you do with all these big ideas, then you have some kind of connection.

"I guess you think the government's not good enough for you, so you're going to save the world with charities and conversations. Every talk starts all wide-eyed, puppy-dog, but ends with you whining like you do all over your Gold Pavilion profile. Whine and bitch, over and over again. Just a spoiled, rich, white boy talking about spoiled, rich, white boy problems. That's all it is.

"And that's another harsh truth you need to accept. You think people need to care more, but you can't force people to care, okay? That's the whole problem with you and your philosophy. You expect people to care. You expect people to appreciate you for all your ideas about creating opportunities instead of dependencies, choosing to come together under true individual liberty, and now the fake beauty of a liberal and a libertarian having a relationship. That's childish.

"You can talk about beauty all you want, but you're this big wad of negativity. All those passive-aggressive lyrics you post about being lonely and wanting to hear back from people, and you didn't get invited to this or that, you can't find someone to jam on guitars, or how everyone likes beer, but you don't. People like what they like, okay? They don't have to be like you. For someone against socialism, you have a strong sense of entitlement.

"And you know what? *You know what?* I like to be around happy people. People that seize the day and suck the marrow out of life. Not people who suck the life out of me. Not people who sit around smoking in junkyards with their one friend from high school. That's pathetic. I want my friends to be people who are happy and know how to have a good time. You don't. In fact, I can't remember one thing you've ever said about being happy or grateful."

"Sarah, come on; I . . . I'm very grateful. I'm overcome by gratitude for . . . like on my profile, all the music I love, and beautiful pictures I post all the time about beau—"

"Beauty and truth and love, right. Love, yeah. I know all about your obsession with me. Well, I'm already seeing someone. That's right. Someone who's strong and knows how to have fun. I need a big, strong man, one who can defend me. You can't. It wouldn't hurt you to work out."

"I . . ." Brandon shook, and his voice cracked. "I also heard that one from the Young Capitalists."

"Well, a broken clock is right twice a day."

"But, how does requiring a big, strong man comport with your feminism?"

"Wow." Sarah threw her hands up. "Really? Wow. Okay. It sits with my feminism just fine. I want a real man, so what? I choose what I want. You don't get to choose."

"I'm not saying I do. I'm talking about the incongruent principles between what you say you value in a mate and the societal values you espouse. If we all pursued superficial qualities and toxic gender roles—"

"Whatever. If you dated me, I'm sure you'd try to turn me into a make-believe girl who will sit around listening to your problems—all weak, sensitive, and dependent. You don't even know me, so how are you supposed to love me?"

"I . . . hm. You know, the entire point of advocating social justice and serving others is loving people we don't know." He looked away. "There's no us and them. There's only you and me. If anything, I'm too independent. I value intellectual honesty over belonging to any ideology. It's because I don't know the answers that I want to collaborate with others. And romantically . . . I spent college alone, because . . . I watch for the right one, one who believes in compassion and . . ."

He thought of the mole in front of her ear and *Aisling*, and then it finally occurred to him that Aisling wasn't there. His concepts had corroded his ideals. He tried to ignore it as reality kept painfully unfolding in front of him.

"I don't claim to know you, Sarah. I . . . want to know you. I want to know you, because I believe in you. I want to really know you, not just—"

"See? That's exactly what I'm talking about. That's creepy and weird and depressing. If you want to connect with people, why don't you try being happy?"

"Because . . . happiness isn't an input. It's an outcome. We should do the right thing, regardless of reward, and either happiness comes or it doesn't. People need to come together, regardless. Reach out to people suffering materially or otherwise. It starts with the individual. It's Ecclesiastes. And the prophets, you know? And the Gospel. Blessed are—"

"Oh, no. Don't you tell me that being a sad sack is a matter of faith." She sat with one arm folded and the other extended with a point. "My faith is mine, not yours. My faith is what makes me happy and a good person. That's what you don't get. That's . . . You know, you're sick. You're a sad sack with no reason to be sad. You've had it easy. You've never had anything bad happen to you in your entire life, rich boy. Even if you did, it would be your fault anyway. Because you're a spoiled little boy. You don't know any real pain. Because if you did, you would get over your petty little issues and be happy."

"Hap . . . happiness and goodness aren't equivalents. Faith is not about comfort and self-congratulation, but . . . doing good for its own sake."

"I'm done." Sarah stood up, pulled her suit jacket together, and buttoned it. She readjusted her red scarf with the gold accents. "You think you have all the answers, but you're still just a spoiled boy who can't even move out of his parents' place after getting a grown-up job. Your intellectual curiosity is a cover for your miserable persona that drains people. That's the only 'do good' that you ever do. What's your obsession with that pretentious phrase, anyway?"

"Sarah, please . . . I really, truly, actually . . ." His voice was stilled by raw, bleeding emotion. His shoulders slumped over and his head hung loose, feeling her scolding glance. Shame burned deep within and emanated outward.

"I really just want to do good, don't you? Isn't that . . .? Wasn't that what you're all about, compassion and understanding? I mean . . . understanding can be unpleasant, so that's why . . ." Brandon looked up into her blank eyes revealing a heart of mordant apathy. He didn't want to see the mole in front of her ear, but he saw it anyway. It was still beautiful, and he was ashamed. "I want to do good, and I want to be home. And you seem—"

"Don't talk about me." She turned away and mumbled as she walked, "You don't know me."

". . . Apparently."

But Brandon already knew that he didn't know her, even as his final word fell behind her. He knew that he knew very little about anything. Like anyone else with any intellectual curiosity, he knew enough to make the smallest sense out of life, no more.

As Sarah let the banner of sleigh bells on the deli's door crash back with a *clang*, he had learned something new—that he had failed to correctly identify the one who would join him in a quixotic professional and personal journey to do good.

And he knew Sarah was right. She was right to impugn his grandiose ideals in their poor realization and execution, as well as his demeanor. This knowledge awakened his soft and intricate dream of two people of very different personalities and political beliefs for their similar upbringings uniting for some noble purpose and ending each day at a small brick house by a beautiful red maple tree. Like a head in the hangman's care, desperate to live, his impetuous coping dream suddenly awoke to the blame and shame made perfect by the final consequence. The dream was dead.

Sitting in a shaking slump, less than a shadow of his minted confidence even minutes ago, Brandon succumbed to what his blind belief hath wrought and ruminated upon her last question and her words. *Needy. Clingy. Awkward.* He ruminated on his new, terrible, and invincible knowledge.

There was nothing to do right now but try not to think. To not think about her words, those words from her mouth, the glossy pink lipstick, the new haircut, all there, a life waiting for a life. And the mole. The mole. The mole and the words.

Fake.

Needy.

Front.

Weakness.

Nervous.

Weird.

Spoiled.

Insecure.

Sensitive.

Awkward.

You believed in her.

Whine.

She didn't believe in you.

Wad of negativity.

Awkward.

She didn't believe in you at all.

Awkward.

Awkward.

Awkward.

End.

End.

End.

End it all.

What he didn't know was that his final consequence was only beginning.

The Morning Star prepared.

***

JANELLE WOKE UP SCREAMING, BUT she couldn't remember why.

"What's your problem?" Caleb asked with his eyes still closed as he stretched his well-sculpted chest.

"Nothing. I must have had a bad dream."

"I'm a light sleeper."

"Sorry, I . . . Sorry. I'll go back to sleep."

"You better. I can't get another ticket driving home with this breath."

Janelle tried to calm down and neither think nor feel. Her heart wouldn't calm down, though.

Through the shadows of her bedroom, she focused her view on the second of two old books on her dresser, frayed and brown, with "*Corinth Press*" in gold lettering, barely visible in the dark.

She reached across the nightstand and picked up the alarm clock. It read 11:14 in dull, teal digits. She set it back down and pulled her arms back inside the covers.

"Mmm . . ." She calmed down with thoughts of emotional security and self-assurance.

A nerve twisted in her chest, but she ignored it.

He was her prince. He was her angel. Of course he was the right one. Of course he was. She let out a slow exhale and backed closer into him, his chest cold and tranquil on her back. "There's no one like you."

"Go back to sleep."

***

ON CHRISTMAS MORNING, THE DAY was darker than the solstice. Gray clouds hung low. They blocked the sun and released flurries. The houses were oddly quiet on this holiday. Strands of little lights adorned a roof here and a doorframe there, illuminating silently in the winter air.

Dipping a spoon into the eggnog and stirring, Brandon wished that alcohol would offer the emotional respite for him as it had for others. The Marcels, Olsens, and Whiteners were all there again, and each of them brought presents and dishes to be shared. A cartoon holiday special played muted on the plasma screen television. He took a quick sip and let it roll over his tongue. Amaretto. He made a mental note to sip it gradually for an hour or so, being careful not to finish it too quickly, or he'd be handed a holiday-themed microbrew from his sister.

He hated beer.

"What's the matter, son?" his mother asked as she picked up piles of boxes and wrapping paper, pushing them away from the front of the recliner. "Are you not liking your ties, your leather planner, or your new guitar book?"

"Nah, it's all nice," Brandon responded, sitting back on the plush couch with the glass in hand. "I actually think those ties are going to look really nice when I head to that conference."

"Oh, good." She sat back in the old recliner and eased backward, gently tugging on the bottom of her glittery holiday sweater. "I figured you could finally use some."

"Yeah."

"Really, what's going on? I know something's been bothering you. You've been more quiet than usual. I figured some holiday cheer would help. Has the job been going well?"

"The job is actually pretty good. Dick has backed off a little since that one report. And Rob seems to think I'm great."

"Oh, that's great. You must have really impressed them. What was the report about?"

"It's about . . ." He thought of a few prepared talking points and elevator speeches that Dick had advised him to use for the conference. Their saccharine taste contrasted hard with Dick's objection to giving Brandon "sugarcoated" performance feedback. Eggnog swirled on Brandon's tongue and through his teeth until the notion of bullshitting his mother was no longer palatable to him. "It's supposed to be about how our training program helps all these down-on-their-luck people get jobs, but our clients might do better going door-to-door."

"What do you mean?"

"Our donors are forking out millions of dollars, not to mention the taxpayers funding the public grants. And for all the money and the stressful work, few of our programs have statistically significant improvements in job offers or skill improvements at any confidence level. The p-values are so high—"

"Son, I'm a public relations officer, not a statistician."

"It means our programs don't work, Mom. The feel-good stuff only *feels* good. Well, to some people, anyway. It doesn't really help our clients."

"Oh. So that's what's bothering you?"

"Actually," he said with a laugh, "that's what should be bothering me. But that's not it."

"I was going to say, big deal. Play the game, like your father says. Your sister would say the same thing."

"Yeah." He went to take another sip but stopped midway and set his glass down on the coffee table coaster. "Maybe faking it and playing the game are kind of . . . the cause of all our economic sorrows. Well, that and the Federal Reserve. Like, it's not about merit, and it's not ultimately about rich and poor. It's about corrupt insiders at all levels versus everyone else. Style versus substance."

"Oh, Brandon." She shook her head. "Sure, it would be nice if things were fair and honest. But you're in your mid-twenties now. You should know better. The world is the way it is, so you need—"

"To get over it. Yeah, I've heard."

"Son," she said, her voice increasing in sternness, "you finally got a good job. Do whatever you want on your own time, just don't blow it, okay? I was getting sick of telling my friends about your dishwashing career. You know how that feels?"

"Mom," he started but couldn't finish. He took a nervous sip and settled back down on the couch. "I am rolling with it. I'm going to have to find a way to make quality control program adjustments on my own, I guess. They're resistant to any change I offer, no matter how I phrase it or how many times I bring it up, so . . . it is what it is."

"That's right. You need to just accept it, for better or for worse."

"Yeah." He lifted his eyebrows and put his glass back down. The familiar urge to scratch his upper left arm came and went as he realized the implications. There was something there. "I think you're right."

"Thank you. Finally!" She cleared her throat and tugged on the bottom of her sweater again. "Are you going to tell me what's really bothering you?"

"Well, Mom," Brandon started, surprised that he felt comfortable again, "if it's not the job, you could probably guess that it's the girl."

"Oh, the girl," she responded. "Of course. Is that Sarah what's-her-face?"

"Sarah Shea-Trivette."

"Sarah Shea-Trivette." She nodded and stared off into no place in particular. "So, what's the matter? Did she not want to add Marcel to her growing list of names?"

Brandon laughed. "I think you'd like her. Big Catholic family. Dad's a professor, mom plays cards at the country club. Sarah's apparently working at Vazio, actually, doing finance stuff."

"Vazio, really? Wow. Maybe she's a keeper, after all. I thought she was into social service stuff like you are."

"I did, too." He picked up his glass and mindlessly looked into its contents, swirling them for lack of anything better to do with his hands. "I thought she took the Catholic social teaching to heart. I thought she was someone . . . I thought she was who she said she was."

"And what have we been talking about? That's life. Was it because you wanted her to get a well-paying job in a charity like you? Those positions are rare, especially early in your career."

"No . . ." His thoughts trailed off. "I think she just didn't like me."

"Talk to your sister about it. She could probably make connections with Sarah at work. That's networking. Just ask your dad."

"She said she was done with me. She's done with me because I'm too insecure and negative, I complain too much, I don't appreciate anything, and—"

"Do you think she's wrong about all that?"

"No, I . . . Well, she is right about a few things, but I think there's a reason that I come across that way. I actually appreciate everything." He sat for a moment and tapped the side of his glass with his fingernail. "Goodness is everywhere. And undermined everywhere. The difference is priorities. It seems like most people go for status, wealth, and style; whereas I think it's more important to focus on meaning, frugality, and substance. There's that style and substance thing again." Brandon took a quick swig and let the amaretto settle on his tongue. "It's not really generational; it's societal. It's like, uh . . . that quote that Germy told me about from . . . Krishnamurti. He said something about it being unhealthy to be well-adjusted to a sick society. People are capable of being loving, creating amazing works of art, and producing prosperity for everyone. Why is it . . . squandered?"

"Brandon, Brandon, Brandon," his mother said with a scoff that he wasn't sure was forced for effect or not. "What are we going to do with you? You scared off a girl with all your deep stuff and explain why it didn't work with all your deep stuff. Get with the program. Let's talk to your sister and see what we can do."

"Mom, I'd—"

"That's how you do things. That's the way things are. Like your father says, in jobs and relationships, it's all networking. Play the game."

"The game is the problem."

His mother threw her hands up. "And what can you do about

that? I can't help you. No one can help you." She sat up in the recliner and got up to join the family in the kitchen. Someone shook a plastic bell and laughed. "You're helpless."

"I'm sorry." Brandon blinked and rubbed his eyes as if something was caught in each of them. The pain in his chest was no longer searing. It had quit trying and had settled into a dull ache, a numbness waiting to freeze or explode.

Everything has a breaking point. Everyone *has a breaking point.*

"I'm sorry for everything."

"Will you stop apologizing? Brandon, come on. You can do better. And I've always tried to break it to you nicely. You should hear what your father thinks of you."

"I know."

***

LEADEN BLACK CORNERS OF THE room gradually gave way on four sides to the soft blue glow of the laptop. This glow was blocked by the silhouette of Brandon and his short mop of bed-headed hair. Before him was the underbelly of communication technology, rolling on each dream to culture's beat. Sounds of his father's television and his mother's shower died down, and now all that could be heard was his own little taps, scroll wheel turning, and clicks.

Brandon stared at his Gold Pavilion feed and clicked "Refresh." He looked at the same updates he saw a few seconds ago, waited a few more seconds, and then clicked "Refresh." He scrolled down and back up again.

In one post, a former classmate from high school had posted pictures of a family Christmas, each laughing and smiling over gag gifts and colorful memorabilia. In another, a restaurant server, who used to bring dishes for him to wash, told the online world about her engagement. In a third post, the guy who used to make plans with Brandon and then invariably abandon them at the last minute had posted an event notice for his indoor volleyball team.

Scroll. Click. Scroll.

Even though Germy and Marianne had made it clear that they wouldn't be around, Brandon texted them anyway. The wayward drift of his incessant compulsion began to tilt toward the last refuge of people like him; people with a high negative correlation between the size of their ideas and the number of people willing to hear them.

In another tab, he reloaded the AlterProgress homepage, looking for new articles about one controversy or another and the vitriolic comment threads that followed. In this sordid side of the underbelly, he already knew that he was driven by desperation, but continuously tried to stay out of reach of despair.

Looking at AlterProgress, Brandon was reminded of hope through Batshitreichwing's message about the power of the individual, still sitting in his inbox from all those months ago. *To truly think for yourself means being prepared to be by yourself.* It had been true politically. And now it was true personally. This was the harsh truth that was actually true, but he still did not know where to go from here. He still didn't know what to do. *Hope* dwindled in nonstop attempts to connect with someone. *Faith* tattered along with the typical. *Love* shattered against the callousness of others.

Scroll. Click. Scroll.

Tinnitus became louder, alternating dull and sharp pain, overtaking him in self-inflicted panic. His palpitations started.

Desperate for peace, he put on his headphones and impulsively clicked "Sacra" from Apocalyptica. Somber electric cellos and the slow drums of this dirge of a song kept pace with his discontent. The strings and drums played deeper and deeper, warning of the times coming upon him.

There was a darkness. It wasn't anything like the peaceful literal darkness in the star-filled skies that sometimes lulled him to sleep at night. It was a darkness with which neither starlight nor daylight could contend, and especially not his monitor's glow. It was within him. It was under his skin. It was under his skin, and he wanted to get rid of it.

He had to focus on the words, even if they didn't do anything for him right now. *Hope. Faith. Love.* They didn't do anything. Not against the other words in his head. He couldn't do anything.

Fear racked his mind and body. The darkness swelled. Perhaps it was a natural conclusion to his litany of failures to connect. Or something worse. Either way, it was all he felt. Dread, panic, and pure fear enveloped him. There was no escape. There was no one to help. He was all alone. Alone and nothing but alone, his very self pulling all the outsides in and threatening to push all the insides out.

The Morning Star rose.

***

IT WAS A BRIGHT AND mild afternoon in Albuquerque on New Year's Eve. There seemed to a faint hint of sulfur in the air. The hotel lobby shimmered in the golden rays of late afternoon with tall, glass ornamental artwork with turquoise highlights to complement the Navajo sand paintings on the wall. The colors of the sand—pale stone, dark red, and oranges of all sorts—were instantly recognizable as colors of the land, even to one who had never been to the Southwest. It looked like something Clint Eastwood would wear to a gunfight.

Figures featured within them seemed more welcoming than they should be. It wasn't right. For all the enchantment of this room, this land, this country, and this world, it seemed that most everything was wrong.

"Here we are," Rob said.

Laying the laptop case on the coffee table, Rob motioned for Dick and Brandon to sit down on the couch across from him. The two middle-aged men wore striped Polo shirts with "Community Training Corps" magnetic nametags hanging on them and khaki pants. Brandon wore a blue button-down shirt with a heather gray undershirt and dark gray slacks. Each put their personal bag on the ground and removed laptops and personal folders.

Dick checked his cell phone for a text from one of his mistresses, and then silenced it and stuffed it into his pocket. He flipped open a binder full of papers and pulled out a pen.

Brandon sat close to the edge of the couch, wrote the date on his notepad, and arranged his printed notes to his side. Sitting up, he scratched the top of his chest and shifted his weight. In the corner of his eye, a glass ornament reflected a ray of the setting sun. Fewer and fewer rays reached across the land, through the windows, and into his eye, and his morsel of hope rolled over the horizon with them.

"I see we got our presentations ready to go," Rob said. "Good. I don't want to have to worry about that later. So, what's our donor strategy? You guys come up with something on the flight?"

Dick tossed a handwritten page on the coffee table. "Here's the talking points. I have the financial figures to show we're ready to expand. Our game plan is to stress that we don't waste time or money on problem clients. Um . . . problem cases. Actually, let's just say we don't waste money. We use their generous support to expand our state-of-the-art training programs to everyone who needs them. With bold investments, we can put the whole state to work."

"Good, good. So, in your elevator talks, you'll make the case that we have the capacity to expand.

"Brandon, my man, how about you? What's your plan?"

"I think honesty . . ." he hesitated. "Honestly, my case should be . . . that we have some positive stories from clients."

Rob raised an eyebrow. *"Some?"*

"Many. Many positive stories from clients. I have a list of blurbs here, some anecdotes . . . I can tell stories about how people are trying new things to find jobs in the region."

"No," Dick interrupted. "State. Statewide. Stay on message. Don't even say region; say state. Every time." He gave Rob a look. "Brandon, I can let you forgetting your nametag slide, but not you going off message like that."

"Statewide, right," Brandon said. His nerves were already piling up. It felt like a permanent weight was forming. "Got it. We'll tell them about how we're matching specific client skills to the job market of the state."

"That's more like it. You better have those specifics ready. Get out there and engage each of them with a big smile. Big smile. None of that twitchy stuff, got it?"

"Got it, Dick." He forced a grin.

"Good," Rob said. "How about our stats, Brandon? Endowment folks like to hear stories with hard numbers. What are you going to tell them about those great findings we have that our programs really are getting people jobs?"

There was a small lump in Brandon's throat that he ignored. "I think . . ." He inadvertently thought about the etymology of that word beginning with *con* and ending with *science*. "We can tell them about the number of people in our programs showing, um . . . readiness, and uh . . . talk about how the pre-post survey results are overall positive."

Rob laughed. "Oh, come on; that's kid stuff. I'm talking about when we actually scientifically validated all our work this year with your analysis. We have statistically significant figures about getting people jobs with every program and module, right?"

"Yeah, I . . ." He looked down. "Yeah, we have statistically significant figures."

"Damn right, we do! I went ahead and forwarded the raw data in a secure email. I'll let you have the honors of telling the foundation folks what it all means. Make that case, Brandon. If you win over one of those foundation bigwigs, we'll have another cool million or two before we even get back home. That's the ticket, my man! That's the ticket."

"Yeah."

"See, Dick? We're in good shape. So, guys, let's cut loose and see how this town brings in the New Year. What do you say?"

"That's what I'm talkin' about," Dick said.

"Oh," Rob said as he patted his pant pockets then reached into his right one, pulling out a key attached to an orange tag with white print. "Brandon, this is for you. Yeah, that's right! When we picked up the two cars at the airport, you probably thought, 'Hey, where's mine?' I could tell you were bummed out about it on the ride over. Well, I'm going to spend my evening at a little place around the corner, so my rental is yours!"

"Oh, really?" Brandon reached over and took the key with a shaking hand, his mind full of dread. "Thank you so much."

"Make sure to call a cab if you have too much fun!"

"Of course, yeah. Thanks, Rob."

"What's the matter? These are top-of-the-line. V6 engines. Lemme tell ya, you're gonna feel good pullin' up to a bar in this black Acura."

"Nah, I . . ." Brandon mentally told himself that he would be capable of simply backing out the car and parking it in a dark corner of the lot and slipping back into his room. The thought of actually driving down the street terrified him. He kept his license for identification purposes, but the most driving he had done in years was slowly driving a drunk Germy home one late night. And he wanted to keep it that way. "Thank you, Rob."

"Oh, you're worried about the driver policy. Such a worrier. I've got it covered, all right? Premium policy and you're on it. You're good. Go have fun! Loosen up, and you'll be a superstar at the conference."

"Ha, yeah." The thought of finding a bar and a fling crossed Brandon's mind. He liked it. Enough alcohol would loosen him, prime him, and sell him. "Sounds good. Thank you."

"There you go. I think we're all set. I can't wait to share your data."

"Oh, that's . . . Okay, yeah, sounds good. Thank you . . . thank you so much, Rob."

"Don't mention it. You've earned it. Get out there and have fun!"

"Will do!"

***

OTHER GOLDEN RAYS OF LATE afternoon cast across the shining royal blue fabric of Janelle's dress. It felt heavenly soft in her hand. She hadn't worn it since her high school graduation party, yet it still fit perfectly. Her dark hair fell past her shoulders in well-prepared waves.

Her legs shifted as her pensiveness grew. With each minute, she felt another impulse to pick at her lip, and each time she remembered she was wearing wet pink lipstick. It was a rare occasion.

She looked at her cell phone, her wall clock, and then back at her cell phone. She drummed her fingers on her knee, the royal blue fabric so soft on the tips.

The two girls who had arrived a few minutes earlier came back to Janelle's room with mixed drinks, iced and azure-hued. Their gossiping passed over her ears. She wondered why these two people from her graduation seminar were the only ones to show up so far from the twenty she had invited on her Gold Pavilion profile. But it wasn't dark yet, and she told herself it was only a matter of time. It was fine if only a few people showed up.

As long as Caleb would come.

"What are you waiting on, girl?"

"Oh, hey. Sorry." All Janelle saw on their faces was eyeliner and unreasonably dark tans. She sat her phone down next to her monitor and mentally told herself to sit up straight.

"You need to come in here and get something. It's your night! Get a drink and relax."

Janelle smiled and stood up, intentionally leaving her cell phone sitting on the desk. She had to be calm. She had to be cool. She had to, and she couldn't, but she would leave the phone there for now and try.

"Girl, I'm sure you want to start out easy. I won't put much rum in this. Just try it out, and you can always get another. Or three. Ha! We're gonna light you up."

The two girls walked into the kitchen and started grabbing cups and bottles, operating quite mechanically under smooth demeanors. It was exceptionally mechanical. And cool. Cold. Glittery and capricious and colder than the Sonoran Desert ever was in the wintertime.

"Here, start out with a shot," the other girl said, handing Janelle a little glass with a maroon mascot on it.

"Actually, I . . . I think I want to take it easy," she responded. "I've, uh . . . I need to drive out and see my brother tomorrow afternoon."

"You'll be fine by then. Promise." She laughed. "You could get wasted and be fine by then; trust me."

Her companion put a yellow plastic cup down and wiped her mouth. "You're the hostess. You have no excuse!"

Janelle smiled. She was about to let her inhibitions go when the question came.

"What are you so nervous about, anyway?"

"I, uh . . . Well, I haven't hosted anything for a long time, and uh . . . hoping things go well with Caleb and his friends."

The girl with the thickest eyeliner looked up and put her cup down. "Caleb?"

"Yeah, Caleb Sterling."

"How do you know him?"

"Well, we're um . . . we're kind of an item now."

The girl with the thickest eyeliner laughed. "You're an item with Caleb Sterling?"

"Yeah . . ." Janelle was caught in the headlights of the words coming for her. "We've been dating for over a month now."

The girl with the thickest eyeliner snickered. "Girl, we . . . Oh, don't you worry now. If that's your thing, we can get you another Caleb or two."

Janelle's face was falling hard. "What do you mean?"

"Caleb's an item for plenty of girls. Hell, he was with . . ." She turned to the other girl who sipped on her drink with a complete vacancy. "What's that girl? That skinny girl that sits next to me. Well, they went home together after our Christmas party." The girl with the thickest eyeliner sniffed and talked slack-jawed. "He's like that. But you're a goodie girl, so I'd get myself a goodie guy if I was you."

The last rays of light disappeared, and Janelle no longer wanted to see them or be seen by anyone. She didn't want to do much of anything. Her rational mind wanted to ask more questions and check profiles on Gold Pavilion, but the truth of the matter was obvious now to her brittle heart. It wasn't necessary. She had successfully deluded herself, and this was her prize. This and the orange bottle laying under her old sweats in the bottom right drawer of her dresser.

The Morning Star shined.

***

BLUE AND ORANGE STREETLIGHTS CUT through the long window blinds of the hotel room as dusk settled. Brandon paced from one side of the room to another, leaving the Wi-Fi-enabled laptop open on his bed. He couldn't stop thinking about the word and what it implied. *Con. . . . Science.* Some part of him knew the dangers, internally and externally, of sending the correct dataset. The panic in his chest and the aural wreckage in his ears were at a fever pitch.

He knew what he had to do. He just didn't want to do it. His arms fell against his shirttails as he watched the glimmer of city lights through the blinds. Lights and light. Artificial and real. *Meaning. Purpose.*

Home. Ais—

Turning back to the glow, Brandon picked up the laptop and sat back on the bed. He propped it in front of him and adjusted the angle of the monitor by a touch. Taking a deep breath, he then clicked through to his email and opened a new message. He copied email addresses for the funders attending the conference from the email on which Rob had copied him. After writing a professional paragraph introduction, Brandon skipped down to write a new paragraph.

> *Dick and Rob,*
>
> *I'm attaching the original dataset to keep you in the loop. I want to make sure our donors and foundation contacts have the most rigorous, accurate, and up-to-date information available from our organization.*
>
> *The previous scratch work you*

> *forwarded from me was sent in error. I apologize. While we were not as pleased with these modest results as we would like to be, I'm certain that sharing them will demonstrate our highest commitment to continuous improvement, following the highest standards of research, data-driven decision making, and programmatic implementation of our findings.*
>
> *Let's catch up at the conference and discuss how to improve our programs based on this data. We welcome your ideas.*
>
> *Thanks!*

Brandon thought he saw the screen flicker, but it was the cursor. The message remained.

Shrill sounds in his ear slowed and became quiet. One heartbeat followed another. It was peaceful.

A ripple of memory came and went. It was something about spilled milk in a classroom. He shrugged off his nerves and considered closing the browser and letting his professional success be.

His finger ambled on the touchpad until the little arrow hovered over the "Send" button. It stopped right in the middle of the *n*, touching upon the letters on either side. In the nanosecond that followed, he realized the meaning of those three letters. Somewhere in his mind, an electron spun one way rather than another.

The Morning Star closed his fists.

Click.

Total mental carnage overcame Brandon. The laptop flew out of his hands and against the wall, bursting and scattering broken keys. Lucid nightmare memories came crashing into reality and wouldn't stop. He shoved his hands over his ears as the shriek became louder than ever before. His tachycardia went faster and faster until it became a blur of arrhythmia. There wasn't anything to see but black behemoths from skies within.

His fists beat against the wall, and he stumbled again. In the mirror above the dresser, he saw his appalling reflection of pouring red eyes and punched it. Cracks splintered across the surface and shards fell onto the floor.

He crashed against the blinds and dropped to his knees. There was something of a scream coming out of his mouth, but it didn't really matter. Nothing really mattered right now except for the awful horror everywhere within him with no way to express it. No way to manage it. No way to get it out.

Except in blood.

There were memories. Once Brandon felt them in their entirety, he stopped thrashing and sat kneeling as a pile of flesh and bone, desperate to escape itself but barely moving.

The memories were reasons. Reasons to negate all other reasons. Stated beliefs, conscious cajoling, and even mere promulgation of the species were no longer valid. Living for the sake of living meant nothing, continuing as a collection of preservatives waiting for expiration. These weren't enough. If they ever were, it didn't matter. The defenses were gone. He had no reason for being.

No.

He remembered.

No.

He remembered everything.

No!

The Morning Star laughed. His long-awaited stratagem proved devastating. He prepared the final strike.

GOD, NO!

***

TEN-YEAR-OLD BRANDON AMBLED down the hallway and skipped down the steps to the garage. His father started the car as his sister sat down in the front seat. The garage door opened noisily to a cloudy morning in late summer. There was a second of silence. Then the engine started. Brandon climbed into the back seat.

"Buckled in?"

Click.

"Got it, Dad."

"Good."

The silver sedan backed out of the garage. Mr. Marcel changed gears and pulled out into the street. They drove quietly through the neighborhood, up a hill, around a corner, and then past the stone pillar entrance. The curbside houses and local stores held the soft, early morning movements of working people.

A few stoplights later, the Marcels merged onto I-40 East toward downtown. They stayed in the right lane most of the way, going down a gradual hill, and then up another. The haze slowly cleared, and a mile before the exit, a few rays of ultraviolet light came through the clouds. They passed into Brandon's eyes for a second. He smiled. And then the rays were gone again.

"How's school going so far, guys?"

"Good," each child murmured as they shifted in their seats.

"Good. A new year. Exciting. Have you decided what you want to be yet?"

"I want to be a nurse," the daughter responded. "I get A's in health and science."

"Yeah, you do," the father responded as he slowed down on the exit ramp. "You know, you could even be a doctor. They make more money, you know."

"Yeah."

"What about you, Brandon? What do you like?"

"I don't know, Dad."

"You get good grades. I bet you could be a businessman like your old man."

"Business is fine." He fumbled with his backpack and looked out the window. "I don't know. I can work wherever as long as I can have a family."

"Whoa, Brandon! You're gettin' way ahead of yourself there." The father laughed. "You don't need to worry about that anytime soon. College, at least. Take care of yourself, right? Always look out for number one."

"I guess."

Mr. Marcel pulled through the office park and around the trees, and there it was, the pale brick building with wide windows and "Saint Monica's School" on the front placard. Students wore white Polo shirts, navy blue slacks, and multicolored backpacks featuring graphics of sports and cartoons. As they lined up against the wall, they chatted and fidgeted restlessly as they waited for their grade to be called. Brandon and his sister had arrived right in time.

"Have a good day, guys."

"You, too, Dad," Brandon's sister responded as she hopped out of the front seat, closed the door, and skipped away.

Brandon pulled his backpack on as he hopped over the car seat and turned to shut the door. "See you, Dad."

"Wait up, Brandon," the father said, turning his freshly shaven face over his perfect Windsor knot. "How's that new teacher of yours? The lawyer's wife. What's her name?"

"Miss Helen?"

"Yeah, Helen. Young thing, real fit. How are you liking her?"

"She's okay. She likes sports guys. She told us yesterday about the triathlon. I don't like all the rules and competing. I like to be all together or alone, like hiking. I like to be free."

"It'll be fine. Though it wouldn't hurt you to play more sports. Keep getting stronger. Miss Amy was really proud of you making up your work after you were sick. I was really proud."

"Thanks, Dad."

"Your mom is really proud of you. She really is, Brandon. She believes in you so much."

"I'm gonna be late!"

"We love you."

"Love you, too."

Brandon ran off to complete the line behind everyone else, pulling on his backpack and standing frail. A tuft of his light brown hair blew in the breeze. He thought he needed to go to the bathroom, but he caught a look from a classmate and forgot about it.

They shuffled through the tall door into the classroom where the walls were decorated with encouraging posters. One said, *"Gopher it!"* with a picture of a gopher. Another featured a child's head surrounded by math symbols and coins, reading, *"Equations make cents!"* The smell of old desks contrasted with that of a new dry erase board. Everyone was chatting. One student told Brandon that her dad bought her a classical guitar. He responded that if he had a guitar, the song he would learn is "Never Going Back Again" by Fleetwood Mac. And then the bell rang.

Miss Helen, tall and toned with short, auburn hair, hobbled in from the hall right before the Morning Prayer and Pledge of Allegiance, still sore from her marathon. She wore her race participation T-shirt with a knee-high skirt. There was something disarming about her youth and casual appearance that quickly departed under her exceptionally authoritative stare and tone of voice.

As the students settled down and took out their workbooks, her eye focused on the child she most anticipated would lengthen her days this school year. A "problem" child. A "bad" child.

Young Brandon felt something strange and uncomfortable while taking the Arithmetic Baseline Test. He felt fear. Math had become difficult for him since the meningitis. It took him longer than any of the other students. He found himself alone as the others ran out for recess, stuck on the last question: Part Eight, Number Thirty. It was a word problem about a doctor named Luke.

Suddenly, Brandon's bowels hurt badly. He looked up at Miss Helen's folded arms and sardonic stare. He put his hand up. "Miss Helen?"

"Yes?" Her dialect was indiscernible. It wasn't high or low or pitchy or befitting any other distinction, nor was it quite plain. It was a voice that sounded like it came from nowhere.

"May I go to the bathroom?"

"Finish your test."

"I'm sorry, Miss Helen, it's just that . . . I have to. I can't concentrate. I want to do well."

"You want to do well? Maybe you would if you didn't daydream through the review. Daydreaming is a bad habit. I don't want to see that anymore."

"I'm sorry. I have to go right now."

"Fine. Use the unisex room around the corner. I don't want you asking for answers in the boys' room. It may be a baseline, but

I won't tolerate a cheater."

"I don't cheat, Miss Helen."

"Hurry. I'm missing my recess, too."

Brandon put his pencil down among dark eraser bits and hopped out of his seat. He walked out of the classroom and around the corner to the single bathroom. He opened the door and reached up to flip the light switch, but the bulb was gone. He blinked into the darkness.

After a second, he stepped into the bathroom and turned to leave the door a crack for the morning light as he unclasped his brown belt, unbuttoned his slacks, and sat down.

A silhouette appeared. He was tall and big. It must have been one of the older students. Maybe an eighth-grader. He blocked out the morning light with a purpose.

Brandon started to speak, but a deep murmur told him to be quiet. The silhouette had already closed the door and turned the lock before Brandon could think to say or do anything else. Brandon blinked again in the darkness for a second, sitting on the toilet in his own confusion and the last seconds of innocence.

Brandon felt a hand pull him up and a feeling in his chest that he had never felt before. It was as if his heart had taken on a life of its own—or a death of its own—thrashing against his chest.

The older boy overpowered, surrounded, and violated. And again. Over and over again. It wouldn't stop. By the time it occurred to Brandon to scream, the other one's hand was over his mouth, far stronger than his own.

"That's good."

It kept happening. Each second was a mind-warping, otherworldly suffering.

There was pain, but not enough. Greater physical pain

would have been vastly preferable. Thoughts of searing self-destruction immediately made it feel better.

The older boy said something about telling anyone and being in deep shit. And for the first time, Brandon thought of cutting his wrists. Maybe then it would be over. It was getting worse and worse and worse and it wouldn't stop. *God WHY?!*

And then it did. A light shuffle, the shadow was gone, the door shut again, and Brandon blinked in the darkness. He sat for a moment, waiting to come back to wherever he was. He felt it. The awful aching and eternal disgust and wanting to tear out of his own skin. He didn't want to feel it. He didn't really want to feel anything. He didn't want to feel anything at all.

His legs managed to stand and move, and so he pulled his ruffled pants up over his shirttails and pulled the zipper with shaking hands, all in the dark. He washed his hands vigorously but forgot to dry them.

Brandon opened the door and let himself back into the light. The now vertiginous light.

When he walked slowly back into the classroom, Miss Helen sat up in her chair and glared at him with a special cruelty. Brandon stood for a second and realized his belt wasn't fully clasped and fixed it. The thought crossed his mind to speak up, but he couldn't.

"What were you doing?" Helen asked, waiting a few bitter seconds for a response.

"I . . . I was . . . The bathroom."

"But what did you do? Don't lie to me."

Brandon stood with a shiver in his lean. He felt empty. It was if he was an inch tall, sitting within a hollowed head, peering out of eye sockets, piloting a factory reject of a child, pulling at whatever controls would respond and expecting their failure.

"I was . . . going to the bathroom."

"Don't you lie to me, Brandon Marcel."

ASHE

"I . . ."

"Were you *masturbating?*"

"I . . . What?"

"I won't tolerate a cheater, and I won't tolerate a liar."

"I don't know what mastering . . . What's . . .?"

Helen sighed. "I can't believe this." She sat up, opened a desk drawer, pulled a manila file folder with "B. Marcel" printed on the tab, and flipped the file open. After a pause and another sigh, she looked up. "I'm not stupid. I know that smell. I know what you were doing. That is very inappropriate. *Very* inappropriate! Do you understand? The Church is against masturbation, Brandon. You could be expelled for this."

"Exp—"

"Are you hard of hearing?"

"No, Miss Helen." That moment, he learned an important lesson: he still had a morsel of self-respect. His conscious mind was already closing down around what happened, and he still couldn't speak of the unspeakable, but a lone fact rattled in his mind. "Someone was there."

"What?"

"Some . . . Someone walked in."

Helen forced a laugh. "I think someone likes to watch a lot of news. You're saying one of our priests is a predator? That's a very serious accusation, Brandon. *Very* serious. And I know for a fact that both of them are at the chapel right now, so I know you're lying to me."

"No, it was a stu—"

"Do you have any idea what you're getting yourself into? Doing that and lying about it to my face? We're talking expulsion. Just wait until I tell your parents about this. Think very carefully about your words before this gets any worse."

"I—"

"You what? I know your type. So self-absorbed that you can't focus while the rest of us are trying to get things done. You break the rules and do sick things because you think you're special and unique. Then you play innocent and point the finger when you get caught. I'm onto you, got it?" Her glare was made of malevolence. "Do you have something else to say?"

"I . . ." Brandon's inability to control his speech to say exactly what had happened struck him as irrelevant. In a world of people, the truth was sometimes only important enough to be used against other people. His own mind worked in tandem with Helen to circumvent the truth. Antibodies of thought were already fast at work in an overprotective attack upon it, locking it away in a subconscious shell that would surely rupture one day. Indeed, tens of thousands of years of humanity's evolution facing civilization's discontents had dictated that the truth would fill Brandon's mind with unbearable fear, trembling, and horror. The truth of what happened and the truth that those entrusted with this little boy's care didn't care to know for their own reasons. He dare not speculate on those reasons. And he dare not incur their wrath if he could avoid it.

Nothing happened. That's it. A lie. A true lie. A lie for truth in name only. Seeming rather than being. Because being was the last thing he wanted now.

A great weight lifted. He let his mind and deference to others take over. It felt better. The precious guardian lie. And now he wanted to keep lying. He wanted to cheat. He wanted to be a problem child. A bad child. Not good. Bad. One *fuck it* was as close to good as he cared about now. He could choose otherwise, but beneath his emotional massacre, he was simply not courageous enough to speak truth to power. Not now, anyway. Now he wanted lies.

"Never mind. I'm sorry. I . . . couldn't . . . stop it."

"That's what I thought. You better let this go while I'm feeling lenient and not wanting to explain this to your parents." Helen picked up his file and pointed a corner at him. "Because, if you bring it up again, there will be hell to pay, I promise you. Hell to pay. I'm watching you." She shoved the file back into the desk drawer as the first classmates opened the door from recess.

***

THROUGH THE DIRE REELING OF utter self-destruction closing the memory, another one surfaced. Aisling had finally broken through.

***

DURING LUNCH ON THAT BLUR of a day, he sat alone by the schoolyard's stone brick wall near the maple tree and thought about dying. Taking a fine silverware knife and slicing his flesh open and dying. He couldn't remember why the thought started, but when he opened his Superman lunchbox and pulled out the peanut butter and jelly sandwich that his mother had made him, he broke down in tears. His body fell against the wall, and he wept.

He beat his fist against the wall, and he didn't want to think about dying anymore.

"What's the matter?" the elderly Sister Ann asked as she came around the corner.

"I don't know."

"Okay." She stood next to him against the wall and put her hand on his shoulder.

He kept his red cheeks buried in his wet hands. Children out on the playground ran after each other and laughed.

"There you are, dear. Let me know what I can do. You'll be okay. Jesus loves you."

"I . . ."

"Do you need to go home?"

282

The last word reverberated through his ears and into his mind, and then he heard something he had never heard before. It was a dissonant hum—his very first tinnitus episode. He tried to rub at it in one ear. It started to fill him with fear and forgotten love. And then, as if it were satiated, it subsided and dissipated. What remained felt like temptation, but at its root, it was something else entirely. It was will. It led inexorably into thoughts that transcended time.

I want to go home. I can't go home like this. I have to be normal. Then others will like me and accept me and care for me, and then I can go home to love. But I'm not normal. I'm too broken and too flawed to be normal.

But then . . . no one is normal. There is no normal. In every house, in every school, in every office, in all these places . . . we are broken. We are separated. We are ill. And we are all a continuous response to the pain.

What do I do with mine? There is a choice. I could let it sit in apathy. I could flee from it in substances. I could fuck it away in sex. I could assault it in violence. I could do everything for myself through social status and physical health and material wealth to become bigger than pain that never goes away. I could remake the world in my image and all my pain can belong to someone else. All things bad. No? No. No.

Then what? What else is there? What is there beyond the beyond? Is there an understanding of understandings? Is there a reason for reasons? Is there a love of love? What is there at the bottom of everything? Nothing. Nothing? I could do nothing. If there's anything to do, there's nothing to do. I should do nothing at all. Or . . .

The child Brandon removed his face from his hands and buried it into Sister Ann's robes and sobbed. She held him gently. Fear dissolved into love again.

When he opened his eyes, he saw something new. Peeking out of her pockets were small pamphlets that read, "For the Mothers of the Plaza de Mayo," with a picture of a woman holding a candle. The veil of dot-matrix printing and production could not obscure the spirit in her eyes; the love for her disappeared child and her yearning for justice. The indelible goodness.

I could do good.

***

JANELLE LEORA LAY FACE-DOWN in a slump on her bed. The party was over, and the last girl had left in a cab. It was quiet now.

Tears flowed silently. The shining royal blue fabric couldn't be seen in the pitch dark. It didn't matter. The shredded skin of her lips and fingers told the story. Her prince never came.

In one hand was her phone, illuminated with Caleb's last text, the word "bitch," among a few others. In the other was the little orange plastic bottle.

She lay face-down and thought of a song and then of a book. Nothing would work. It didn't matter. She was looking for a feeling or a reason, but there were none. She awaited the results of the race between her will and oblivion. One way or another, it would end tonight. With her small, soft, shredded fingers, she pulled the bottle closer.

***

WHEN THE ADULT BRANDON CAME to, he found a shard of the broken mirror in his right hand, pushed against his left wrist. A tiny pool of blood had formed at the point. The pain was a comfort. The flow was a comfort. It was all so familiar. It assured him of a home in hell.

The mordant chaos wouldn't stop. He wanted to slice apart his arms and bury the shards in his guts. He wanted everything around and inside his heart to be mush. He wanted to be completely emptied. His heart was a mockery of romantic comedy kisses and the smell of old cabins in the woods. He wanted it gone. He had every feeling and every reason overflowing. The thoughts wouldn't stop.

284

I am shit. I am different, weird, bad, slobby, dishonest, inappropriate, weak, naïve, and I have not developed conclusions, and I am no analyst, and I am awkward. I am so awkward and wrong and a beta and a liar and a cheater. She said it, and he said it. They have authority, and I have this shard. Their power and my power. This is all I can do.

I can't go home. I can't because others who have the apron and penguin . . . Aisling? But Sarah said it. I believed in her. She did not believe in me. But mom does. I am spoiled and needy and a big wad of negativity. That is all that I am. There is no LOVE. A book for a girl.

I am a pain that needs to stop. I am a canteen of shit in a desert of lies. It needs to empty all out and stop.

Her fingertips on her ear. What do I do? I need to release it and make it stop.

A box of cereal for a boy. There is a crack of ultraviolet light and AISLING.

I want to make it stop, and it will all go away, and everyone will be happy, so happy because happiness . . . there is a reason.

What do I do? END IT!

A reason for reasons, but I am a different and bad and awkward piece of shit that needs to stop. There is something I have to do, but I want it to be over now. I don't know the mothers or their children, and I don't want to see her eyes. I can do nothing for anyone. It is undeniably true that everyone wants me to go away. END IT ALL and then AISLING thinks the real undeniable truth that that spirit in her eyes . . .

END IT. Something happened at Janelle's party. Now she . . . no. She is loved, and she might need to be shown love, and everyone needs her. END IT NOW, YOU FUCK. She was there for me. Oh God, she was always there, and I wasn't there for her, and she LOVES, and the whole world is burning. I can feel nothing; others burn, but she doesn't know it, and she blocked my number, but she needs to know it, just as I don't know I have every reason to DIE except the reason of reasons, the real undeniable truth that . . . that . . . yes, Aisling. It is indelible. It is. IT IS.

Brandon looked up and blinked through wet, bloodshot eyes. He dropped the shard and stood up, tall and strong. Between gnarled blinds, he saw something wonderful.

High above the barren land, the moon shined bright, framed forever by resplendent stars. He reached out as if the points of blazing light were already within his hand, drawing paths from his grasp to beyond infinitude.

Could it be? . . . Yes. It must be. This is a night for joy. This is a night for a miracle. Faith does not come without its solemn purpose. Each day and every day, and every night and right now. For above and below the starry canopy there is a reason for reasons and a LOVE OF LOVES.

He knew what he had to do.

Brandon pulled down his shirt sleeve. The blue fabric absorbed the blood at his wrist as he pulled out his wallet and tossed three hundred dollar bills on the dresser. He picked up the key attached to the orange tag with white print. Throwing on his black peacoat, he tapped his pockets to make sure he had his cell phone and charger.

The hotel room door closed behind Brandon as he dashed down the stairwell and into the brisk, desert dusk. He found the black Acura in the parking lot, unlocked the door, and fell into the driver's seat. His physical heart galloped with fear. His spiritual heart outran it.

He took out his cell phone and opened the Map App, typing "Cactus Wren Park" as the destination. It was almost five hundred miles away. His chest jumped again. He refocused again. On the screen, he saw that he would be taking I-40 West. He smiled. It was time for a new song.

Brandon used the mp3 function to turn on The Killers' *Day and Age* album and clicked to "A Dustland Fairytale." His heart beat faster as he turned on the ignition and looked carefully to make sure he put the gear in reverse. He backed the rental car slowly out of its parking space, listening to instructions in one ear and the start of a magnificent song in the other. He turned carefully onto the main road and eased through one stoplight and another. Cars passed him on either side. It was all dreadful and horrendous, but so it went.

Up ahead, he saw the perpendicular highway. He put on the turn signal and eased into the right lane. The wheels hit the entrance ramp, and he accelerated, faster and faster, pushing the pedal against his nerves. He had to get there. Fear shook his chest and hands, but he had to get there. He'd go just over the speed limit the whole way, but he would get there that night.

And so Brandon merged onto I-40 West and drove into the night, with the stars above him and the road beneath him.

January

THE SWEAT OF BRANDON'S PALMS had soaked the fabric of the steering wheel as he careened down the high grades and harrowing curves of I-17 South near Black Canyon. *You can't control it. You are powerless.*

The night-shrouded natural ridges around him reminded him of the unnatural ridges on him, each beckoning to him.

This is stupid. Pathetic.

With the back of a truck fast approaching ahead, he put on his turn signal and passed on the left. Aisling was with him.

No, it isn't.

Returning to the right lane, he saw the crest of the hill at the tip of the headlight beams.

Here we go.

The car flew over the hill and resumed its deep descent. He could feel shaking through the brake pedal, and so he eased off it.

Far below at the distant bottom, he caught his first glimpse of the giant cluster of light in the middle of the desert night. *There she is.* In the corner of his left eye, a tall ridge melded with the darkness, as did the deep chasm in the corner of his right eye.

You're a flick of the wrist away. Do it. END IT NOW, YOU SHIT!

A lone firework shot into the sky and burst in red and

white above the city.

Almost there. I'm not late. Not yet.

The car continued the steep descent until the land flattened out like hard wrinkles meeting a burning iron. Brandon switched gears and put his foot back on the acceleration. Traffic suddenly increased. The shadowed landscape on either side of him opened up to street lights. He was on the outskirts now.

Faster.

Beneath the highway lights, the V6 engine carried him closer and closer, passing into suburban neighborhoods. More cars merged onto the highway. Brandon exhaled against his grave nerves. His playlist had looped back around to The Killers. And then the Map App spoke for the first time in hours to alert him of an upcoming turn onto another highway. His grip tightened.

***

JANELLE'S GRIP TIGHTENED AS SHE pushed her other palm on the white top and twisted. Hours of distraction and her own spirit finally gave way. The little pieces of her proposed end huddled together within. She looked down into the bottle and wondered if there was something she was supposed to think or feel.

You bitch.

She sniffed and turned the bottle to an angle and let one fall into her palm.

Take it.

The cylindrical knife. Solvent of death for her solute of life. The solution to all but sin and a cure for all the feelings within.

He never came.

It rolled around and found itself pinched between her thumb and index finger.

And he will die, and then you will have no family, and you never will, you bitch.

She closed her eyes, and a tear rolled out and fell on her empty

289

bed.

Take it.

There was something like a belief that lingered and kept the pills stowed.

Do you see what faith does?

She opened her eyes.

It's time to die.

Her fist closed around the pill, and she made another choice for just that next second.

It's time to hope. Someone cares. Maybe . . .

***

THE ACURA'S HEADLIGHTS CAST ACROSS the empty exit ramp then slowed to a stop at the light. It was quiet and getting quieter among the closely packed neighborhoods.

This is stupid.

Brandon cracked his knuckles and checked the map on his phone.

She doesn't care.

He was a couple of miles away now.

Pull over and stop, you dumb shit. You don't belong here. You don't belong anywhere.

He looked up into bone dry air and into the face of the Morning Star and stared him down. The light turned green.

Be right there, hon.

***

A FEW MORE TEARS FELL onto the bed as Janelle lost all remnant thoughts of family and friends, with all of her life leading into this empty bedroom.

She picked up the bottle again and thought that the pain would never stop. Eternal separation. A reality that showed no sign of ending, only repeating into isolation and misery because the world had not seen how it needed her.

Not yet.

***

BRANDON TURNED INTO THE CURB and slammed on the brakes across the street from Cactus Wren Park. He parked, jerked the key out, threw the car door open, and then dashed across the yard rocks of the darkest house on the street.

YOU FUCK!

His hand curled into a ball.

***

JANELLE'S HAND CURLED AROUND THE bottle and emptied its dozen contents into her other hand. It seemed so natural. The off-white little chemicals rolled around and invited her to her last act.

Do it. Take them.

She lifted her hand.

TAKE THEM ALL!

The many little deaths pushed against her mouth and one rolled inside.

There is still . . .

In the tears, misery, humiliation, empty bed, empty heart, and every perceptible thought to end her reality, she chose again to wait a single second longer.

And then she heard something strange. The mortal moment disintegrated into a sound.

It was a knock.

Janelle ran down the hall to her door and looked through the crack. It was Brandon. Through all disbelief, they were there for each other. She swung the door open and they met with the greatest embrace. Love could not escape them. He held her, and Aisling held him.

Starlight glowed. Mercy reigned. The truth always was and always would be.

***

"THIS ISN'T OVER."

"You've lost."

"You will, too."

"I've nothing more to do."

"Why?"

"He knows he is loved."

And the angel stood before God.

February

JEREMY KNEW HIS OFFICE JOB would last about as long as his most recent relationship. He despised formal collaboration and held a special contempt for sitting quietly at a cube, especially when snow flurries flew like ashes outside.

After he saw a job posted online for contracting work at a construction company, he went into his boss's office and submitted his notice. That night, his parents were furious. They screamed at him about how Grayson had very prestigious and lucrative opportunities because Grayson had a real degree and his act together.

What Jeremy didn't know was that, at the end of the month, he would meet Syandene and they would have a relationship that wouldn't end until an elderly death did them part. And his new enthusiasm would eventually lead the construction company to promote him to the head of Demolition. The fierce effectiveness of his work filled a need in the market. Jeremy proceeded to employ twelve workers, half of whom would not have had opportunities otherwise. Under his productive destruction, the company received the highest industry ratings in project turnaround and employee satisfaction in the state. Jeremy found that falling asleep next to Syandene after a day of blowing things up restored his sense of family.

***

MARIANNE KNEW SHE COULDN'T PROVIDE for

Brant on her current wages, and so, on Valentine's Day, she met with her mother to make a plan to get her certification. But even after earning the certification, she still couldn't find a better paying job. It was the reality of the Great Recession and its long aftermath. Life seemed like work and more work, but she held it all together with a tattooed hand and made sure to kiss Brant goodnight every night.

What Marianne didn't know was that, despite toiling in stress and never settling down or getting married, her son Brant and, later, her daughter Angela would defy the stigmas and statistics to make stellar accomplishments. Brant would become an advanced paramedic and save forty-two lives more than if another had been in his place. Angela would graduate from a biochemistry program and join a team that pioneered a vaccine for a disease sooner than if another had been in her place, saving countless more. Their mother reached old age, weary but immensely proud.

***

JANELLE KNEW THAT THIS WAS not the time for romance, and so she let Valentine's Day come and go as uneventfully as she had every year before. Chris slowly improved mentally and physically, and toward the end of the month, she met with a nonprofit group that specialized in veteran care. He seemed to get better almost immediately.

What Janelle didn't know was that her understanding of mental health and boundless compassion would inspire her to lead that group into starting a new creative writing program for veterans with mental health issues. The program became a national standard, replete with anecdotal and scientific accolades. She not only saved lives that would not have been saved otherwise; she helped them find their meaning, just as they helped her to find her own. Those lives touched other lives, and those touched other lives still, and on and on and on.

And on a clear, warm day years later, she met a United States Marine Corps Staff Sergeant with a scruffy face and a big laugh. He wasn't the best poet, but he was the best guy.

Her prince had arrived. And yet, she was already a queen.

March

BRANDON WOKE UP PEACEFULLY, HIS cat purring next to him. Pangs of nervousness for that day and the rest of his life started, so he sat up and reached for his dusty Martin acoustic. He slipped the pick out from between the strings, checked the tuning, and started strumming an A minor quick and steady. He fingered the D, Fmaj7, and G chords and kept strumming spiritedly yet somberly as the lyrics came to him. It was Johnny Cash's version of U2's "One" from the *American III: Solitary Man* album. He found himself singing in his own botched baritone, each line fading into existence. The song played on in his head throughout the overcast day and forevermore.

***

"GOOD TO SEE YOU AGAIN, Brandon."

"Good to see you, Conrad!"

The two shook hands and sat down in the cramped office with files and supply boxes piled around them. Brandon sat up straight and tall in his crisp charcoal suit atop a French blue shirt and forest green tie. He folded his hands on his notepad.

Conrad took off his thick glasses, wiped them with his shirttail, and then put them back on to review Brandon's résumé again. He scratched his short gray beard on his chin and cleared his throat. "It's good to see ya, and . . . I hear ya on why you're here. You want to be a little more . . . mission achievement than just expansion, right? That's too bad about CTC, really."

"It is," Brandon responded. "It is. Once the Board saw my reports, my position was defunded. I wished CTC used the data to improve the programs instead of only sharing the positive numbers to get more funding. I honestly didn't mean to rock the boat, but they apparently expected me to conform to that way of doing things, and I couldn't do it in good conscience."

"Not surprised. Dick seemed . . . overconfident when I met him at the state conference. I don't get people like him who turn away from the facts. Anyway, I liked the volunteer work you've done for us. Just knowing our donation inflow helps us know what supplies we need to order and knowing our client trends help us to prepare for the next month. And yeah, your crack at our monthly report dataset . . . it's the best of our applicants, I gotta say. Vicki was impressed, too."

"Oh, thank you, Conrad! Glad to hear that. Vicki's great. I admire her program management style. She anticipates client needs and finds the resources to match it. Efficient."

"That she is. Keeps me in check. Sometimes at lunch, I get on my liberal soapbox, and she reminds me that not everyone is going to agree with me."

"Yep. Different beliefs . . . sometimes come together to do good work. It's . . ." Brandon looked away and thought of Sarah, Batshitreichwing, Randall, and then turned back around to Conrad. ". . . a beautiful thing. Labels and parties work for short-cuts about ideological identification, but they're not the point. The collaborative ideals and results are the point. More than our abstracted beliefs, and especially everyone's pride and tribalism around their labels."

"Hm. I catch your drift. No point in keeping our doors open if we can't see the results ourselves, right? So, uh . . . hm. I wanted to ask this on the phone, but it's . . . I don't know."

"What's on your mind?"

"It's, um . . . you know, the pantry coordinator job is kind of, uh . . . entry level. Lots of food intake from donors, monthly outputs and outcomes reports, and making grocery sacks for clients."

"That's good," Brandon said with a small nod. "I'm confident I could optimize donor intake strategies and use our data to find ways to maximize our service delivery."

"I'm sure you could, but what I'm saying is . . . I know you had a good living over at CTC, and we don't have that kind of budget, so . . . well, the thing is that this position is more toward the, uh . . . lower compensation. It's a little over half of what CTC paid you." He looked down, nodded, and then looked up with excitement. "But we have good health insurance!"

Brandon smiled. "That sounds just right to me."

"Are you sure? I don't want you to run off in six months or—"

"I understand your concern. But I think this position will be a great way for me to flex my microeconomics, program evaluation, and needs assessment to see if we can be more targeted in our outreach to find and implement the precise services to maximize the probability of client self-sufficiency. This is precisely the kind of experience I seek for the next few years."

"Sure, you've got skill and heart, but just to press the salary point . . . come on; someone with your background should want more. I have a contact for a position over at—"

"Thanks, but nah. Living with my parents may not be the most glamorous life, but there's nothing like family, you know? The bus route comes here, too. Works great. I'd be delighted."

"Fine, fine," Conrad said as he threw up his callused but gentle hands. "I mean, hey, I'd love to have you. And, you know, however long you stick around and help us serve our clients . . . at least you get to do some good, right?"

Brandon grinned. "Exactly."

***

BRANDON KNEW IT WOULD TAKE more than one paper grocery bag. On another overcast afternoon after paid hours, the last of the donors and volunteers had left and quiet reigned among the shelves of non-perishable food items. Standing over the stacking table, Brandon rolled up the long sleeves of his gray T-shirt and reached into a folded bag to pull it apart.

Just as he reached for a can of green peas, he heard the eight-bit chime of his cell phone indicating a text received. It was Janelle. She liked his playlist and would share it with the guys. Brandon smiled and put the phone back in his pocket.

He thought about packing up and leaving for the day. Then he heard the A minor chord start in his mind's ear and felt the lyrics in his chest. He stared through his life and back again. An electron spun. And with eternity within him, he made the supreme act of individual choice. He picked up the can of green peas and placed it into a corner of the bag.

What Brandon didn't know was whether or not that can of peas would make any more of a difference than the rest of his fading dreams. Most prominent among them was to find a wife and start a family so that he could finally come home. He believed this dream was where reason and emotion would meet for him.

But it wasn't.

In truth, he never needed a companion. And so he would never have one. He would find his home after the end of his days. After all, because of that one can of peas at the bottom of the paper bag, just one item under his new method of client needs analysis and pantry organization for maximum service delivery, ten-year-old Tim Kameda would have nourishment for his placement test that he would not have had otherwise.

One.

Tim didn't know that Maria Dean had depression. His loving hug at the school retreat stayed with her when her fair-weathered friends did not. It gave her a hope that she would not have had otherwise.

One.

Maria didn't know that Jayla Weber's new product model would provide the specific component needed to meet the annual target. By giving Jayla one more chance to improve performance, Maria had saved the upstart company. This had also assured Jayla's family financial security that they would not have had otherwise.

One.

Jayla didn't know that her son Eric would keep up with the piano lessons long after her death. It was an overcast day before the vernal equinox when he approached the small keyboard in the main hall of the convalescent home. He didn't know whether or not people down the hall were listening, but he was content to play by himself. The notes rang true from Eric's weathered-dry fingers. He played a song in C minor, and then one in D major, and then *one* last song in A minor. It was just three songs that afternoon the day before his death, but in those songs, there was a good beyond death. And it would not have been otherwise. And it would be forever.

One.

About the Author

Patrick Ashe is a writer and rock musician with over a decade of experience in nonprofit program evaluation. He is an Eagle Scout, graduate of Appalachian State and Indiana University, and an instructor at the University of North Carolina at Chapel Hill. After studying and working in five states, he resides with his family in his hometown of Winston-Salem. He is the author of *Upon This Pale Hill* (2020) and *Typical Tragedies: A Book of Poetry* (2020).

patrick.ashe41@gmail.com
https://www.facebook.com/PatrickAshe41
https://twitter.com/PatrickAshe41
https://www.instagram.com/PatrickAshe41

Made in the USA
Monee, IL
01 October 2020

43716573R00184